"What is a kiss?"

Unthinking of her words, Rose prattled on, too relieved that he was believing her tale. "It was such a small gift to him. You yourself—" she turned on him "—are not above offering the kiss of peace."

"What is a kiss?" Gaston groaned. "I'll show you...."

Before Rose knew what was happening, she was pulled into the circle of his strong arms. His dark head bent to hers...

Catherine Archer has been hooked on historical romance since reading *Jane Eyre* at the age of twelve. She has an avid interest in history, particularly the medieval period. A homemaker and mother, Catherine lives with her husband, three children and dog in Alberta, Canada, where the long winters give this American transplant plenty of time to write.

ROSE AMONG THORNS

Catherine Archer

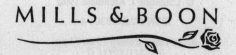

MILLS & BOON

To my grandmother,
who taught me that it was all right to dream;
To my parents,
who said, "You have to work for your dreams";
To my husband, who said, "Go to work";
And to Jenny, who taught me to rework.

*MILLS & BOON, the Rose Device and LEGACY OF LOVE
are trademarks of the publisher.
Harlequin Mills & Boon Limited,
Eton House, 18-24 Paradise Road, Richmond, Surrey TW9 1SR*

© Catherine J. Archibald 1992

ISBN 0 263 79304 4

*Set in Times Roman 10 on 11 pt.
04-9511-89531 C*

*Printed in Great Britain by
BPC Paperbacks Ltd*

Chapter One

Rural England
Spring, 1067

Rose looked down from the palisade, a gentle breeze ruffling the soft auburn curls at her temples. She ran her gaze over the broad strip of grass that had been cleared of trees around the outside of the tall rough-hewn wall, then down to the bottom of the slope where the forest grew thick and verdant. She narrowed her wide-set green eyes, trying to penetrate the dense growth, looking for some overt sign that the Normans had actually come to her shire.

She shivered with apprehension and wrapped her arms around her slender form. Foreboding welled up inside her, making her heart beat with a sickening, irregular rhythm. Dear God, she thought frantically, I must not let anyone see how frightened I am.

Taking a deep breath, she willed herself to calm. The months since first her father's, and then her brother's, death had seen Rose take a very tenuous hold on the leadership of Carlisle. It was difficult for the villeins to place their trust in an untried girl of eighteen.

"What are we to do?" Alfred asked beside her, startling Rose out of her reverie. "Joseph rode into the keep just moments ago. He said he spotted fifteen knights, my lady. And they are but four hours from Carlisle.''

She almost gasped aloud. Fifteen mounted men. Her father and her brother had been the only men to go from Carlisle on horseback. The animals were not nearly so abundant in England as they must be in Normandy. Besides, her lips thinned with contempt for the enemy, Saxons preferred to fight on foot.

Rose turned to face the small, hunch-shouldered reeve, hiding her anxiety behind a mask of self-confidence. Alfred reminded her of nothing more than a scared rabbit, standing there with his thin nose twitching, wringing his bony hands.

She was careful to keep any hint of emotion from her voice, fearing she would betray her own agitation. ''We have no choice but to grant them admittance. We could not defend ourselves against such a large retinue of knights.''

''But, lady, fifteen mounted men,'' Alfred's narrow lips worked nervously, ''and many more foot soldiers, as many as fifty. What are we to do?'' he muttered again.

Rose's fine features softened with pity for the reeve as she patted his shoulder, feeling the jutting bones beneath her fingers. But there was nothing she could do to lessen the sting of her words; Alfred knew her intent. ''We will do what we must. Gather the people together. I must speak with them before the invaders arrive.''

''Some of the men will not take this lightly, lady.'' Alfred spoke haltingly, ''Men like Hugh and John who were at the Battle of Hastings with your father. If only your brother, Edmund, was here.''

Rose drew herself up to her full height. She might not have been groomed to act as thane to her people, but her veins ran with her father's blood, too. ''Edmund is not here, I am.'' She closed her eyes and took a deep calming breath. When she spoke, her voice was even, though her hands were clenched. ''My heart goes out to all who have been affected by this war, but I will not allow the fighting to continue at

Carlisle. The Normans have won. The Bastard William has taken the throne, and we are only fools to attempt resistance.''

Alfred took a step backward. "I meant no offence. I only sought to inform you of the feelings of your vassals.''

Rose slowly lowered her hands to her sides. "I understand, Alfred, and I thank you for the warning. But I will find some way to make them see that to try fighting the Normans would be nothing short of suicide. Hurry now, there is not much time.''

Alfred tried one last suggestion. "What of your cousin Robert? We could send a message to Brentwood, asking him to come. Under his leadership the men could fight....''

Rose knew a moment of sorrow in thinking about how her proud cousin would react to the Norman yoke, but she cast it aside. Her lips set in a stubborn line, as they always did when she had made up her mind about something. "If Robert is wise, he will see the necessity of surrender. If only for the sake of his mother and sister. Go now, my patience has been sorely tried.''

Alfred dipped his head rhythmically, without meeting her gaze. "I will see that everyone is gathered in the Great Hall.''

Rose nodded in dismissal and moved to the rough-hewn ladder to climb down. She gathered her long skirt into one hand while hanging on with the other, climbing nimbly to the ground. She crossed the courtyard quickly, chickens and goats scattering before her.

Until a few short months ago, Rose had paid little heed to the problems of leadership. Not that she had been pampered and idle; they were simple folk and there was always work to be done. She knew well how to run a household, much about healing lore, and had even been taught to read and do sums.

Up until this point the people of Carlisle had been willing to follow her lead. But now, when it mattered so very much, Rose was unsure of what their reaction might be to her plans.

Unbidden, she felt a rising resentment against her father and brother.

It had been bad enough when her brother Edmund had left Carlisle to fight the Danes. But only a few short weeks after his departure, her father had gone to join the king's army when the Normans had taken advantage of the Saxon defeat at Stamfordbridge to launch their attack.

For weeks, Rose had heard nothing. Then word had come that both her father and brother had perished in the fighting, Edmund at Stamfordbridge, her father at Hastings.

Laughing, dancing Edmund. How she wished he were here.

Edmund was the one who should have been thane after her father. He would have known what to say to the people. They would have followed him without dissension.

As she moved through the courtyard, Rose forced herself to meet the anxious faces with equanimity. Sunlight caught in the bright auburn of her hair as she raised her head high. Could she make her people see that she wanted only what was best for them? She had to. It was their only hope of survival.

The Great Hall was filled with people of every station and corner of the shire. All eyes turned to her and the hum of conversation died, the silence hanging flat and discordant in the air. Each person, from the well-to-do farmers and tradesmen to the lowliest serf, waited for her to offer assurance that their world was not about to collapse.

Rose felt her throat go tight with dread, threatening to suffocate her. Her palms grew clammy and cold. She wiped them on the skirt of her tunic. On legs that felt as if they were boneless, she moved through the room. The crowd parted for her, each set of eyes fixed on her slender form as she made her way to the fire pit at the center of the high-beamed room. A trestle table had been set beside the now-empty pit. Strong hands reached out to assist her as she climbed onto the table. She was grateful for the help.

Standing there above them, she felt small and alone in the midst of so many. The faces around her reflected her own apprehension and magnified it tenfold. As Rose saw the depth of their fear and how they looked to her for guidance, her own fear drained away, seeping from her like water from a cupped hand. In its place grew a courage born of acceptance. She had not wanted the responsibility of this position, but she would acquiesce to the higher power that had directed her fate to this moment.

When Rose spoke, her voice emerged clear and distinct. "You have all known since good King Harold's death that we have a new ruler. And yet, we have felt relatively safe here at Carlisle, far from London. We all prayed that we would go unnoticed. Our wishes have been to no avail. A party of Norman knights is, even as I speak, approaching Carlisle." She paused. "I ask you not to take up arms against them."

Rose heard a low mutter spread through the crowd. She could see a few of the men exchanging furtive glances of discord.

Rushing to forestall any dissension, Rose continued briskly. "I know it is difficult for you to give up all you have to these invaders, but that is what I must ask you to do."

Several men began to shake their heads, some laying hands to their dagger hilts.

Rose raised her hands and the room grew silent again. "We must submit to the Norman yoke peacefully. To resist would mean disaster for us all."

"Lady Rose," a giant of a man called as he stepped forward through the crowd.

"You wish to say something, Hugh?"

The blacksmith's face was stained dark from many years of standing over the heat of his forge. A leather jerkin stretched tight over his massive chest and the sleeves of his woolen shirt were rolled up to reveal his hamlike forearms.

"I say we fight. They are not so many that we must stand back and let them take what is ours."

A murmur of agreement spread through the assemblage, growing louder as it passed along. Rose could see the determination on the faces of the men. She also read fear in the eyes of the women as they watched fathers, husbands and sons.

Compassion for her people made Rose glance away. She had no wish to see them frightened and humbled. But Carlisle must survive. She forced herself to go on. "Hugh speaks the truth," she said clearly. "These men have no right to take what is ours, yet the fact remains that they will take what they want. Even if we found some way to ward off these knights who come today, William the Conqueror would only send more in their place. Next time it would not be fifteen mounted knights but twenty, and after that thirty. They would keep coming until no one is left alive and not one stick is left standing at Carlisle."

"At least we would die like men!" came a voice from the crowd.

"And what of your wives and children?" Rose said, swinging around to point at the man. "Would you have them die like men, too?"

Singled out by her scorn, the unfortunate fellow ducked his head down and slunk back, cowed.

A woman sobbed and clutched her baby to her breast.

Rose pressed on. "You who hope to keep what belongs to you will end by losing all. Is what you consider doing worth the risks? Who, better than I, knows what can be lost to these demons? Both my father and brother lie dead in graves so far from here I can not even go to spill my grief." Saying the words made the wound bleed as if fresh, and she swallowed convulsively, steeling herself to go on.

Hearing more sobs coming from the crowd, Rose raised her clenched fists high to her breast. "Must all of us suffer yet more grief before there is an end to this killing?" Her eyes grew cold and she shook her fist. "I, too, balk at the thought of Norman rule, but what is done is done. We must accept our lot and go on.''

Rose saw indecision in the upturned faces around her. She remained silent, waiting, giving them time to reason out her words. The silence held, and one by one heads nodded as the people began to see the wisdom of what she said. Relief swelled in her chest, releasing the tight band that had prevented her from taking a breath.

The smith spoke again, his deep voice rumbling out. "How are we to know these Normans will not put our families to the sword even if we don't resist them? They've given us no reason to trust them.''

"Hugh's right,'' came another voice to her left. "What is there to stop these Normans from making war on us, even if we do as you say?''

Rose whirled in irritation. "They have no reason to act against us. Who would plant the crops? Who would man the forge? Who would care for the horses? Don't you see?'' She held out her hands, her voice and posture imploring them to listen. "The Normans need you. Soldiers are adept at making war and taking from others, but they know little of raising food, tending flocks—all the things done by the common folk every day.''

A couple stepped closer to the trestle table, looking up at her anxiously. It was John, a farmer with four children. His wife, Mart, who was expecting their fifth, stood close at his side. "Lady Rose, I want to believe what you say is true. We all do.'' He gestured with rough, work-worn hands. "But you must understand that it tears a man's insides,'' he said as he rubbed his hand over the coarsely woven wool that covered his belly. "'Twill be too hard to accept one of these foreigners as our thane after your father, Good Walter, was cut down by the men we would now call our masters. This goes against all that is holy.''

With tears in her eyes, Mart took her husband's arm. "Lady Rose, what will we do?''

Rose closed her eyes and prayed for guidance. She knew she could give no guarantees. The future was too uncertain. She opened her eyes, answering them honestly. "I know not what my position here will be." Rose raised her right hand high over her head and crossed herself with her left, her voice ringing out clearly with the strength of her vow, "but I swear as long as there is breath in my body, I will work toward the good of Carlisle and its people."

In the stillness that followed, she could hear the sound of her own blood pounding in her ears. The people knew she had just made them a solemn pledge before God.

Finally, when she felt as if she would faint from standing there so vulnerable and alone, a woman stepped forward and bowed formally, then turned and walked from the Great Hall. After her came her husband. Then the people came in a steady stream, each to bow and leave.

They were accepting her as their overlord, not formally, with pledges of homage, as they had to her father or as they would have to Edmund. But they were deferring to her judgment; they respected and believed in her.

Her heart swelled with pride. But this new confidence was a double-edged sword. With this honor there came the responsibility of living up to her oath. She had no way of knowing what the Normans would do when they arrived. Rose only knew that she must do as she had promised. She must help her villeins in any way she could.

When only the serfs remained in the vast room, Maida, the cook, stepped forward. "What should we do, my lady?"

"You must go about your work. We will prepare food for these conquerors and a place to rest."

Maida folded her tiny hands over her apron, which was stretched taut over the wide girth of her stomach. She smiled, her pink cheeks rounding despite the disquiet in her blue eyes. "I never met a man who was not more amiable with his belly full."

Knowing the words were said to bolster her, Rose drew herself up straight. If Maida could see her uncertainty, then others could. ''We must put our faith in God and pray that all will be well. Go now and ready the guest bower for their leader. It is the best we can offer.''

The cook started off, then pivoted around on surprisingly small feet clad in worn leather. ''Shall I have more wine and ale brought up from the cellar?''

Rose nodded and answered with more self-assurance. ''Yes, of course. We shall do our best to tame the beast.'' She addressed the other servants, ''Go now. There are many tasks to be done.''

As the last of them left the Great Hall, she sighed and weakly sat down on the tabletop. Rose slid to the floor, only to find that her legs would not support her weight. Holding on to the edge of the table, she made her way to a bench, then slowly sank down onto it.

What was she going to do? The Normans had not even arrived and already she was so terrified she could barely control it. What would she do when confronted with the reality of their presence? She must collect herself and face them with a vestige of courage, if not for her own sake then for the sake of her vassals.

A group of armored, mounted men burst from the trees and galloped up the hill, their horses racing at a breakneck pace. They cried out victoriously to one another on seeing the keep laid out before them. One of the steeds, a gleaming white stallion, broke from the others and easily outdistanced them.

The rider, Gaston, his narrow hips hugging close to the saddle, leaned his wide shoulders forward, exalting in the surging power of the animal beneath him. Great clumps of earth and grass were thrown up behind Pegasus's pounding hooves, wafting the fresh scent of spring through the knight's visor.

The palisade surrounding the keep was tall and sturdy in appearance, even though it was fashioned of wood. Whole logs had been used and not even a hint of light could be seen at their joinings. But when he saw the open gate, his lips twisted with disdain. How could these Saxons pay so little heed to security? He did not slow the pace of his mount until he was inside the protective palisade.

There were a number of serfs working about the courtyard, but none moved to check him. They simply stopped and stared at the fearsome sight of a mounted knight upon his war-horse.

Gaston pulled up his mount in derision. There would be no fighting done today. When Hubert, his older half brother had suggested that he, Gaston, and the other mounted knights ride on ahead of the rest of the army, Gaston had wondered at his wisdom. It was only after they had ridden though forests and passed tilled fields the whole day long without incident that Gaston had come to relax. But he was surprised to enter the keep without challenge.

He pushed up his helmet and wiped his brow as he eyed the staring serfs with amusement. Since the Battle of Hastings, Gaston had, on many occasions, argued with the other knights over the worth of the Saxon warriors. He had developed a grudging respect for the bravery of foot soldiers who had faced mounted knights so fearlessly. Hubert could only decry them for being so unprepared in the face of their enemy.

Now Gaston began to wonder if Hubert had been right all along. What manner of men were these Saxons who did not even attempt to defend themselves from aggression?

Then Gaston remembered what King William had told them about Carlisle. The lord of the fief and his son had both been killed; only a young daughter was left.

Gaston knew from dealing with his own sister, Marguerite, that this girl would have little, if any, knowledge of defense. He smiled softly. When he had last seen Marguerite a year ago, her only concern had been with making a match that was both advantageous and romantically satisfying. She had spent a whole afternoon regaling him with her plans to marry a wealthy and handsome knight who lived nearby. It was a measure of his love for her that he had withheld the pessimistic comment that had sprung to mind. The idea of romantic love was best left to bards and young maids. Gaston had long since learned that love served a momentary need, both for the man and the woman.

The other mounted men quickly entered the palisade behind him. Gaston de Thorne's handsome features twisted with distaste as the knights galloped around the enclosure, uttering fierce battle cries and laughing cruelly while the poor frightened serfs raced about screaming.

Farm animals scattered. Many of the chickens were not quick enough to elude the flashing hooves, and feathers flew like leaves in a wind. Several dogs, hurrying to investigate the fracas, dived, barking, betwixt the wheeling stallions. One, a spotted mutt, yelped as he flew through the air after a well-positioned kick hit him in the side.

The other men reveled in the destruction they were causing. Gaston's own brother, Hubert, wore an expression of wicked glee on his rugged face as he spurred his stallion toward a fleeing serf. There would be no point in reminding Hubert he was destroying his own property. As usual, he would do as he pleased.

Gaston noticed that the courtyard seemed to be clearing. There were few people left besides the ones cornered by the mounted men, and these serfs dodged back and forth trying to escape. The others had run toward a large building set in the center of the courtyard. Its oaken door stood wide open, just as the gate had been agape.

Even a woman should have the sense to close the door of the hall when the keep was being set upon. Gaston began to wonder if she might be addled. If he weren't so disgusted with watching the unnecessary havoc his brother and the other men were wreaking, he would have laughed. It would serve Hubert well should the girl prove to be dull witted; he had been too quick to accept the king's offer of lands and a bride for services rendered.

Gaston himself was not ready to take up farming. There were too many experiences left to be tasted.

Soon the courtyard was empty of any moving thing save the men on their horses. The serfs had fled, and any surviving animals had gone to hide under whatever cover they could find.

Gaston watched as his brother turned his stallion to the open door through which the people had disappeared.

"Wait!" Gaston shouted as an alarm sounded in his mind. He spurred his mount forward. "It may be a trap."

Hubert and the other men halted their heaving steeds, their gauntleted hands going to their sides automatically. Each knight closed his fingers around the hilt of his sword. Cautiously they prodded their horses forward.

Gaston rode up close to the building, placed his helmet on the pommel of his saddle and dismounted. He waited for Hubert and the others to do the same before going any further. Helmets were not as effective when a man needed to see everything around him clearly.

Hubert and the other knights dropped to the ground. The sunlight flashed off fifteen swords as they were pulled from their sheaths.

Gaston tested the weight of his own sword in his hand. It felt good, an extension of himself. The enormous ruby that was set into the hilt glowed as if in expectation. The weapon had been a gift from his uncle, the Duke of Etienne, on the day he had earned his knighthood. The sword had protected Gaston against many enemies and he sent up a quick prayer for his good fortune to continue.

Hubert stepped forward cautiously, surprisingly agile for one so large. Gaston took his right side and Pierre his left, the other knights closing in behind, ready for battle.

The inside of the building was dark after the brightness outside. Gaston blinked rapidly, trying to see through the gloom, all the while ready for whatever might await him. After a few moments his vision cleared and he stood up straight, slowly lowering his sword to his side.

The hall was a long room with a high ceiling. The fire pit burned at the center of the chamber, in the Saxon fashion, the smoke escaping through a small hole in the ceiling. All the tables and benches had been cleared from the middle of the room to rest against the rough walls.

At the far end of the hall were the people of the keep, all crowded together in a little huddle. Their faces, which were turned toward the fifteen knights, were filled with fear and loathing.

Suddenly, into the stillness, a rumbling sound burst from the depths of Hubert's chest, a great guffaw of laughter that filled the room. "And these are the Saxons you would have me believe are so brave and cunning, Gaston? Look at them there," he pointed a thick finger. "They run like frightened children rather than defending their home, as real men would do."

A slight, feminine figure stepped forward from the crowd before Gaston could comment. An older woman moved to stop her by placing a hand on her arm, to no avail.

All thoughts of his brother's opinion of the Saxons flew from Gaston's mind. His attention was centered on the woman approaching them. She was little more than a maid. Her fair skin was smooth and the color of cream. Deliberately she came, her head held high on her slender neck. The hem of her forest-green gown brushed the sweet-smelling rushes on the floor with a gentle swishing sound that reminded him of the wind in autumn leaves. The heavy fabric of the gown clung to her full breasts and narrow hips. A belt of silver links hung about her waist, emphasizing its smallness. Wisps of bright hair, the color of a chestnut mare's coat, curled around her face and a thick braid hung down her back to her hips, swaying behind her as she moved toward them with unconsciously sensual grace.

Gaston felt a stirring warmth in his loins as his gaze lingered on the gentle sway of her hips. She came to a halt before him, sweeping the floor in a deep curtsy. At the same time, she looked down and tilted her head forward, only enough for the barest of civility. When she raised her head to face the menacing knights, Gaston saw a flicker of fear in her gaze, but only for a moment before she conquered her terror and her eyes flashed bright green defiance.

Admiration for such a brave spirit swept over Gaston even as he acknowledged to himself that his physical reaction to her was startling in its intensity. He felt his heart begin to pump hard and fast against his chest in reaction to this little beauty. Such a mixture of loveliness and strength of character would be a prize well worth having.

"And who might you be, damsel?" Hubert asked, startling Gaston back to reality. Hubert sheathed his sword in an action of calculated indifference.

"I am Rose of Carlisle," her voice rang out firm and sure in the vastness of the hall.

Gaston, remembering he still held his own weapon in his hands, returned it with practiced ease to its scabbard.

Hubert's gaze raked the young woman before him with scorn. "Well, Rose of Carlisle, I am your new lord, Hubert de Thorne." Hubert took a step toward her, folding his arms across his massive chest. His chin jutted out proudly as he gazed down at her, awaiting her reaction to his statement.

She stood her ground and tilted her head back to glare up at the towering giant. "By whose order?"

As Hubert bent over the fragile form of the girl, his eyes were hard as granite on hers and Gaston wanted to reach out and pull his brother away. Instead he clenched his teeth, his hands curling into fists; this was not his affair. He had no right. The woman was nothing to him.

"By the order of His Majesty, William the Conqueror, who rules by divine right, I have come to take these lands—" he made a sweeping gesture "—and you with them."

Gaston felt a twinge of pain at these words, but he gave no hint of this. It was ludicrous for him to be thinking this way. If he needed a woman he would have no problem in finding one. Even the Saxon women he had come into contact with had been eager enough to share his bed.

Deliberately casual, he crossed his arms over his chest, his features an unreadable granite mask.

"What do you mean, Sir Knight? I am a freeborn woman. Surely not even William would enslave freeborn gentlewomen."

Gaston could see the erratic beating of the pulse in her long slender throat. No matter that he told himself he was a fool, he had a sudden urge to put his lips to the spot and feel for himself the pounding of her blood; to claim this woman as his own before them all.

For the first time in his twenty-seven years, Gaston found himself feeling jealousy over a woman.

Now he very much regretted declining William's offer of properties. But what matter, he reminded himself bluntly, the lands would have meant nothing if this woman came not with them.

"I mean I have been instructed to take you to wife, along with claiming the lands that have been awarded to me," Hubert said in answer to her query. He smiled thinly, seemingly gratified that he had beaten the girl when she shrank away from him with a quickly indrawn breath. He nodded his head in satisfaction.

Her hand fluttered to her breast and Gaston's ensnared gaze followed. He blinked, reminding himself that his thoughts had strayed where they dare not go. By order of the king, this woman would be his brother's wife. It was a cardinal sin for him to think of her in this way.

Rose recovered her composure quickly. "Good sir, you have a strange manner of greeting. You near frightened the serfs to death. Have you a purpose for behaving this way?" She stared up at him, unafraid, a slight frown marring her delicate brow.

Hubert scowled down at her fiercely. "What right have you to question me, wench? I am lord here and I will do as I see fit. If you must know—" his strong teeth showed in another smile that did not reach his eyes "—I wanted to test the mettle of my new holders. I fear I found them lacking."

"In what way have you found us lacking, my lord?" she asked, holding his eyes with her own. Her voice was loud enough to be heard by all and, yet, controlled.

Gaston wondered if this slip of a girl could make Hubert see what a fierce spirit burned inside the defeated Saxons. Never had he seen a woman who did not cower before his brother's anger. He was hard-pressed to keep up his pose of indifference.

Contrary to Gaston's hopes, Rose's defiance only served to infuriate Hubert further, his scowling countenance darkening to blackest thunder. His brows pulled together in a straight line over his nose and his lips curled in an expression of rage. "In every way!" he bellowed.

Raising her chin even higher, Rose gazed up at the fearsome knight, refusing to be intimidated.

Watching her, it was hard for Gaston to imagine any queen being more regal.

Hubert raised a clenched fist, sputtering in his wrath.

Acting on instinct, with no thought in mind save protecting her, Gaston stepped to the fore. "I am Gaston de Thorne." A faint scent of wildflowers came to him and he wanted to breathe in her nearness. But he made himself go on without pause. "Know you not that you should have a guard posted at all times? The gate was left open when we arrived with no one to mark our coming. This is a dangerous time to treat security with such contempt." He took her arm, turning her to face him in the hope of preventing her from further provoking Hubert. Her defiance would only end in disaster; Gaston had seen his brother lose his temper before.

Rose looked up at Gaston in irritation, then became still as her eyes locked on his for a moment that seemed to hang suspended in time. He felt a tightness in his chest as the others faded, leaving only the two of them, their eyes, their souls, held in silent communication. Then her lids drooped down and she took a deep breath, letting it out slowly on a sigh. When she opened her eyes again, her gaze was clear and Gaston could almost believe he had imagined the look of wonder he had seen there.

"There was no one at the gate," she said stiffly, "because we were all busy preparing for your arrival." Was Gaston mistaken, or was her voice a little more breathless now? "We had not expected you for most of another hour. It was also reported that you were a much larger party." Her gaze swept over the knights.

"You knew an army was approaching and you busied yourselves to make a welcome for us?" Hubert asked, incredulous at what he considered their stupidity.

Her tone was antagonistic. "What would you have us do, resist you so you would have some excuse to put our men to the sword and our homes to the torch?" She jerked away from Gaston and folded her arms over her chest. She stared up at the two towering knights with contempt in her lovely eyes.

So, Gaston thought, the girl was clever as well as beautiful. Her words made sense. But while he admired her mettle, he knew she had gone too far.

Gaston's mother, Marie de Thorne had made certain her sons were schooled in the ways of chivalry, even Hubert and Leo, the eldest, who were not hers by birth. Gentlewomen were to be honored and protected.

But this... this was too much. If Rose of Carlisle did not cease in her defiance of him, Hubert would be forced to chasten her. His honor before his men would demand it.

"You speak without thinking," Gaston warned quietly, attempting to forestall her. He could not bear to see Rose punished even as he understood his brother's need to do so.

"I speak without thinking?" Rose put her hands on her hips. "It is you Normans who have acted without thinking."

Before Gaston could react, Hubert's hand snaked out to connect with the soft flesh of her cheek. The sound of the contact shattered the stillness of the hall and left a silence more deafening than any noise.

Chapter Two

Reeling from the force of the blow and the shock that coursed through her system, Rose stumbled. She would have fallen had not Gaston reached out and caught her to him. Even in her dazed state, Rose sensed the protection and comfort he offered.

The moment Gaston had stepped forward, her world had tilted crazily, refusing to right itself as she gazed up into grey eyes that held all the cool mystery of a morning mist. His face could have been chiseled from marble, so perfect were his features, with a straight nose and sensual lips that drew her eyes. A lock of raven-black hair fell across his forehead in a stubborn curl that made this powerful man seem somehow vulnerable in her sight. She felt this even though her head reached no higher than his wide shoulders and he stood before her, garbed in mail, his weapons hanging from his belt.

She tried to still the shaking in her limbs and failed. No one, other than her mother, had ever struck her. Rose put her hand to her burning cheek, feeling the hot sting of tears well up behind her lids. She blinked, refusing to cry before these Norman savages.

The temptation to yield to the safe haven offered by Gaston's encircling arms was great. Some inner sense told her she could lean on this man and trust him to care for her, care for her people.

But she couldn't allow herself this luxury; she knew her instincts about the man holding her could not be right. He, or one of his kind, was responsible for her father's death. He was her enemy, a Norman.

And the huge hulking beast who had struck her claimed her for his own. It was upon him she must center her thoughts. Rose looked up at Gaston, who stood so close she could see the coarseness of the stubble that grew along his strong jaw. The observation was disturbingly intimate, and she felt the hairs prickle on the back of her neck. *I am behaving and thinking like a fool,* she told herself reproachfully.

Gathering what little strength she could summon, Rose tried to push herself away from him.

Automatically he reacted by tightening his hold of her. Gaston felt an uncomfortable stab of bitterness at her rejection. But his heart softened when he looked down, taking in her glazed expression and the red print darkening on her cheek.

Hubert was beginning to sputter and Gaston knew he could not protect her for much longer. He looked about them for some kind of distraction. If Hubert could be diverted for a moment his temper would cool. Over Rose's shoulder he took note that a woman had left the group at the other end of the hall and was coming toward them.

It was the same woman who had attempted to keep Rose from coming forward when they had arrived. Her round bulk tottered toward them with delicate mincing steps.

Leaning over the girl with a gentle squeeze of her shoulders, Gaston whispered a vehement admonition, so low that no one else could hear. "Know you that Hubert has killed strong men with one blow. If he had meant to harm you, you would have fared far worse than you have. My brother had no choice but to chastise you. You goaded him before his men." Gaston kept his tone gruff in the hope of making her see reason. Rose must not defy Hubert further, for her own well being. "Now, woman, hold your tongue."

Gaston glanced at Hubert, whose lips were puckered in anger. Why, he asked himself, was he protecting this girl? The chit was nothing to him. Until a few short moments ago he had never seen her. It was not as if she were the most beautiful woman he had ever beheld. Oh, she was lovely enough, but there was something else that drew him to her. Mayhap it was the unquenchable essence of courage he sensed in her. Gaston did not know. He only knew that he felt compelled to protect her, even from his brother.

More loudly, so the others could hear, Gaston reprimanded, "What mean you, damsel, to speak so to your lord?" Belying the harshness of his words, Gaston's thumb moved soothingly over the smooth skin of her collarbone.

Rose looked up with a jolt of surprise at the intimate touch. Why was she allowing this man who was her enemy to hold her in this way?

Somehow she knew that the strength to stand on her own must come from inside herself. Anger rose from her stomach like soured wine. It was directed toward herself for her weakness and toward the man who held her, for having witnessed her humiliation. The anger gave her courage and she pulled away, drawing herself up straighter. Rose felt the arms supporting her loosen, albeit with seeming reluctance, and the tall knight stepped away from her, his gaze warning her to caution.

Why had he come to her aid? Even as she hated him for who he was, her eyes searched his compelling grey ones. Then she frowned, disgusted with herself. She cared not why the Norman had helped her. Rose wanted nothing from him or any other Norman. These men had ridden into Carlisle, flaunting their dominance and terrorizing her people.

When the Normans had first entered the hall, Rose had known real fear for the first time. The huge knights in their full chain mail had caused fear to claw its way to her throat in a silent scream.

But she had gone forward, had forced herself to confront their leader, though her heart pounded so loudly she
was sure it could be heard by all.

"My poor lamb."

Rose heard Maida's voice behind her, tinged with derision that was directed at Hubert de Thorne. She turned to
the cook quickly, thinking to forestall her from saying more.
She did not wish for Maida to suffer for coming to her aid.
Taking the plump hand that Maida held out to her, Rose
squeezed it gently. "I am fine."

Maida raised her other hand and brushed at the fine ten-
drils of hair that fell across Rose's cheek. "Luckily the skin
has not been broken," she clucked.

Looking up, Rose found the knight Gaston watching her
with dark eyes. She turned away abruptly, rejecting his attention.

Rose realized that she must force herself to think clearly.
Somehow she must try to right any damage done by her defiance. Hubert's anger would ill serve her people.

She gave Maida's hand one more squeeze for reassurance
and released it. Rose knew what she had to do. She need not
feel herself above the things she asked of her villeins.

Hubert shifted impatiently, all this dallying was making
him restless. He was not accustomed to accepting defiance
from anyone, least of all a slip of a girl. A grunt of irritation sounded in his throat and he moved to stand between
Rose and Gaston. Must he do more to show the wench that
he meant to make her obey him? He looked down at her and
his eyes took on a licentious gleam as they roved over the
luscious curves of her young body. Once he had gained
control over this and the other two fiefs he had been
granted, he would see this wench wed and well bedded.

Unaware of Hubert's thoughts, Rose took a deep breath
to compose herself, then gathered the skirt of her gown in
her hands and sank down into a deep curtsy to her lord. This
time her eyes remained discreetly lowered and her head tilted
humbly on her neck. The thick rope of auburn hair fell

across her shoulder to brush the rushes on the floor. "My lord," she said slowly, "forgive me for my insolence. My concern for my people made me foolish and I spoke without thinking." Once the words were out, Rose had to bite her lip to keep from decrying them. It went against everything in her to abase herself before this Norman.

Hubert seemed surprised by the sudden change in her demeanor but did not disguise his approval, even though he scowled down at her for a moment longer. Puffing out his chest and taking his leisure, he walked around her slender form. Having completed the circle, he stopped, spread his feet wide and put his hands on his hips as he studied her.

Watching the man's feet, Rose could not help thinking that he was a much larger and more feral version of the rooster that strode though the yard, lording it over the hens. Well, this man would find out that she was no hen to be ordered about at his command. Hubert de Thorne would see what she was made of.

At last he spoke. "Rise then, Rose of Carlisle. We will make an attempt to forget this beginning and start afresh, as long as you are willing to keep your tongue in check from now on."

She rose gracefully to stand before him, her hands clasped together and her eyes downcast. She was the picture of meek obedience.

Feeling the power of his gaze, Rose flicked a glance toward Gaston. He was watching her intently, his eyes narrowed. Rose had the feeling that he was not fooled by her act of being well chastened. She thought she saw a glimmer of warning in the cool depths of his eyes, and her chin tilted haughtily before she looked away.

It was well she turned her attention back to Hubert. Gaston's admiring reaction to the gesture would only have unsettled her more.

"Methinks I am most pleased with Carlisle," Hubert told her with a condescending smile. "I hope the other two fiefs I have been granted yield me as much."

"Other fiefs?" Rose asked.

"Mayhill and Brentwood. I must be about claiming all my property without delay."

Rose felt the blood drain from her face. Not Brentwood! Her cousin Robert was thane at Brentwood and he hated the Normans with a passion unequaled. When Robert had come from Hastings with news of her father's death, he had told Rose he would not rest while Brentwood was taken, no matter what the cost.

Robert's sister, Elspith, and his mother, Iris, would be terrified, even though they had Robert to guide them. Rose could only pray that Robert would not bring harm upon them in his fight to resist the Normans. Neither of them were strong. Especially her aunt Iris, who was a helpless and ineffectual woman.

And Elspith—Elspith was Rose's closest friend. Although the girl was older than her by two years, Rose had always felt that she must look after her gently reared cousin. While Rose had been climbing trees and trailing after Edmund and Robert, her cousin had been choosing ribbons and laces to adorn the many gowns her father bought for her.

Rose could only pray Robert had taken them away from Brentwood, though she knew he had not. It was not in her cousin's nature to accept the Norman rule. Her one hope was to get a message to him. Mayhap he would listen to reason.

Looking up into Hubert's arrogant face, Rose did not know how she was going to help her cousins, or for that matter, herself. She felt hope draining from her like the color from boiling beets.

How could she bring herself to marry this Norman? The very thought was repulsive to her. He had already shown himself to be cruel and totally uncaring toward her and her people.

Rose fought hard against the panic that threatened; fought hard and won. For the moment. She would do what she must. Her vow to her people would not be broken.

Dear Lord, she cried silently, *what is to become of us?*

Looking around herself, Rose could hardly believe that only seven days had passed. The entire atmosphere of her home had changed. The quiet activity of the courtyard had become a bustling hive of energy. Everyone went about their tasks with added vigor, from the villeins who came and went, down to the meanest serf. Hubert's presence seemed to goad them into doing more than they had ever done before. It was as if they must show him what they were made of, thus bringing him down from the heights of his contempt.

Rose felt only resentment for Hubert's ambitions, though she had to admit he expected no less of his own men. There were always several soldiers in the area of the yard that had been set up for arms practice. Even Hubert and Gaston spent as much time as they could honing their skills. The air was rarely clear of the metallic clash of sword against sword or shield. And often Rose would hear a grunt of pain when a man did not react quite as fast as his opponent.

If Gaston drove himself just as diligently as Hubert, it was because he chose to do so. He answered to no one, and Hubert's men obeyed Gaston as if he were Hubert.

The two of them were everywhere about the fief. They spent long hours talking with the farmers about the soils and with the tradespeople about their goods. They passed their evenings in the Great Hall with Alfred, the reeve, going over the accounts.

Clearly the Normans did not wish to ruin Carlisle, but this did not lessen Rose's animosity toward them.

Rose could not think of Hubert as a husband or of their impending marriage with anything but dread. Fortunately, he was too busy to expend even a small portion of his time in wooing her. Just thinking of him made her limbs quake and her throat too dry for speech.

To make matters worse, when she closed her eyes at night, it was a pair of black-lashed, misty grey eyes that filled her thoughts and kept her tossing and turning into the night.

In the courtyard, on the training field, in the Great Hall, her gaze would find him. There was no use denying that there was something in the tall slender knight that drew her, just as Hubert repelled her.

For his part, Gaston appeared not to be aware of her; for this, Rose was thankful. It would have been beyond bearing to have him know how she watched him.

As she stood in the courtyard and studied the scene of almost frenzied activity before her, Rose knew that by swearing to help her people, she had taken upon herself more than she had ever imagined.

Then, over the usual din, she heard the guard at the gate shout out a challenge. One of Hubert's first commands had been that a man be stationed there at all times.

She hurried across the courtyard, curious to find out who the arrival might be.

Immediately Rose recognized Will, one of the serfs from Brentwood. The mare he rode was lathered as though she had been pressed hard, and Will slumped in the saddle, his breath coming quickly through parted lips.

Rose ran the last few steps as he swayed. She reached up her arms to help him to the ground even as she heard the men from the practice field come running across the green toward them.

"Lady Rose," Will panted, "I have come from Sir Pierre, the knight who Lord de Thorne sent to Brentwood. He instructed me to deliver this message." He reached inside his jerkin and pulled out a rolled parchment.

Without giving herself time to think, Rose took the missive and hurriedly pushed it up the sleeve of her gown. The furtive action was completed none too quickly, as the foot soldiers arrived to see what was happening.

"Is something amiss here?" asked a short bulky man with thinning grey hair that grew in thick tufts about his ears.

Rose recognized him as Fontour, Hubert's master-at-arms. He squatted down beside her on his short muscular legs.

"No, nothing is wrong," Rose answered hastily, feeling the scratch of the parchment on her arm. "This man has ridden hard from Brentwood with a message for Lord de Thorne. Since both he and Sir Gaston have gone out to inspect the fields I suggest that we let Will rest and have something to eat before he is questioned."

Fontour stared into Will's pale face for a moment. He rose with the grace of an acrobat and shrugged his wide shoulders.

Rose looked down to hide her relief. Helping Will to his feet, she led him to the Great Hall.

After making sure he was served both food and wine, Rose went to the far end of the hall and sank down onto a bench facing the doorway.

Quickly Rose took out the roll of precious paper; to her surprise it wasn't even sealed.

She unrolled the parchment with shaking fingers. The message was short and succinct. It requested that Hubert send troops to the village of Brentwood, as a band of Saxons were raiding the fief at regular intervals and none of the villagers would give any clue as to who the renegades might be. Sir Pierre felt that the villagers' attitude made it clear that they were protecting someone.

She knew that the raiders could only be led by her cousin Robert. His hatred of the conquerors would surely end in his death. Her frustration with Robert knew no bounds. It was one thing for him to risk his own life, but what of his mother and Elspith?

Soon after arriving at Carlisle, Sir Pierre had gone to Brentwood as Hubert's agent. His reports told them that neither the young lord nor his family were to be found.

Until now, Rose had held out a faint hope that Robert had escaped to Scotland or Wales with his mother and sister. But he had not. Robert meant to thwart the Normans at every turn.

Rose had a deep-seated hatred of futility. When people lived close to the land as her family had, they learned that energy was best spent in producing something—crops, cloth, meat. What Robert was doing could come to no good.

When Robert was caught—which he surely would be—would his mother and Elspith be taken with him? Would Hubert be cruel enough to sentence them to the same fate as Robert? Rose could not but believe it would be so. She was certain Hubert would be merciless in his desire to utterly dominate those under him. It mattered not that they were innocent women who had taken no willing part in what they did. Rose shut her eyes and offered up a fervent prayer that wherever the two women were they would be safe from harm. Surely God could not allow them to suffer for Robert's mistakes.

Hubert was a man to be feared by all, including herself. If he found out Rose had taken the parchment, he would strike like a bird or prey, punishing her with calculated indifference. She, like any of his other subjects, was to be brought to heel with all possible speed.

Going to where Will was seated, Rose bent over him. "Are you feeling a little more rested now?" she asked in a tone that was loud enough to be overheard by those near. At the same time, under the guise of her concern, Rose took the roll of parchment from her sleeve and passed it back to him. Leaning even closer, she whispered, "Do you have any idea how Robert might be reached?"

Will gave no sign that he had heard, just sat there, looking as if he wished for her to leave him in peace. Then he nodded, so quickly that unless someone was watching him closely they wouldn't have noticed.

A soft sigh of relief escaped her lips. "Tell him then that what he is doing is sheer folly. If he has no care for himself, then he must surely think of his mother and Elspith. They do not deserve to live the life of outlaws."

From behind her came an unmistakable deep voice. "Lady Rose."

Gaston.

Rose's heart jumped with a sickening jolt. She had no idea what conclusions Gaston might have drawn from her quiet conversation with Will. She had returned the message with little time to spare.

He went on. "I was told a messenger had arrived from Brentwood."

She whirled around to face him, anxiety making her uncommonly sharp. "Sir Knight, must you always creep about?"

His black brows arched upward, and he looked down at her with amusement. "Damsel, I do not creep. Were you not otherwise occupied, you would have heard my approach."

Rose flushed, then raised her chin. She had once heard her father tell Edmund that it was best to get the enemy on the defensive. She answered him boldly to hide her agitation. "We did not expect your return until evening. Did Hubert send his toady to spy upon me?"

Gaston's lips tightened and he turned to Will. "You are the messenger?"

At Will's nod he made an abrupt gesture. "Go."

Will lost no time in obeying.

Gaston moved toward Rose, forcing her up against the table. When he stopped, her position of leaning backward was uncomfortable at best. His gaze moved slowly over her face, then down the line of her throat. Only the tightness in his jaw betrayed his reaction to her insult. "My horse threw a shoe. I am no man's toady."

She knew he spoke the truth, but deep inside she was secretly gladdened at ruffling his damnable self-possession. "You leap like a frightened fawn at his every whim."

When Gaston's grey eyes began to twinkle with mirth, she knew she had gone too far. The comparison was completely ludicrous. Chagrined, she bit her lower lip.

He bent closer, smiling. "You prick me, little Rose, with your words."

His breath was warm on her face, and her heartbeat doubled. She put her hands on the tabletop to keep herself from toppling backward. "Nay, Sir Knight. It is you Thornes who prick me till I bleed."

The pun was well aimed, and Gaston's expression showed his appreciation of her cleverness. But he was not going to allow her to get the best of him. His gaze moved over her with leisurely admiration.

With his index finger he traced the curve of her cheek, and she thought she must surely faint from lack of breath. Rose closed her eyes to block out the sight of his too-compelling eyes.

He whispered, "You speak so vehemently, little one. You may choose to offer up your blood most willingly. Great pleasure can be gained in the sacrifice."

Her body flushed with unbearable heat, and her eyes flew open. The soft words brought intimate images of herself and Gaston. To cover her confusion, she replied with outrage. "That is something you will never know, Norman."

Recoiling as if she had struck him, Gaston moved back. "I but spoke of my brother. Forgive me, if I led you to believe otherwise."

As he turned away, striding to the door, Rose wondered who he was trying to convince—her, or himself.

Later that same day, Hubert summoned Rose to the guest bower. She found him seated in a chair before the empty hearth. Gaston stood at his side.

She had not been here since the two men had taken up residence. Every available surface was covered with some sort of weapon or piece of armor. The bed closest to the fire was unmade. The other bed was neat, the furs pulled straight, a black cape folded across the foot. She recognized the cape as belonging to Gaston.

Her gaze came to rest on the sheet of parchment in Hubert's hand. It was the message Will had brought from Brentwood.

Rose was intensely aware of Gaston. Her tongue flicked out to moisten her dry lips. Had Gaston seen her give the message back to Will? Why had he not challenged her then? She grasped her hands together to still their trembling, telling herself they knew nothing.

But she couldn't meet Gaston's gaze with her own, sure he would read her guilt.

Hubert reread the letter with a thoughtful frown, then handed it to Gaston.

"Your decision is made?" Gaston asked, scanning the page.

"I must go to Brentwood," Hubert answered. He stood and leaned over Gaston's shoulder, his gaze running over the words on the page once again. "The situation warrants my personal attention."

This brought no real fear for her family. Rose knew Robert could easily stay out of Hubert's reach with his knowledge of the area around Brentwood. Hubert was of no immediate threat to Robert. It would be some time before he knew the countryside well enough to have much chance of capturing her wily cousin.

It was the deprivations of living in the forest that gave Rose cause for concern. How long could her aunt Iris and cousin Elspith manage? Rose did have a plan, but first Will must take her message to Robert. Only if she met Robert face-to-face could she hope to convince him.

Rose carefully kept her expression blank when Hubert raised his eyes to her face. He watched her intently for a moment, then he said, "Lady, would you be so good as to see that enough food is packed for myself and fourteen of my men to last us several days?"

Relief flooded through her. He did not know she had read the letter. "Of course, my lord," Rose answered, tipping her head forward slightly. Hubert nodded back absently, dismissing her. Rose turned to walk away.

"Several days?" she heard Gaston ask, as her heart sang at the thought of Hubert's departure. "Would it be wise for so many of us to be gone for several days?'' Her steps lagged. Cautiously she looked back at the men, hoping Gaston would not try to convince Hubert to remain at Carlisle. The scowl on the elder brother's face heartened her.

Hubert would do as he pleased, just as he always did. For once, Rose could find no fault in her intended husband's stubborn ways.

With quickened steps, Rose went out into the sunshine in search of Maida. The cook would be invaluable in helping her to prepare for Hubert's journey.

When Rose had gone, Hubert turned to his brother. "You will not be going with me, Gaston."

Gaston quirked a brow as his lips turned upward in irony. Though he knew Rose's accusation of the morning to be a falsehood, Hubert's manner rankled. There was a hint of steel in his tone. "I will not be going with you? Since when have you decided where I will or will not go?"

Hubert glanced up, surprised. "I meant not to give you an order. I but think of the most practical plan."

Gaston made no reply, feeling ridiculous for having taken umbrage. It was just Hubert's way to say things plainly. Both of them knew the younger man was free to come and go as he pleased. The fact was, Gaston knew he did not want to be alone with Rose.

Over the days they had been at Carlisle, Gaston had willingly worked himself to exhaustion, hoping that this would rid his dreams of a shadowy form cloaked only in a glorious auburn mane. The hazy figure in his dreams could have been any red-haired woman. But the eyes were those of the Lady of Carlisle, long lashed and green as jade. The winsome expression in them turned his blood to liquid flame.

Even now he had to force his attention to what Hubert was saying as the erotic vision fired his senses.

"I believe our purpose would be best served if you were to remain at Carlisle." Rhythmically Hubert tapped his lips as he thought for a moment. "I trust that wench not one jot.

She seems over clever to me. It would not do to have her here for long without supervision."

"God's blood!" Gaston exclaimed, allowing anger to act as his shield. He clenched his hands into fists at his sides. He did not mean to remain at Carlisle. "The woman was in charge of the whole fief before we arrived a week ago. I trust she would manage quite well for a few days." He braced his long legs wide apart and glared at his brother.

Obviously misunderstanding the reason for Gaston's anger, Hubert said, "I know that acting the lord was not what you had in mind for yourself, else you would have accepted the king's offered reward, as I did. I am well aware of how capable Lady Rose is, but I do not want her to think she will be given the authority she once had. From what I have learned from the reeve, Alfred, she has been responsible for more than she should be. Why, that little woman could likely give us inventory on every commodity in this fief. Were it not for her fear of reprisals on her people, I would not trust the very food I take from the table. For a maiden she is far too forward for her own good." He eyed Gaston sagely.

"That may be so, Hubert, but I have no wish to sit here coddling a female. I can go to Brentwood in your stead. She is, after all, your intended bride." The muscle in his jaw flexed with the effort it cost him to speak normally.

He couldn't stay here alone with the Lady of Carlisle, not for a week, not for a day. He was far too susceptible to her magic. She had only to look at him and his pulse quickened.

Hubert shook his head. "I must find these rebels myself. They will know that I am no man to sit back and let others act as my strength."

"Would it not be just as effective a lesson if I brought the culprits here to you?" Gaston said, trying to be reasonable.

"It will not serve." Hubert thumped the wall with his fist. "And beyond that," his tone grew wistful, "I will be the

man tied to this place for life. When you grow tired of playing the lord, you may follow where your fancy leads."

Gaston frowned. He had no wish to burn so Hubert could
have one last taste of freedom. If Gaston hadn't been so
disturbed, he would have thought this situation amusing
indeed. Hubert was now balking at his domesticity, when
Gaston, who had wanted his freedom, could only envy his
older brother. He countered, "Leave one of the other
knights."

"Who?" Hubert scowled. "Pierre is at Brentwood and
Gerard is at Mayhill. Besides, you are the most knowledge-
able among us as far as building the wall is concerned. You
know William himself suggested we begin work immediately, if we found the fortifications here lacking. I, for one,
do not feel secure with this hovel of wood and plaster to
guard us against enemies. The only sensible precaution the
former Lord of Carlisle took was to build the escape tunnel
under the back of the palisade." Hubert gave a disparaging
laugh. "At least then they could run."

Hubert's superior manner rankled, but Gaston made no
comment. If he continued to resist Hubert's plans, he
needed to offer some better arguments than the ones thus
far.

Under any other circumstances he might have stayed
gladly. The week he had spent at Carlisle had taught him he
would adapt readily to the role of lord. It gave him great
satisfaction to see the changes they had made at Carlisle
beginning to work.

But his satisfaction in the work faded into the back-
ground when compared with the overpowering reality of his
growing desire for Rose.

Gaston stiffened his broad shoulders. He would not be
bested by something so trivial as lust for a woman. He ignored the ache near his heart at the use of such a term for his
feeling toward Rose.

What Hubert asked of him was not illogical. He would be
the one responsible for maintaining authority when Gaston

had gone. Even as he acknowledged Hubert's reasonings, Gaston's nod was hesitant as he looked into his brother's penetrating gaze.

As Hubert clapped him on the back, Gaston tried to convince himself the arrangement would not be so difficult. He would simply avoid her. Carlisle was a spacious property.

Chapter Three

Rose wavered at the entrance to the Great Hall, seeing all
the folk gathered for the evening meal.

Since the previous afternoon, when Hubert had instructed her to make arrangements for his trip, she had
barely had time to think, let alone partake of any food. She
wanted nothing to delay Hubert's departure. In his impatience to go to Brentwood, Hubert and his men had traveled ahead of the wagons. Rather than stay at the keep, the
Norman meant to place himself in the midst of the raiders'
own domain.

The aroma of savory stew and fresh bread drifted to her,
and the answering pang in her stomach decided her. Going
to one of the benches placed beside the trestle tables, Rose
wearily sank down.

The room was abuzz with chatter, and Rose took note that
the faces around her seemed more cheered than they had for
quite some time. No doubt everyone was as heartened by
Hubert's absence as she.

At least she should have felt heartened. But the events of
the day had conspired against her. As soon as Hubert had
ridden through the gate, leaving her anything but downcast, things had begun to go awry. The jam had boiled over,
a dog had upset a pot of wool that was being dyed, and
Maida had found weevils in a barrel of flour.

Even though she was tired, hungry and discouraged, her eyes scanned the room with a strange mixture of yearning and despair. If she were honest with herself, she must admit the greatest portion of her reluctance to enter the hall had stemmed from knowing Gaston would be here.

Their day's responsibilities had kept them apart, but she knew neither her own duties nor Gaston's work on the stone wall could keep them separated indefinitely.

Her hand brushed idly against the fine wool of her skirt and she looked down. The lilac underdress and fine white tunic were among her best. Spent as she was, she had changed for the meal after telling herself the clean garments would freshen her. She let out a heavy sigh, knowing there was no use lying to herself. Never had she worn this gown for Hubert.

Silently Rose cursed herself. She should not have come here tonight. Her exhaustion made her vulnerable, and she had not the strength to resist her fascination for the handsome knight.

When Hubert was present, he insisted that she sit beside him and share his trencher, as was the Norman custom. Thus far, Rose had not opposed this, for it had given her an opportunity to listen to the men's conversations. And since most of the talk at table concerned Carlisle and its people, she had been content to do as Hubert bid.

Now that Hubert was gone, she could return to dining with the other women, in the Saxon way.

The sound of male voices drew her attention and stayed her action. The sight of Gaston leading a group of men into the room held her gaze captive. His hands shaped the air around him as he spoke, emphasizing his words, and the ebony curl had fallen forward on his brow. He was so tall that he stood half a head higher than the other men and his wide shoulders dwarfed theirs, yet none came close to matching the easy grace of his movements.

Rose closed her eyes, shutting out the sight of him, telling herself he was a Norman. But, even as she hated him for what he was, some force inside her drove her to this terrible...wonderful awareness of him. She longed for those eyes, so clear and deep, to look at her as they had the first morning, to see inside her and find the place where she was all giving, all woman. That moment had been so brief but so compelling it had changed her for all time.

She was unable to look away as he strode across the room, his short tunic exposing the strong muscles of his legs as he moved. He was confident and sure, but without any of the vainglorious self-importance that Hubert often displayed. Why, sweet Jesus, if she must marry a Norman, why could it not have been this one?

Rose gasped softly at the traitorous path of her own thoughts. What matter which one she was bound to? she asked herself angrily. Neither was any better than the other. They were both warriors who cared only for their own gains.

She must remember to whom her loyalty belonged. Her own wise, courageous and noble father was dead because of these invaders. Her father had taught her how important it was to live with duty and honor. He was the one by which she measured every other man. Never could she let herself forget that.

At that moment, Gaston threw back his head and laughed, exposing the strong, tanned column of his throat. His laughter was a deep rich sound that vibrated pleasurably along her nerve ends. And even as her conscious mind denounced Gaston, her heart began to beat a little faster as her body reacted to him in its own way.

She watched as he went to the head table with Sir Jean and Sir Eustace, two of the three knights Hubert had left at Carlisle. The men took their places as they continued to talk, Gaston settling himself in Hubert's accustomed seat.

Feeling that she was too conspicuous in her present position, Rose began to make her way to the women's tables.

"Lady?"

There was no mistaking his low-timbred voice and Rose stopped. Without turning to face him, she answered, "Yes, Sir Gaston."

"Will you not join us for the meal?"

"I thought to leave you to the company of your friends," she answered softly, turning around to face him. Gaston was standing so close that she had to look up to face him, and Rose took a step backward. She wondered how he could have come to her so quickly, so silently. Her eyes strayed over the wide expanse of his chest, resting for a moment on the few dark hairs that showed at the open edge of his tunic. A hint of pink stole over her cheeks and she hurriedly looked away.

"We would be grateful for your presence," he replied easily. His words were full of courtly grace, but his eyes were rainwater cool as he gazed down at her.

Rose realized everyone else was seated and waiting for her and Gaston to take their places. Now was not the time, with every eye upon them, to challenge his request.

Rose answered with a slight inclination of her head. "I accept your kind invitation, Sir Gaston."

He smiled politely, not meeting her gaze. "My thanks."

Rose turned and preceded him to the table, feeling all eyes on them as they made their way across the room. She kept her back straight, not wanting anyone to guess at the turmoil inside her. She had no idea how she could get through this meal at Gaston's side.

Rose took her usual seat next to Hubert's, acutely aware that it was not he who took the place at her side.

Gaston cut a slice of thick crusty bread with his knife. His movements were deft as he fashioned a trencher from the bread and ladled savory stew into it. This done, he leaned back and courteously waited for Rose to take her choice of meat.

She reached out with the little knife she used for eating and took a piece. Bringing the bit to her mouth, she nibbled at it with her even white teeth. The stew was delicious,

flavored with herbs from Rose's own garden. But even that
was not enough to rekindle the hunger that had deserted her
the moment Gaston had come into the hall. Her exhaustion
was replaced by a nervous kind of energy that tingled along
her spine, leaving her feeling edgy.

In her agitation, she didn't notice that Gaston was very
careful not to touch her in any way as he began to eat.

Every time Gaston turned toward her, he caught the scent
of wildflowers that lingered about her. He wondered at the
wisdom of insisting she dine with them, as Hubert would
wish, even as his eyes were drawn to her bright hair. It shone
with glossy vitality against the soft lilac of her gown. Fine
beads of perspiration appeared above his upper lip.

A serf came with two pitchers of wine. Rose poured from
the smaller one, which was watered; she needed all her wits
about her tonight.

Gaston took the larger jug and placed it on the table in
front of him, ignoring the serf's look of surprise as she went
to get more.

On previous nights, Sir Gaston had proved to be a very
moderate drinker, unlike some of the other Normans.

Sir Eustace and Sir Jean both hooted with laughter at
Gaston's action and shouted for the woman to hurry, then
ridiculed their friend for his boorishness in taking all for
himself.

"Don't forget you have much work to do on the wall tomorrow," Sir Eustace warned with a wink.

Gaston turned his cool gaze upon his friend. "I believe I
will prove equal to my responsibilities. I have drunk more
than this small amount—" he pointed to the pitcher "—and
still carried out my duties. Either of you have yet to see me
dragged aboard a ship because I was too ill to walk." He
nodded toward Sir Eustace with a narrow smile.

Sir Eustace turned a mottled red as Sir Jean guffawed
loudly and slapped him on the back. "He refers to the last
night we spent at Saint Valery." Jean pointed toward
Gaston. "The only reason you weren't getting thoroughly

drunk with the rest of us was that you had finally taken pity on the mayor's daughter and accepted her offer to—'' Jean's voice rose and he fluttered his stubby black lashes ''—'comfort a brave knight who might perish in the war.' ''

Gaston's smile faded and he scowled at the two of them. Now it was Eustace's turn to laugh.

As Sir Jean had begun his story, Rose's astonished gaze had flown to Gaston's face to gauge his reaction. Intense discomfiture played over his features as his friend spoke. She experienced a smug sense of satisfaction at seeing Gaston made uncomfortable. He always appeared to be so remote and in control of himself, while she had only to be near him to forget everything, even that he was her enemy.

But when Sir Jean had continued, speaking of the mayor's daughter, her enjoyment disappeared, to be replaced by a frown of displeasure. What did Sir Jean mean about Gaston taking pity on the girl? Was he so accustomed to women's attentions that they meant so little to him?

Her face flushed scarlet and she lowered her gaze as Gaston glanced down at her. She could not bring herself to look at him. Was that how he would see her? As one of the many who threw themselves at his feet? Her hands clenched into tight fists, the knuckles white as shame washed over her in a flood of self-recrimination. What a silly fool she was!

Her throat was dry with self-loathing and she felt the sharp prickle of tears behind her lowered lids. Rose reached forward to pick up her drinking horn hoping the wine might soothe her aching throat.

Gaston chose that same moment to spear a piece of meat with his knife, and their hands brushed together with the lightest of contacts, no more than the touch of two leaves brought together by a whisper of breeze.

Rose jerked away. The warm, firm flesh of his hand left an invisible circle of heat. A strange languidness traveled though her, settling low in her stomach. Rather than soothing, the sensation was oddly unnerving, and she shifted restlessly. Taking a deep breath, Rose looked up from under her lashes to see if Gaston had taken note of her agitation.

As her gaze met his, Rose drew in a sharp breath of surprise. Gaston's eyes were no longer cool. The misty orbs had darkened to smoke, and a hint of blue flame smoldered deep inside them like the hottest point of a fire. She sensed a hunger that shocked even as it thrilled her. Her heart beat with a quick rhythm that made her blood race in answer to his hunger. The urge to reach out and touch the smooth angles of his face was overwhelming. Rose reached toward him, her fingers spread in unwitting appeal.

Sensing her intent, Gaston moved his arm to block the motion, stretching his own hand toward the trencher of stew, as if that had been his only intention. Never could he allow her to show her feelings to anyone but himself. If Hubert came to believe Rose had betrayed him, he would be merciless.

Gaston's gentle gaze met hers, warning her to heed her actions.

Rose blinked and drew back, clasping her hands together in her lap. She ran her tongue over her dry lips and tried to slow the frantic beating of her heart.

Once again, as on that first day when he had helped her to stand after Hubert had hit her, Gaston had saved her from making a fool of herself.

She risked a quick glance toward Sir Jean and Sir Eustace. They were still telling stories of the time they had spent on the coast of Normandy before the invasion of England. Neither of them had taken note of what had passed between her and Gaston. She closed her lids for a moment in silent shame.

As if nothing had happened, Gaston went on speaking with his friends, adding his tales to theirs. Rose was amazed at how easily he joined in their light banter, while she was still struggling to gain control of her wayward emotions.

But Rose knew, no matter how well he was able to hide it, Gaston was not as indifferent to her as she had thought. Not that this knowledge was welcome to her. On the contrary. She knew it would now be even harder for her to hide her own feelings for him.

What her feelings were toward Gaston she wasn't sure. They were nothing she could put a name to. Hating him as she must because he was a Norman, and so her enemy, didn't seem to lessen her reactions to him in the least.

The rest of the meal passed in a daze, as exhaustion and despair overtook her. Never had she felt so wonderful—and wretched—as when she was with Gaston de Thorne.

She could not help comparing her life now with the way it had been the last time spring had graced the countryside with its bounty. Then she might have been tempted to linger in the Great Hall and listen to the talk of past battles and tales of the great Saxon heroes who had fought and sometimes died. If the people were fortunate, a passing bard might stop, on a warm summer evening, to sing for his supper. These nights were special and long remembered by all the people who would gather and listen to the minstrel's songs far into the night. If Rose had grown sleepy, her brother, Edmund, would have willingly offered a strong shoulder. Dear, beloved Edmund. How she missed him.

Now those days were gone forever, like so much flotsam. The Normans had taken everything from her, and this she could not forget or forgive, even if a pair of black-fringed eyes made her heart beat faster. Too much of herself was owed to the memory of those times past. She would steel herself against the Normans, especially the one who had begun to make her aware of herself as a woman.

Chapter Four

Gaston stood up and stretched his arms high over his head. His shoulders felt stiff from lifting the huge blocks of stone that would form the base of the new wall.

Looking up at the sun, he could see the day was fast approaching the noon hour. He grimaced just as a loud grumble came from his belly.

A wry smile touched his lips. What would the other men say if they knew he was dreading mealtime because of a girl-woman? Gaston shook his head at his own cowardice—he who had faced the fiercest warriors on the battlefield without flinching.

His knowledge of architecture tied him to the keep—and to Rose. If only his mother had not sent him to the monastery to become a priest, he would not be in his present predicament. As a boy in the friary he had become interested in building. When his aptitude for design had been discovered, he had even studied under the master, Father Rudolfo. Gaston had been well on his way to following in the old priest's footsteps when he learned his handsome face and reserved manner made him appealing to women.

Gaston had been only fifteen years old, and no saint. He could not resist what the women around him seemed so eager to provide. When the wife of a local count had offered him her all, he had not had the fortitude to refuse her.

When Gaston's activities were discovered, Father Rudolfo had realized the young man was not suited for the austere, scholarly life of a monk.

Thus, Gaston had been returned to the family estates to renew his prowess with weapons and warfare. As time passed, Gaston had never regretted not joining the priesthood; he was simply too fond of the world and its pleasures.

One pleasure in particular intrigued him—Rose of Carlisle. In her he saw none of the artifice that was so much a part of other women he had known. Her feelings were easy to read, be they good or bad.

Bending down, he set once more to the task he had appointed himself. There was no need for him to work among the men carrying the stones. The physical labor helped keep his mind from wandering to a pair of wide green eyes that sometimes flashed like lightning reflected in a dark forest pool.

He hefted a massive stone block from the wagon and carried it to the pile next to the working masons.

His actions last eve had been a mistake. His only thought as he insisted Rose dine with him and the other knights had been Hubert's wish that Rose become accustomed to the Norman ways. He had been careful not to show how deeply her very nearness affected him.

Just the touch of their two hands had been enough to make his senses spark with a sweet rush of heat.

He shook his head, trying to concentrate on his work. Gaston could only hope Hubert would not be gone long. Even a few days alone with Lady Rose would be a torturous test of his will.

"Sir Gaston!" shrilled a high voice.

Gaston straightened and put up a hand to shield his eyes from the glare of the sun. A young, stubby-legged boy was running full tilt down the hill from Carlisle. His round cheeks were flushed with effort as he puffed along.

As the child drew near to him, Gaston was unable to restrain a grin. "What is it, boy?"

The child came to a halt, panting. "The Lady Rose sent me to fetch you, sir."

A frown replaced Gaston's grin and the boy began to twist the front of his tunic in his chubby hands.

When he saw the apprehension on the child's face, Gaston's brow smoothed. He had not meant to frighten the child. The knight reached down and ruffled the shock of pale blond hair. "Did your lady deign to mention why she had need of me?"

The boy's words tumbled over one another in his nervousness as he answered. "Daniel, the farmer, has come with his daughter, Evelyn. I think he is angry." He stopped then, afraid to go any further about matters he didn't fully understand.

Why must Rose bother him with trifles? Gaston couldn't suppress a grunt of exasperation as he stepped over the low rim of stone and mortar that would be the wall.

As he strode up the gentle incline, his irritation began to cool. The damsel had done right in sending for him. Hubert was adamant in his belief that the people must be taught to come to himself or Gaston. When the farmer saw that Rose deferred to Gaston in this matter, he would come to him or Hubert in the future.

By the time Gaston entered the gate, he was feeling quite charitable toward Rose. However, he was surprised she was accepting her position so quickly. Not since that first day had she shown more than rare glimpses of the woman who had defied Hubert so bravely. He had thought her spirit was much stronger. It appeared as if she might become just the sort of wife his half brother desired.

Striding through the door of the Great Hall, it was only a moment before Gaston realized something was wrong. The usual hum of conversation was absent and the servants were hovering at the perimeter of the room, watching the three people at its center like wolves around a campfire. Gaston's uneasiness grew.

Rose turned from the other two and walked toward him as he approached. As always, her beauty struck him in the chest like a blow from a morning star. He noticed with concern that her fair complexion was pale with strain and she kept her gaze lowered as she stopped before him. Her hands worked nervously at the amber ribbon she wore at the end of her thick braid.

He forced himself to pay attention to the couple she had been talking to. Without looking at Rose, he asked, "Why did you send for me, damsel?"

The man was tall and stout, with a grey beard covering most of his face. His dark eyes watched the Norman knight with unconcealed hatred. Gaston's gaze slid past him to the girl a half step behind him. An ill-made gown hugged close to the ample curve of her breasts and hips. The hood of her mantle was pulled up to cover her head, obscuring her face from Gaston's view.

He turned his attention back to Rose as she raised her lids to look at him. He saw that her eyes were dark as eastern jade and full of reproach. She gestured toward the pair with a slender white hand. Her voice dripped censure. "Daniel has brought his daughter here to demand satisfaction from one of your... Hubert's men."

Bristling at her tone, Gaston's backbone stiffened. But as she continued to stare at him as if he were some vile thing that had just crawled out of a swamp, he felt a tug of amusement. If he hadn't been so preoccupied with gaping at her, Rose's animosity would not have struck so deep. And here indeed was a glimmer of the spirited woman who so fascinated him. Schooling his features to reveal nothing but polite interest, Gaston moved to stand beside the man. "How may I be of assistance?" he asked evenly.

The farmer's gaze flicked to Rose, who nodded toward Gaston. Taking a deep breath, Daniel said, "It's my girl, Evelyn." He took hold of her arm and pulled his daughter

forward so Gaston could see her. Her hood fell back to reveal a delicately lovely face, surrounded by a spill of bright
gold hair. Daniel's brows were pulled together in a straight
line of disapproval as he glared at his daughter. "I found her
out in the shed with a Norman."

Gaston smiled slowly, putting his hands on his lean hips
as the remainder of his tension eased. "And what would you
have me do, good sir? It sounds as if things have progressed well without my assistance. Even a Norman would
have difficulty in resisting such beauty."

Rose gasped in outrage.

He had not meant to be so crude, but he refused to take
the situation too seriously. Gaston did not intend for this
incident to be used to incite further animosity between
Norman and Saxon. Hubert had expressly forbidden his
men to take any women against their will, and this was
widely known. If Daniel had come here with the idea of ril-
ing the people of Carlisle against the Normans because of
his daughter's indiscretion, Gaston must stop it now.

Gaston rubbed his chin thoughtfully before he spoke.
"You may have heard that my brother has ordered stiff
punishment for any man caught violating a woman on one
of his holdings. He made no such provision where the
woman is willing." He watched closely for the man's response.

Daniel's eyes, when they met Gaston's, were bright with
fury. "The man escaped before I could get a close look at
him, and the girl will not talk. I have even beaten her and
still she refuses to tell me anything."

Rose spoke up, her voice as cold as a breath of ice. "Under Saxon law, this man would be responsible for paying the
bride price, whether Evelyn went to him willingly or not."

When he turned to face her, Gaston's expression was cool.
"Saxon law is no longer in effect here." Secretly he enjoyed the flash of fire in her eyes at this reminder.

Looking at the girl's down-bent head, Gaston said, "Evelyn?"

She raised her head, her lovely blue eyes shimmering with tears. "Yes, my lord."

Gaston's tone as he took her arm was low and soothing. "I would speak with you." Without waiting for a reply, he drew her with him to the far corner of the hall.

Rose had known from the moment Gaston looked upon Evelyn's lush curves and lovely face that he desired her. He had all but said so when he said no man could resist her. Did Gaston believe Evelyn would be willing to accept him as well as her other Norman lover? The gall of the man, Rose fumed silently. How could she ever have believed herself attracted to him? He was as wicked as the rest of his fellows. He was even more vile because he had begun to make Rose believe he was different, gentler.

She looked to where Gaston stood with the girl. Disgust left a bad taste in her mouth as she watched him take her hand and gaze down into her guileless blue eyes. Blue eyes, was that what he preferred? His other had moved up to hold her slight shoulder. By the True Cross, must he fondle the girl before them all?

It was doubly clear to Rose that Gaston would have no objection to becoming Evelyn's next lover.

And Evelyn, the slut, could she not see what a fool she was making of herself? Had she no more sense than to carry on like this with Gaston, here in the hall, before the very eyes of her father?

Rose took a deep breath and dragged her eyes away from the little tableau, unable to bear the sight of them together for another moment. She turned her attention to a knot in one of the beams that supported the roof.

"Do you believe Sir Gaston can convince her to name the man?" Daniel wondered aloud.

"I...I do not know." In her anger, she had forgotten the farmer. Rose turned to look into his worried eyes. Surprisingly, he only seemed concerned that his daughter might refuse to speak out.

Was he blind? Could he not see what was happening across the room? In a moment the two would be in each other's arms.

She glanced toward the serfs, who were now talking quietly amongst themselves. They did not appear to see what was going on, either.

Rose bit her lower lip. Was she the one who was mistaken? She watched as Gaston released the girl's hand and beckoned to the serf, Rob. Evelyn stood respectfully at his side, her eyes downcast, as he spoke with the servant. Rob nodded to whatever Gaston said, and hurried from the hall.

Gaston swung around and came toward Rose and Daniel. Evelyn was forced to take two steps to each one of his long strides in order to keep up with him.

Rose felt her face grow hot with embarrassment. She realized what she was experiencing was nothing more than unfounded jealousy. A jealousy she had no right to feel. Even if Gaston had desired Evelyn, he was a man, free to choose whatever woman he wished. It was Rose who was bound to another.

As Evelyn came toward them, Rose wondered at the expression of happiness on her face. She was watching Gaston's broad back with something akin to hero worship.

Unbidden, Rose experienced a new wave of jealously as she watched Gaston smile openly at the girl. He was so undeniably handsome, his easy charm enough to turn any maid's head. Never was he thus with Rose.

Daniel was not blind to the easy camaraderie between his daughter and the knight, and shuffled his feet unhappily.

The two came to a halt, and Gaston put his hands on Evelyn's shoulders, giving her a gentle nudge toward her father.

Gaston planted his feet wide apart and crossed his arms over his wide chest. When Hubert took up this stance, he brayed like an ass. Not so Gaston; he spoke calmly, his voice cool. His very lack of expression let the farmer know the matter was done. "I have come to a decision."

"She has given you the name?" Daniel asked, his head high as he strove to retain some dignity.

"She has," Gaston answered levelly. He gave Evelyn a look of encouragement when she took a half step back toward him, then added, "I want you to know I have taken your daughter's wishes into account."

"What have you decided then, Sir Gaston?" Rose forced herself to ask. Her lips felt tight and her head was beginning to ache with strain. How arrogant this Norman was to go before the girl's own father and dictate as if he were God himself. Could he not leave them some measure of self-respect? "I await your pronouncement with bated breath." She did not even try to disguise her sarcasm.

Gaston's lips thinned and a muscle pulsed in his lean jaw, but he did not reprimand her. "There will be a marriage between the Norman soldier, Jacques, and the Saxon woman, Evelyn." He purposely raised his voice so all present would hear him.

Rose's mind reeled with shock. This she had not expected. She opened her mouth to protest, as did Evelyn's father. But they were stilled by a quelling glance from the knight.

Her eyes flashing defiance, Rose glared up at Gaston. What right had he to deal such a blow? To tie Evelyn to one of the invading savages was too large a price to pay.

At that moment a commotion drew their attention to the entrance at the front of the hall. A young Norman had entered. He came straight across the room to Gaston's side, his head held high.

Glancing toward Evelyn to gauge her reaction, Rose was surprised to see the light of joy in her blue eyes. It was true that the fellow was attractive with his sun-streaked brown hair and rugged good looks. Yet Rose couldn't understand how she could welcome him so readily. He was one of the men who had come to take their land; their freedom. Had the girl no sense of loyalty to her own kind?

She watched as the pair linked hands, their faces glowing.

Something, some unknown force, compelled her to look up, and as she did her gaze collided with Gaston's. His grey eyes were dark as smoke, magnetic, pulling her inside. The deep, wanting hunger in him was more seductive than any honeyed words or caresses could ever be. Her body trembled in response. Then, taking a ragged breath, he blinked and the hypnotic force was gone. It was replaced by a regret that left her shaken. Regret that what they felt was wrong for more reasons than there were stars in the heavens.

Unable to bear any more, Rose turned away. Her emotions were battered beyond anything she had ever experienced. She felt as though she had been suspended for one brief moment in a soft cloud, then had suddenly fallen through into the icy cold water of a mountain lake.

When she dared glance at Gaston again, he had turned and was talking to the soldier, Jacques. From the look of him it appeared the young man was well pleased with Gaston's decision.

Rose put her hand to her aching forehead. She was so confused by her own feelings, she did not know what to do. All she was sure of was that it was a mistake to allow the couple to marry. Evelyn would learn to regret her folly all too soon, Rose was certain, for this man was her enemy.

A sound at the door drew her eyes. This time a serf entered, leading the village priest. She felt a tiny ember of hope. Surely, if anyone could stop this travesty, Father Liam would do so. He was not only Rose's priest but her friend and teacher. It was to him she had gone to learn Latin, philosophy and all else she knew about the world. It was through him, as well as her parents, that she had developed her sense of right and wrong. She could only believe he would see the wrong in this marriage.

Father Liam hurried forward, his feet long and narrow beneath the hem of his black robes, as was the rest of him.

His brisk strides belied the white hair and fragile skin, which were evidence of his advancing age. He raised his slender, long-fingered hands in a gesture of concern as he came up to the little group.

"Rob has told me of a marriage between these two." His kind, light blue eyes rested first on Evelyn, then Jacques. "Before I can go forward with the ceremony, I must speak privately with Evelyn." His voice was rich and deep, and his gaze as it met Gaston's was adamant.

Rose wanted to cry her triumph aloud. Now Evelyn would refuse to marry the Norman.

"Of course." Gaston nodded with barely raised brows. Having met the priest on his visits to the village, Gaston already knew the older man and respected his need to see that all was well before performing the marriage. He motioned for Jacques to follow him as he went a short distance away from them.

Rose looked on as Father Liam put his hands on either side of Evelyn's face and stared into her eyes. "Are you certain you want to go forward with this wedding?"

Unhesitatingly Evelyn answered, "Yes, Father. I want, very much, to become Jacques's wife." Her face was alight with confidence as she gazed up at the priest.

Father Liam nodded, bringing his hands down to his sides as he stepped back. "We shall go on with the ceremony."

Rose shut her eyes on the misery that filled her. Father Liam would not prevent this farce.

The brief ceremony was performed without any of the usual Saxon rituals. No spear was passed to Evelyn to remind her she was her husband's partner in time of danger. Evelyn's father did not give the bride's shoe to Jacques so that he might touch it to her forehead to indicate that she'd now follow her husband's wishes. Daniel stood to the side, looking helpless and defeated.

Watching the cheerful faces of Jacques's fellow soldiers, who had assembled for the wedding, Rose felt utterly alone.

As Father Liam pronounced the blessing, the soldiers let out a cheer of approval. The tables were set out and the guests settled in for an impromptu feast. Cold meats and cheeses were piled on till the tables groaned with the weight. Wine flowed.

Gaston looked on, pleased at this first riotous joining of Norman and Saxon. Though he did notice that most of the Saxons were women, many of them from the village, the more spirits were drunk the less defined the line between peoples became. More than one woman allowed herself to be led from the hall, squealing not with fear but laughter.

Rose swung around, intent on leaving the hall. She could not watch for another moment.

Once outside, she was surprised to find that dusk had fallen. She'd had no idea so much time had passed.

"Lady Rose."

She came to an abrupt halt as a strong hand closed on her shoulder from behind.

"Yes." She did not turn to face Gaston.

"This first marriage between our two peoples is a memorable occasion."

Her voice was bitter as a December wind. "You have my assurance, Sir Knight, I shall never forget this day."

With a growl of impatience, he took her arm and pulled her around the corner of the hall. His grey eyes were dark as the smoke that rises from damp wood. "Why must you set yourself against us at every turn?"

Why could Rose not accept them? If he did not miss the mark, more than one Norman-Saxon babe would make its way into the world nine months from this night. He continued in a lighter tone, hoping to make her see the situation as it was. "Can you not accept that Evelyn desired this marriage? She sees Jacques as a man first and a Norman second."

She jerked back from him and came up against the wall. She felt trapped and helpless. Something in her broke like a freshly opened wound, her resentment pouring from her.

"Why must I? You have taken everything we owned and still that was not enough. You must also take our very hearts and souls. Are we to be left with nothing?"

"The girl's love was not taken. It was given freely." His words hung sharp and hurtful in the warm night air.

"Evelyn will come to rue her choice, I have no doubt," Rose spat, turning to go past him.

Gaston raised his arms to block her path from either side. Catching her breath, Rose looked up at him, her heart pounding as she realized how near he was. She could feel the warmth of his chest and her gaze strayed to a pulse beat at the base of his throat. He smelled of dust and sweat and a musky maleness that made her slightly dizzy.

His tone was low and husky. "A heart can not be stolen, it must be given." He searched the furious beauty of her face for any sign of yielding.

She forced herself to focus on the wrenching pain of her anger. "When I see a Norman I see an enemy. One of your kind murdered my father. When I look into a Norman's face, I ask myself, Is he the one?" Unwelcome tears glittered in her green eyes.

Gaston bent close to her. "Your father's death was not a personal thing against him as a man. In battle a man seeks only to keep himself alive." He shrugged. "It is war."

She dashed a tear away with the back of her hand. "We did not come looking for your war. I will never forgive your kind for what they have done to me and mine."

He reached out and took her hand in one of his, bringing it to his chest. "Feel my heart beating beneath your hand. Yes, I am a Norman, but I am flesh and blood. Man, not monster."

She felt the solid muscle under her quivering fingers and flushed with heat. He was so close she could feel the hair at her temples stir as he exhaled. Holy Mary, it was hard to breathe, and she felt as weak as a newborn lamb. Why did he prod her so? She shook her head as if she could deny the throbbing call of her blood.

"No." Rose raised her tormented gaze to look at him.

There was so much sorrow in her, he wished there was some way to ease her hurt. Never before had he felt such a need to protect. If only there was some way he could show her she had nothing to fear. Without pausing to consider his actions, he tipped his head and covered her mouth with his.

For Rose time stopped. There was nothing but the feel of Gaston's smooth, questing mouth. Without thinking, she moved her lips under his. A heady sweet wonder filled her as her head spun and the world tilted.

It was her easy compliance that brought Gaston to his senses. With a groan he drew back from her, holding tightly to her hand, which still covered his heart. "You see, I am no monster." Even as he said the words, he hated himself and knew he had not kissed her to prove his point but because he could not stop himself.

For a moment Rose seemed confused, then her eyes darkened with pain and she beat at his chest with her free hand. She was sobbing in earnest now. "Let me go. Is this how you would treat your brother's wife?"

Gaston's head jerked back as if she had slapped him. He released his hold on her and stepped back. "I...forgive me. I but sought to comfort you."

In Rose's stomach was an aching knot of misery. He had only been making his case by kissing her and she had responded like a lovesick adolescent. "'Tis a strange sort of comfort you offer, Norman."

She turned and ran from him.

Raising his hand as if to call her back, Gaston paused then brought it to his side. He had no right. Hubert was to be her husband and it was he who must teach her about men.

Gaston, like Hubert, could have taken the reward William offered. But he had declined, laughingly telling his king he had all he wanted, for the moment, in a ready sword and a sure arm.

Now he regretted that decision; regretted that he had not accepted the king's offer of lands. If he had accepted, he would now be working toward his own future and the lives of his people. Then Gaston shrugged. It was no matter now. Carlisle and Rose belonged to Hubert.

Chapter Five

Rose was determined to weed her garden. Since the coming of the Normans it had been sadly neglected; the weeds were thriving, threatening to choke the small plants.

Looking around herself, she knew it would be hard for anyone to believe that anything of importance grew here. But somewhere in the confusion grew the sage, parsley, sweet basil, dill, garlic and a myriad of other roots and flowering plants she had cultivated.

Her feet sank into the dark earth, which gave off a rich musty scent. Bending to her task, Rose began to weed the garden with vigor. But even the physical labor could not keep her mind from straying where it should not. Although she had managed to avoid Gaston quite successfully since the day of the wedding, he had not been forgotten. He was always there at the edge of her thoughts. Sometimes, when her guard was lowered, she would remember the way her body reacted to his kiss. Just the memory of the expression in his hungry eyes was enough to bring a rush of scarlet color to her cheeks. Even now, as she relived the moment when his lips had touched hers, her pulse beat quickened until it was like the steady thrum of a hummingbird's wings.

Giving a groan of frustration at her own inability to control her thoughts, Rose gave a vicious tug, her hand coming up full of both weeds and tiny dill plants.

"Sweet Mother of God," she swore, tossing the clump of dirt and plants away. Was she losing her mind, that she could not concentrate on even the simplest of tasks?

Why did Gaston not leave her alone, him with his talk of men and war? Rose did not wish to see him or any other Norman as anything besides her enemy.

But he had made her see things differently, no matter how she fought him. Was it not true that Gaston had taken Evelyn's own wishes into account when he made the decision for Evelyn and Jacques to marry? And was he not fair and just to her people, as well as his own? The villeins came to him less warily now with their disputes and problems.

If only she did not find him so devastatingly attractive, she might better be able to judge her own perceptions.

With renewed resolve, Rose bent and went on working, determined to keep her mind on what she was doing.

Gaston strode through the courtyard, then around the outside of the Great Hall to the back.

The guard on the palisade had reported sighting a group of men at the edge of the forest to the north.

Thinking to have the matter dealt with most readily, Gaston meant to investigate himself. He was certain there could be no real danger. A group of men was working on the base of the stone wall not a hundred yards from the edge of the forest.

The Saxon escape tunnel would be the quickest way to gain the outside.

Almost against his will, Gaston's eyes searched among the many people working in the courtyard for a thatch of bright auburn hair. Not seeing Rose, he had to force down a stab of disappointment. He then chided himself for his foolishness in seeking her. He should be heartened that she was avoiding him as he was her.

In the days since the wedding, they had exchanged few words, and those with the barest of civility. He reached up to scratch his head where the sun had warmed it, wondering that the maid could remain so angry for so long. He had done his utmost for Evelyn, given the circumstances.

A frown darkened his wide brow. There was naught to be gained in trying to understand the vixen. He could easily go mad attempting to do so.

He was just skirting the little patch of garden at the back of the keep when the sight of the woman working there gave him pause. Though her back was to him, the curve of her waist and hip were arrestingly familiar.

This was no serf woman, but Rose. His eyes had lingered too many times on that shapely backside for him to mistake her. She turned slightly as she worked, and he could see a strand of silken flame had escaped the cloth she had tied over her hair, the covering having been washed so many times there was no hint as to the color it might once have been. Her gown, too, was threadbare and lacking in color, but Gaston found no complaint, for the thin fabric did little to hide the pert swell of her bottom.

Forgetting for the moment that he had other matters to attend, Gaston moved to lean against a sturdy post close by. He crossed his arms over his wide chest, a gleam of appreciation in his smoky grey eyes.

He smiled. It was good to watch her unaware. Too often in his presence she was stiff and unyielding, allowing none of her warmth and softness to show. Not knowing how long he stood there enjoying the sight of her, Gaston was content to do so.

The fluid grace of her motions was so unconsciously sensual, even at this most menial of tasks. She bent and straightened . . . bent and straightened . . . her movements continuous in their flow, her hands patting tenderly at the earth around the small living things she tended.

Then she stood up, putting her hands to the small of her back. His eyes darkened with undisguised hunger when Rose stretched her arms high over her head, the motion pulling her gown taut over her high full breasts.

* * *

Rose stretched her aching muscles, breathing deeply of the pungent scent given off by the mixture of herbs. The neat rows of plants behind her gave Rose a sense of accomplishment. They now had a clear path to the sun and rain. She glanced over her left shoulder to see how much she had left to do.

What she saw made her stiffen, and she brought her arms down to her sides.

Her pleasure in her work and the warmth of the day were gone as if they had never been; it was as if she had no right to find joy in even these small things. Why could he not leave her in peace? she wondered, looking across the narrow strip of earth that separated them.

Her eyes took in the relaxed length of his tall frame where he leaned so casually against the pole that was used to prop open the cellar door. His attitude of complete self-assurance and the warm admiration in his eyes irritated her beyond measure. She wanted to wipe that smirk from his handsome face. Who was he to stand there staring as if... as if he might devour her? Rose flushed and turned away.

Bending, she went back to her work, hoping Gaston might go away if she ignored him.

Gaston did not move. She was totally conscious of him and his long bare legs crossed at the ankle. She had only to turn her head slightly to have a clear view of them.

Out of the corner of her eye, she saw him stand up and come toward her. When he stopped beside her, Rose felt his gaze as real as a touch on her skin. Her pulse throbbed like a battle drum.

"Good morrow, Lady Rose." His voice was low and rich as fresh cream, seeming somehow intimate here in this garden with growing things around them and the soft earth beneath their feet.

Rose stood, keeping her gaze lowered to the supple leather of his ankle-high boots, unable at this moment to look directly into the eyes of this all-too-fascinating man. "Good morrow, my lord.'' Raising her gaze to peer across the courtyard beyond him, Rose realized they were the only two people in sight. Her breath came a little more quickly.

"Why do you toil here?" He gestured about them.

Rose's gaze swept over the garden, then back to Gaston's feet. Her eyes wandered up his long legs, to his strong thighs. The muscle in his thigh tightened then rippled as he shifted his foot, and Rose felt an almost overwhelming urge to touch him.

Obviously Gaston grew tired of waiting for an answer, for he asked, "Can you not appoint someone to this task?"

Realizing she had been staring, Rose flushed and looked up at Gaston, then wished she hadn't when she saw the knowing expression on his face. Her gaze flew back to his feet as she answered hurriedly, "There is no one. None of the serfs seem to know the difference betwixt the herbs and the weeds." She gave a nervous laugh as she lifted her hands, palms up, and shrugged.

Gaston's voice remained neutral, though his eyes never left her down-bent head. "I believe there is one amongst Hubert's men who may know something of gardening. If you would like, I would find out and send him to you?" He found it hard to attend to his own words, wanted to reach out and take that ridiculous covering from her hair. It was nothing short of a sin to hide such beauty.

Of all things she had expected he might say, this offer of help was not numbered amongst them. Her pleasure shone in her eyes as she looked up at him. "That would be very kind of you, Sir Gaston."

He smiled down into their emerald depths. "It is only a small service to offer such a lovely lady."

A smile of sweet gratitude curved her pink lips and Gaston's breath caught in his throat. It was the first genuine smile he had ever seen on her face, and he was made to wonder what Rose had been like before these troubles had come upon her.

There was a smear of earth on her cheek and he raised his hand to brush it from the creamy perfection of her skin. Her flesh was smooth as velvet under his gentle fingers. He knew again the same rush of wanting that had made him kiss her before. He lowered his lids and swallowed convulsively.

Looking at Rose, Gaston saw that her eyes had darkened to deepest jade, soft and luminescent. Her skin glowed with a warm pearly light and she leaned toward him with parted lips, too innocent to hide her response. It was Rose's lack of guile that made him see what he was doing with infinite clarity. He was the more experienced. She only followed his lead. He must be the one to control what lay between them.

Gaston snatched his hand away like a cat that has touched glowing coals. He stepped back from her, his hands curling into tight fists at his sides. He stared into the distance, focusing his thoughts on the mundane, his voice cold with the fierce effort to conquer his emotions. "Surely someone was responsible for tending this garden before you."

Rose blinked in surprise, then turned away, stung by his abrupt change in manner. It was as if the past few moments had never been. Each time he switched so suddenly from that mood of compellingly seductive warmth to cold formality, she told herself she would not fall under his spell again.

Then Gaston would look at her with his heart in his eyes and his gentle ways would override her defenses. She clenched her teeth to hold back a moan of despair, feeling powerless in the face of her attraction to him.

She saw he was still waiting for an answer. What manner of man was he to run so hot and cold? "My mother tended this garden herself." Her voice was dull with hurt. "She used many of these plants in her medicines and was considered a gifted healer. When she died, three winters ago, I took over her duties. Though I am not my mother's equal, I have some skill as a healer. Mother did her best to teach me all she knew, and I do have her charts to assist me."

Gaston raised his black brows in surprise. "You are able to read then?"

Biting her lips in consternation, Rose answered hurriedly. "Enough to understand the charts." She remembered the day Will had come with the message from Brentwood. Gaston had shown more than a slight interest in her conversation with the young man. She did not now wish him to connect her with the message from Sir Pierre. If only he would not stand so close. His wide shoulders filled her view and made it hard for her to think clearly.

"That is a very unusual skill in a woman," he said thoughtfully. "Your father must have been an exceptional man to allow his daughter to be tutored as he would a son."

As always, the gentler side of Gaston's nature caught her off guard. Her gaze lingered on the strong line of his jaw, outlined against the blue of the sky.

"He was," she answered softly, unsure as to why she went on. "My father was a very special man. He had a way of making people love him. It was as if he was the center of everything, the light we all basked in. Even my mother lived in his shadow, and she was a woman of great strength. It was mother who taught me to read with the help of Father Liam, who had taught her. Father Liam often said I was a better student than…Edmund…he was ever off to the forest climbing trees. Edmund was so like Father, a natural leader of men. Father couldn't help loving him best. No one could. I was only—" she shrugged "—myself." Though she spoke matter-of-factly, the memories brought her sadness. She had so badly wanted to please her father.

Gaston turned to her, his clear grey eyes unreadable. "Mayhap you do not allow yourself your due." With that he swung around and strode away.

Rose's gaze followed him with a mixture of relief and regret. What did he mean? Gaston was just too unpredictable for her peace of mind.

Rose shivered as he disappeared down the underground tunnel. Preoccupied as she was, she wondered why he chose that route when he could go through the gate.

Rose had disliked the tunnel from the day her father had shown it to her as a child. It was narrow and dark as a moonless night all the way to the outside, because the exit was obscured by an overhanging rock covered in greenery. There had been the sound of squeaks and scurryings all along the way. Once she had even felt the brush of something against her foot. It had taken a long while before her father had been able to get her to go on. Once the two of them emerged through the opening in the forest, the man had been unable to convince his daughter to return to the keep in the same fashion.

As far as Rose was concerned, the tunnel could be sealed off for all time.

Before Hubert had gone away, he had made a point of telling everyone who would attend him that the tunnel was of no use now that he was lord. He could defend his property so there was no need of an escape route.

Hubert, Rose frowned. She tried not to think of him at all. And it had proved much easier than she had imagined to set her intended bridegroom from her mind.

It was a slimmer, more sensitive man who gave her such cause for anguish. No matter how she became angered with him, he remained in her thoughts.

She lifted her hand to her cheek. Rose could still feel the touch of his hand on her skin. The caress had been so gentle that the slight roughness of his long fingers had been pleasant. If only she could put his image aside as easily as she did Hubert's, her life would be so much simpler.

The sun had not risen much further in the sky when Rose heard a cry go up from the guard at the gate.

She, as well as everyone else who was within hearing distance, ran toward the sound. Standing at the edge of the crowd as she wiped her soiled hands on her skirt, Rose saw

Gaston and another man come through the gate, bearing a stretcher between them.

Hurrying forward, Rose asked, "What has happened?"

Gaston's expression was grim. "Claude was carrying a message from Hubert. He was attacked in the forest and brought here to Carlisle where his body might be found. Fortunately for him, one of the palisade guards saw something that made him suspicious and reported it to me." His lips twisted and his eyes darkened with regret. "Unfortunately, I did not believe these outlaws would be so bold as to attempt any mischief so close to the keep. I allowed myself to dally before I investigated the sighting. My self-indulgence may have cost Claude his life."

Suddenly Rose was sure Gaston had been delayed by stopping to speak with her. She knew an intense longing to tell him the fault for this did not lie with him. But she held her tongue. It was not her place to offer comfort to Gaston de Thorne.

Instead she would help in the way she knew best. Rose glanced around the sea of faces surrounding them, her eyes stopping on the servant, Kev. "Kev, fetch my bag of medicines and bring it to the guest bower. Quickly," she added when he hesitated. "And Mary," she called out, spotting a serving girl, "bring water."

Mary did not move and Rose turned to see Kev, too, simply standing there. "What has addled your wits?" Rose's voice was raised in exasperation.

Neither serf spoke. Then Rose understood. They did not wish to prolong the life of this, or any other, Norman. Rose stood up straight, her head held high. "Do you dare to disobey me?"

"But, Lady Rose . . ." Kev began.

"Nay, do not say it," she threatened. "We can not stand by and do nothing when we might help, no matter what manner of man he might be."

Still they hesitated.

Rose stood her ground, her eyes fairly shooting sparks of outrage. "Am I not still your lady?"

With that, the two exchanged a look and moved as if by one mind to do as they had been bid.

Gaston spoke softly. "My thanks."

Rose swung around to look up at him. "Do not offer your thanks yet, my lord. Let us see to the wound. He must be taken to the guest bower immediately." She urged them forward with a wave of her hands and followed close behind.

As they moved to the guest bower, Rose wondered briefly that Gaston had not checked her in any way. Hubert had made it clear before he left that Rose was not to give commands.

Then she heard the other man carrying the litter hesitantly ask, "The Saxon woman will attend Claude?"

Gaston's answer was firm, brooking no argument. "There is no other."

The man's distrust of her was sobering. The Normans were in an odd position here, that of having to trust their enemy. It gave her pause for thought.

But she had no time to think on this as she raced ahead to open the door of the bower.

"Come, Lyle, we will put him in Hubert's bed," Gaston directed, pausing beside the bed so Rose could remove the mail shirt that lay across the end.

"Carefully," Rose warned as they laid the stretcher on the bed.

Gaston and Lyle pulled out the two rough wooden poles from the makeshift litter. Handing the other man his pole, Gaston said, "You may go." The suspicious way Lyle watched Rose told Gaston he would be of little help now.

As she went to drop the mail shirt upon the other bed, Rose saw that certain changes had been made in the room. The chamber had been cleaned and tidied, though there was still a jumble of items on Hubert's chest. Upon the chest beside Gaston's bed was a folded tunic, a shell comb and a sharpening stone.

The door opened and Mary appeared, carrying two buckets of water.

"Bring them here," Rose ordered, going to Hubert's chest and unceremoniously dumping his belongings onto the floor. She took one of the buckets and washed her soiled hands. "Go fetch more water," she told Mary, handing her the bucket of dirty water, "and put some on to boil. Also, I will need plenty of clean cloth. Now hurry." Mary obeyed.

Gaston moved aside as she came to stand beside him.

A grimace crossed Rose's brow when she saw the way Claude's leather tunic was soaked dark with blood. "Give me your knife," she told Gaston. She took the knife, grateful for its well-honed edge, and began to cut away the tunic.

After only a minute, Gaston took the blade away and finished the task for her. What they saw as they pulled away the cloth made both of them gasp.

The wound was deep, long and narrow, such as a sword might make, extending from Claude's shoulder down his side.

Gaston paled at the extent of the injury. He turned to Rose with questioning eyes.

Rose looked away. The wound was serious, and in a bad place. They both knew such an injury could be crippling, even if she managed to save the man's life. In the event that infection set in, the arm would have to be removed, and a soldier with one arm was not of much value to his liege lord.

"You told me you have some skill with healing," Gaston spoke with forced calm. "Can you help Claude?"

Rose closed her eyes and prayed, drawing on the reservoir of strength that sustained her in times of real adversity. When she answered, her voice was filled with determination. "I will do what I can."

Already blood was seeping out to cover the bed.

"Where is Mary with those cloths?" Rose muttered. "And where is Kev with my bag?" She would surely have to chide him for his sloth.

Gaston's voice was deep and comforting beside her. "What can I do?"

She showed him. "You can place your hands here . . . and here. If we can hold the wound closed, it will lessen the bleeding."

She watched as Gaston put his two strong hands on either side of the gaping wound and pushed it together.

At that moment, Mary rushed into the room. She had Rose's bag in one hand and the clean cloths in the other. Behind her was Kev with the water.

"Get the fire going," Rose told him, going to Mary.

Kev glanced over at the bed, saw the amount of blood that stained the covers and left, his face a sickly grey.

As the door slammed behind the young man, Rose snapped, "I wanted him to light the fire."

Mary passed the bag of medicines to her mistress. Her eyes carefully avoided the wound after one quick glance. "How may I help?"

Rose began to remove smaller bags from the large one. She told Mary, "Tear some strips of cloth after you build the fire."

Mary went to the fire pit and soon had a blaze going. She placed a pot of water over the flames to heat.

Rose took the small bowl she used for mixing medications and put bits of different herbs and powders into it. She instructed the serving girl, "Bring me some water. It need not boil for this infusion."

Gaston's lips were tight with the strain of holding the wound for so long. He watched warily as Rose stirred the mixture. "What are you giving him?"

Rose looked down at the bowl of medicine, her teeth worrying her bottom lip as she concentrated on adding exact amounts of each ingredient. "Dried peony, garlic, sage, and hemlock." At Gaston's quickly indrawn breath she rushed on, "I will need to clean and stitch the wound. If he should wake and resist us, that task would be made most difficult." She paused, her gaze resting on Gaston's. "It is true that hemlock is poisonous, but if given in a correct amount, it will only bring on a deep sleep. I will not tell you there is no danger. The difference between a lethal dose and one that produces unconsciousness is slight. I can only tell you I have studied my mother's charts and believe I know how much to administer." She waited.

Gaston nodded slowly, his pained expression telling her he had little choice but to trust her.

Rose bent to her work.

Long moments later, she came toward the bed, holding the bowl between her cupped hands. She nodded and Gaston raised the wounded soldier as gently as he could. Even so, the injured man moaned in agony.

Grinding his own teeth in sympathy, Gaston knew Rose had been right. Claude could not withstand the pain of stitching the wound without some aid. He was too weak from loss of blood.

While Gaston held his head, Rose gave the soldier the infusion.

They stepped back to wait, both of them holding their breath as they watched to see if the mixture would bring sleep or death.

To Gaston's relief the man began to breathe more easily after a few minutes. He turned to Rose with a smile of genuine warmth, and her shoulders visibly relaxed.

Taking another pouch from her bag, Rose told Mary, "Bring some of the boiling water."

Mary hastened to obey.

Rose rinsed her bowl, then filled it with boiling water and sprinkled some dried leaves into it. She let this steep for a time then carried it to the bed. It gave off a not-unpleasant odor, almost like that of dried grass.

Bending forward, Rose poured some of the liquid into the wound. The soldier groaned and tried to roll away. Her face was set in an expressionless mask. Even though she knew she must sometimes inflict hurt on someone to help them get well, it never got easier. "Please hold him," she said, without looking up at the knight at her side.

Taking a firm hold of Claude's shoulders, Gaston pinned the man to the bed. "What is this concoction?"

Her voice emerged in a calm monotone, as if she were giving a lesson. "An infusion of marjoram. It will cleanse and purify the wound."

Setting the bowl aside, Rose turned to Mary. "It is time."

Mary hurried forward with a needle and a length of thread. Rose took them and passed the thread through the hole with practiced speed.

Bending over her patient, Rose focused on the gruesome cut. Bile rose in her throat and nostrils, acrid and sour. But she swallowed it back, concentrating all her strength on the task at hand. Taking a deep, steadying breath, she pierced the flesh with the needle.

Claude began to thrash in earnest, surprisingly strong after having lost so much blood. Even the hemlock she had given him could not totally block out the pain.

Her voice was a mere whisper. "You must hold him still. I can give him no more of the medication."

Gaston's only reply was to bear down on the man with his powerful arms.

Rose continued.

After a time, sweat began to drip from Gaston's face and dot the other man's chest. It was hot in the room, and Claude fought their ministrations greatly. But Gaston said nothing, holding his countryman with steely strength until Claude, thankfully, was still. Whether it be from the drugs he had been given, or exhaustion, Rose was grateful.

At long last, Rose tied off the last stitch and straightened from her stooped position. She wiped the beads of perspiration from her brow with the back of her hand and sighed wearily. "We will wait now to see what will happen. Whether he lives or dies is in God's hands."

Stepping away from the bed, Gaston shifted his stiff neck and shoulders. He turned to Mary. "Fetch your mistress a glass of wine."

The maid rushed to obey.

Rose walked a few steps and slumped onto a bench that sat beside the wall.

Gaston went to her side and took Rose's arm, raising her up. With gentle care, he led her to one of the chairs beside the fire. "You will be more comfortable here."

Rose sank down gratefully, putting her head in her hands. She was weary beyond bearing. Tending that wound was one of the hardest things she had ever done, knowing as she did that she held a man's life in her hands. A strange quavering began in her limbs, and she lowered her hands to tuck them under her thighs.

Gaston's voice was soft. "Are you well?"

She refused to look up at him, determined not to let him see how shaken she was. "I am fine." She made a half-hearted attempt to smile in his general direction.

The door opened, and Mary entered the bower, a flask and two cups in her hands. Gaston took them from her with a nod. "You may go now."

Mary cast her mistress a long look, then turned to study the tall knight. His concern for her lady was most evident. Slowly the maid nodded, a knowing look in her eyes.

When Gaston scowled darkly at her presumption, she swung around and made a hasty exit.

Going to Rose's side, Gaston poured a cup of wine and handed it to her. She quickly drained the flagon, then held it out for more.

As Gaston refilled her cup, he noticed that her hand was trembling.

This time when Rose raised the cup to her mouth, she drank more slowly. She leaned back and closed her eyes.

Thoughtfully Gaston traced the decorative stem of his cup with long fingers. "You are very gifted."

She was silent for so long he thought she meant to leave his comment unanswered. Then she spoke, her voice weary beyond measure. "I have never sewn such a wound before."

Opening her eyes to look at him, she seemed to read the surprise in his face. "Oh, yes, I've tended cuts, set a few bones, even delivered a child. But nothing compared to this." Rose gestured toward the bed with a shudder. "I could see all the way to the bone."

Squatting down, Gaston leaned toward her, his arm resting on the chair at her side. "Why did you come forward?"

She looked at her cup, finding him too close for her peace of mind. Their experience, fighting the dark specter of death together, had created an almost tangible bond between them—a bond she was unwilling to acknowledge. She shrugged her slight shoulders, trying to lean away from him. "Why did I come forward? There was no one else. Was I to let a man die, when I have the knowledge to save him?"

Gaston's reply was deep and low, forcing an air of intimacy between them. "Even if he is a Norman?"

She shrugged again, taking a nervous breath. "He is a man."

His breath was warm on her cheek. "So you will admit that a Norman is only a man."

As if she had no control of her own will, Rose turned to face him. Mere inches separated them. His eyes watched her with an intensity that told her he was speaking of more than saving Claude.

Words tumbled from her lips in agitation at his closeness. "When a Norman is ill and needs help. I would not allow a hound to lay suffering, when I could help it."

His eyes, so liquid, so coolly fascinating, challenged her to review her own beliefs, to see his truth. "But Claude is not a hound. He is one of your enemy. A man who might have struck down your father on the battlefield."

She put her hands over her eyes to block out the sight of him. "I do not know." She shook her head in confusion. "I don't want to think. I am so weary."

His strong hands took hold of hers and gently but insistently forced them down.

She was compelled to look at his face, his eyes. The grey depths were filled with concern, and more. A spark of something she could not fully understand.

His voice emerged in a husky whisper, filled with warmth and comfort. "You are exhausted." Slowly he raised her to her feet, his gaze never leaving hers. "Forgive my lack of understanding."

The hour had grown late and the dimness in the rest of the room created a small intimate circle where they stood in the warm glow of the flames. The attention of each of them was totally focused on the other as the firelight flickered across their faces.

Rose's head was spinning, though she knew it was not from being tired. She was completely aware of Gaston as a man. His sensitivity and kindness toward her were more heady than wine. The goodness in him was breaking through the wall of reserve she had erected around herself.

She had felt so completely alone. Now Gaston was giving her what she most needed—someone who cared.

Closing her eyes, she leaned forward, resting her forehead against the solid strength of his chest. Rose sighed with pleasure when his arms came around her, drawing her close. This was where she was meant to be, for now and always.

"Little flower," he murmured. He brushed his cheek over the softness of her hair, which was molten in the firelight.

She sighed his name. "Gaston."

He put his hand under her chin and raised her face, his expression tender. "You must seek your bed. I will look after the patient until you have rested."

A frown appeared on her brow. Rose felt slightly befuddled and wondered if it was the wine. "Are you certain? He must be watched at all times."

Gaston answered with a smile. ''I will stay here until you return. Now get some rest.''

Her gaze was so grateful, so trusting. He bent his head to offer a kiss of peace. He meant it as nothing more than a sign of their newly found harmony.

But as his lips touched hers, their mouths barely brushing, a spark ignited between them. Rose felt the white heat of it in the pit of her belly and gasped aloud.

She sprang away from him, her green eyes dark with the force of her response and her disillusionment. ''How could you? Fool that I am for trusting you. I would do well to remember you are my enemy.''

Gaston held out his hand in appeal. ''I meant nothing more than to offer you the kiss of peace, as one might a brother. I would do you no harm, Lady Rose. I intended nothing more than comfort.''

There was a sheen to her eyes as she held back tears. ''''Tis indeed a strange comfort you offer, brother. First you kiss me to prove you are a man, and now you want me to believe you kiss me to show you are a brother. You must forgive me if I grow confused.'' She groaned as she turned her back to him and ran from the bower.

Chapter Six

From where she stood on the palisade, Rose could see the
men working on the wall. It was easy to pick Gaston out in
the midst of the group. His height and glossy black hair set
him apart.

From this distance she felt safe to allow her gaze to linger
on the knight. A fortnight had passed since Claude had been
injured, a fortnight since Gaston had kissed her. Rose's
mistrust of her own wayward emotions had erected a barrier between them.

At least her patient was faring well. He was beginning to
heal, though his gratitude toward her was a little overwhelming. He seemed to feel this recovery was completely
due to her meager skills.

His assumption was overgenerous. Rose had worked hard
to save Claude's life, but it was his own strong will to survive that had healed him.

Even Gaston encouraged Claude in this misconception,
adding his own assurances that indeed Rose had performed
a miracle.

For her part, Rose believed Gaston wished to make much
of her efforts so she would not forget she had saved the life
of a Norman.

She rubbed the heel of her palm over her puckered brow.
Contrary to her own desires, she was beginning to see the

Normans as more than savages. After spending so much time with Claude, she was growing to know him well.

Rose had tried to maintain a coolness between herself and her patient, but Claude's naturally gregarious nature had worn down her defenses. His ready smile and cheery tales of life in Normandy made it impossible for her to remain distant.

Yet she couldn't forget the Normans' propensity to take what they wanted without caring for the rights of others.

Rose shook her head as if to clear it. There was nothing to be gained by dwelling on her troubles. No matter what she believed, the Normans were here to stay. With a deep sigh, she looked out, her gaze following the path of a robin as it streaked across the blue of the sky. If only she were free as the robins to come and go as she would.

Her gaze stilled and she squinted into the distance.

Off past the small village nestled at the bottom of the hill, a column of smoke rose into the sky.

"Fire!" she screamed.

The men working on the stone wall stopped to look up.

She pointed to the trail of smoke, crying out again, "Fire!"

They turned to look, their hands coming up to shade their eyes from the sun.

Gaston was the first to react, breaking into a run. The other men followed on his heels.

Rose turned and hurried to the ladder. She scraped her palms on the rough wood as she scrambled down, but paid no heed. All hands would be needed to help put out the blaze, or if need be, to treat any victims.

The guard at the gate shouted to her as she ran out, but she only called up to him to send more men to help.

Quickly he ran to do as she bid.

By the time Rose reached the village, she had a stitch in her side, but she didn't stop. She barely slowed as she called out to the people she passed, telling them to bring buckets and follow her.

When Rose arrived at the small farm, which lay not far from the village, she was gasping with the effort to breathe and her side ached unbearably.

The farmyard was in chaos. A cow lay dead in the yard, a pack of dogs fighting over it. A group of young boys raced back and forth, getting in the way, and Rose wondered why someone didn't make them stop. A woman was loudly crying into her dirty apron. The air was thick with acrid smoke.

Yet, amid the chaos there was order. Soldiers and Saxons were working together as they carried buckets of water to throw on the flames that ate at the roof of the cottage.

Rose searched for Gaston in the crowd. Hearing his deep voice during a lull in the noise, she followed the sound.

She found him standing at the side of the burning cottage. Some of the people from the village had arrived and he was directing them as to what needed to be done.

She ran to him. "What happened? Did someone leave the fire unattended? Where are Nigel and his family?"

His face was set in grim lines. "This fire was no accident."

"What do you mean?" she grabbed his arm. "Where is the family?"

"Dead."

"All dead?"

He nodded curtly. "Yes."

"I want to see them," she cried. "How could they all be dead?"

Gaston turned away. "I have had the bodies removed."

"I don't understand."

"The raiders Hubert is hunting were here. They killed the family who lived here and set fire to the buildings." His voice was expressionless. He couldn't forget the sight of the slaughtered bodies. He only hoped they had died relatively quickly.

"Oh, dear God." Rose blanched and swayed. "That can't be." Something was dreadfully wrong. Robert would never do such a thing. "I want to see them," she insisted.

The cottage was a great blazing torch now, and he ordered the men to fall back. There was no point in continuing to try to save it.

It was only after everyone was safely back from the fire that Gaston answered her. His tone had a note of finality. "I'm afraid I can not allow you to see the bodies."

Though she was impressed with his leadership in this situation, Rose could not allow Gaston to usurp her rights as Lady of Carlisle. Rose drew herself up. "How dare you deny me?"

Gaston swung around to face her, his eyes hard. "These people died after being tortured. My only thought was to spare you the grief of seeing what has been done to them, not to deny you your rights as their lady."

Rose put a hand to her forehead. "I . . . I . . . how can this be?" She swayed.

He reached out to steady her. Realizing Rose would not want her people to see her like this, Gaston drew her away from the crowd. The small shed that had housed the farmer's cow and other small animals was also blazing. He led her past the structure and sat her down on a wide tree stump.

Gaston squatted down next to her, taking her cold hand in his. "I know you are distraught, but you must have no fear for yourself or your people. Hubert is out looking for these very men, and capture them he will."

"You don't understand." Rose looked away, biting her lower lip. It was impossible to believe Robert had committed such unspeakable evil. He would not torture her villeins.

"I know they are not my people," Gaston went on, misunderstanding her reason for distress, "but I have come to respect you Saxons in the short time I have been here. Even though I didn't know Nigel and his family, I too regret their deaths."

"Were these devils still here when you arrived?" Rose asked him.

"The men were here"—Gaston frowned in self-derision—"but we had come on foot and could only catch one of them as the rest rode away." He looked down at their clasped hands. "That man was inadvertently killed."

Gaston had managed to reach the raider before he could get onto his mount. A struggle had ensued, during which the raider had fallen, hitting his head hard upon a rock. The man had died instantly, leaving Gaston frustrated, with no one to punish for the horrible cruelties wrought. And many unanswered questions.

"All dead." Rose put her arms around herself and rocked back on the stump. "It happened so quickly."

Gaston could give no satisfactory reply. All he could do was try to prevent it from happening again. He stood. "I plan to take some men out and see if we can find any sign of these villains. The closer we follow, the more chance we have of finding them."

Rose nodded, rising. "Of course." She looked up at Gaston, the warmth and trust in her eyes giving away more than she knew. "I want to thank you for your care of my people."

"They are my people now, too," he answered.

A large vat steamed over the fire pit. A solution of the deepest blue had been readied for dying the cloth Rose dropped into the vat. It was the best of the season's wool and would be made into the finest of garments.

She had begun this task, hoping the activity would help keep her mind from the events of the previous day. Gaston and the other men had not been able to find even one sign of the men who had killed Nigel and his family.

Her frustration was compounded by the fact that this wool would probably be used to make her wedding garments. She had an urge to turn the whole thing over onto the ground and watch it sink out of sight.

"Lady Rose," came a male voice from behind her.

Intent on her task, she did not look around as she answered. "Yes."

"Lady Rose!"

She clenched her teeth in irritation. "Yes." She swung around to face a man dressed in the rough tunic of a farmer. He was not one of the men of Carlisle. Putting her hands to her hips, Rose studied the craggy lines of his face, thinking as she did so that he seemed somehow familiar.

Suddenly, as if a candle had been lit in her mind, she remembered. His name was Ulrick and he had long been one of her cousin Robert's men.

Thick grey brows pulled together over his dark eyes as Ulrick saw the recognition in her gaze.

As she opened her mouth to greet him, he raised a hand and peered about them cautiously. His voice was as rough as the lines of his face. "I have a message for you."

"A message," Rose whispered, hurriedly wiping her hands on the apron tied about her waist. She glanced around to see if they were watched. No one seemed to have marked their conversation. Only the women working with her would know that Ulrick was not of Carlisle, and they went diligently about their work. They would give no sign that might alert the guard on the palisade walk above them to Ulrick's presence. Rose offered up a quick prayer of thanks that her women were so quick-witted.

Then she felt a passing moment of regret. The people, once common working folk, had learned too much of stealth. An innocence had gone that would never be returned.

"Come with me," she said aloud, shaking off her melancholy. Ulrick must surely have news of Robert and Elspith. That was cause to rejoice, she told herself as she moved away from the group around the fire.

Ulrick came with her, keeping close behind as she hurried across the courtyard.

Seeing a soldier sitting in the afternoon sunshine, polishing his armor, Rose slowed her steps. This would not do. She was going to draw attention to the two of them if she did not take hold of herself.

After glancing up briefly, the soldier went back to cleaning the links of his chain mail.

More slowly, Rose lead the Saxon to a deserted spot behind the Great Hall. She turned on the man with ill-concealed anxiousness. "What have you to tell me?"

Ulrick took one more careful look around to make sure they were, indeed, alone before speaking. "I have a message from Lord Robert."

Rose's heart stopped, then started again with a sickening thud. After all these weeks of silence, would Robert contact her unless something were dreadfully wrong? Why now, after the distressing events of yesterday? Could she be mistaken in trying to convince herself he had not been involved in the deaths of her vassals? She had so many unanswered questions.

Only Robert had the answers.

Ulrick went on. "Lord Robert wants you to meet with him tonight."

Her heart swelled with hope. Surely Robert would not meet with her if he had done her people such wrongs. Rose raised her gaze to Ulrick's. "Then he is well?"

The man looked a little taken aback at the question. "Yes, lady, when last I saw him this morning."

Rose grasped his arm in excitement. "Lady Iris and Lady Elspith, are they also well?"

Ulrick stepped back, studying the grounds for observers.

Rose released his arm quickly, cursing herself for her lack of control. She must not be seen to be overly familiar with a vassal. Nothing must mark Ulrick's presence in any way. She swallowed to moisten her dry throat, then asked more calmly. "Are they well?"

Ulrick did not meet her eyes. "To the best of my knowledge, lady, but I can not say more. I am only to tell you that Lord Robert wishes to meet with you in the West Wood tonight."

"Where?" she asked, realizing she would get no more information at the moment.

Ulrick answered gruffly. "At the place were the stream widens into a pond."

Rose nodded, knowing the place well. She, Edmund, Robert and Elspith had often gone there to play in the summers when her cousins would come to visit. Robert would know Rose could find her way there, even in the dark.

Looking over at Ulrick, Rose saw that he was obviously uncomfortable with standing here in the open. He shifted his weight nervously from foot to foot as he kept his gaze moving continuously around them.

"Will you need my help in getting out of Carlisle?" she asked him.

His expression took on all the clever cunning of a fox. "No, lady. I have my own way."

"Then I will not keep you longer. I know the danger. Thank you for coming here. God's speed to you...." she finished, her voice trailing off as she watched him walk away unnoticed.

Rose folded her hands under her chin, her brow puckered in thought. Had Robert learned of what had happened to Nigel's family and wished to help? She refused even to acknowledge that he could have been a party to it.

It was possible her cousin knew nothing of yesterday's events. He might have encountered Hubert's army and realized that he had no chance against such a knight. What could she do if Robert wanted her to help him? She had little or no authority now the Normans had come.

Rose shook her head. There was little sense in speculating. She would see Robert tonight and then she would know the truth.

She needed to concentrate on getting out of the keep undetected. The guard at the gate had grown more lax during daylight hours as people came and went from village, farm and keep. But at night no one was allowed to leave or enter without first being questioned.

Her eyes came to rest on the little mound that marked the opening of the tunnel. There was no guard posted there. It would be nothing short of suicide for a hostile army to enter that way. It was too narrow for more than one man to traverse at a time. Invaders would be cut down, as they came through the opening. The tunnel had been built for escape, not attack.

And escape was just what she planned to do.

Then she halted her own headlong thoughts. Gaston. He would be hard to fool. He watched her every move, making sure she behaved in a way that Hubert would approve.

Drawing herself up to her full height, she took a deep breath. She would not let him prevent her from going. There had to be a way.

In her accustomed place beside Gaston at dinner that evening, Rose said little. She did not want to draw attention to herself. If she attempted to make conversation, the men would surely take note of her growing agitation.

Rose had no room for error.

If anyone should mark her leaving, not only she but Robert would be in danger. Hubert would think nothing of having her punished if he felt Rose had betrayed him. He would not care for the fact that she must do all she could for her family. She could not turn away from her own blood.

Gaston spoke beside her. "Claude was very tired from getting up today, but after he had rested again, he said it had made him a bit stronger."

Rose looked up, her eyes puzzled as she attempted to concentrate on Gaston's words. She had been too absorbed in her own thoughts to listen. "What did you say, sir?"

Gaston studied her closely. Lady Rose seemed very distracted this evening. "I was saying that Claude is doing well." This was the second time he had spoken and not received an answer.

The curiosity in Gaston's expression was clearly evident, and she cursed herself for being foolish. "Yes, he is." She nodded enthusiastically. Bending forward, she picked up her goblet and took a sip of wine. Had she really thought that keeping silent would prevent Gaston from noticing her preoccupation? He was far too observant.

"He thinks of you as a sorceress." Gaston grinned down at her, his eyes hooded. "I would not doubt that the man is a little in love with you."

Rose rushed in hastily. "That is ridiculous. He is only grateful that I was able to save his arm."

The grin faded as Gaston bent closer to her, his voice low. "The fact that you are also a very lovely woman may play some small part in his admiration."

Rose looked up in surprise, her green eyes round with confusion as she searched his painfully handsome face for some clue as to his true feelings. Why did he play these games with her? She felt like a small animal caught between the paws of some larger predator as she waited for him to decide what to do with her.

Gaston's eyes were languid and she could gauge nothing from his expression. She turned away, worn out with trying to read meaning into his meaningless remarks. "Forgive me, sir, for being a simple country maid. I can not fathom the reason for your flattery. Mayhap were I more sophisticated, I would take such remarks as my due."

His deep laugh rang out, causing several heads to turn, and Rose was mesmerized by the sparkle in his grey eyes. "Country maid you may be, but never simple." His tone lowered so only she could hear, and his gaze captured hers. "Did you but want, you could cleave my heart with one angry word."

Her heart fluttered in her chest, though she knew this exchange was only court banter. She forced herself to look away and gave a shaky laugh. "Please, sir, do not go on. At least I am not so innocent as to take your empty flattery seriously."

He leaned closer. "Were you not so innocent, you would realize just how deeply the words ring true."

Her breath caught and she glanced toward him, but he had turned to answer one of the other knights.

Rose did her best to finish her meal, though her stomach rebelled with each bite. She would need her strength if she were to outwit this Norman tonight.

Later, when the residents of Carlisle had long since taken to their beds, Rose left her bower. As she made her way across the grounds she could see the sentry where he paced the wall, silhouetted against the moonlight. A hint of dampness was in the air, and she wondered at it as she looked up into the clear night sky bright with a multitude of stars.

When she reached the tunnel, it took all her strength to lift the heavy door, the muscles in her arms screaming at the effort she made. Letting the door fall to the ground, she wiped the beads of sweat on her forehead with the back of her sleeve.

With a deep breath for courage, she entered the tunnel. It was dark and if she held out her arms, she could touch the walls on either side of her at the same time. It smelled of damp earth and was thick with the scent of furry little bodies. She shuddered as she heard the little squeaking and scurrying sounds the mice made as they hurried ahead of her.

The opening on the outside seemed a very long way from where she had entered, but finally she came out into the fresh night air. Taking a deep breath to clear her lungs of the stale musty smell, Rose stepped out onto the hillside. Here at the back of Carlisle, the hill was much steeper and she looked up at the palisade, which seemed far above her.

Rose turned and scrambled down the slope to the edge of the forest, holding her breath as she waited for an outcry from the palisade behind her.

It was a relief to enter the enveloping safety of the wood. The moonlight shone in silvery beams of light through the trees, and a gentle wind ruffled the leaves over her head. Her leather-shod feet sank into the thick carpet of humus on the forest floor and she smiled, feeling at home. Rose had spent too many hours roaming this wood for plants to feel frightened.

In a short time she was at the stream. She saw no sign of Robert and for a moment she was afraid he had changed his mind. But she calmed herself. If he were not coming, Robert would have sent word to her.

A slight stirring to Rose's right made her turn. A man stepped from behind a tree, the hood of his mantle pulled up to obscure his face.

She needed only study him for a moment before the lithe grace of his movements gave Robert away. She ran forward, hurtling herself into his outstretched arms. He pulled her close to his comforting warmth. Her throat ached with the joy of seeing him again, and she found herself unable to ask him about the raid, afraid he would think she accused.

She cried against his shoulder. ''Robert, Robert! For a moment I feared you would not come.''

His dear, familiar voice rumbled under her ear. ''I waited only to see you were not followed.'' His arms tightened and he put his cheek down on her soft hair. ''It is good to see you, little cousin. Elspith and I have both missed you. It has been too long since we last met.''

She pushed back to look at him. ''Is Elspith well?'' Her eyes were dark with concern in the moonlight.

''As well as can be expected with our home taken and none of the comforts a lady should have.'' He pulled her back into his arms with a growl of anger.

''And your lady mother?''

He gave a choking gasp. ''Dead.''

Rose simply stood there for a long moment. Her own dear mother's sister. Gone. ''But how?''

His tone was hard to mask his sorrow. ''Illness. She could not stand the deprivations.'' His clipped answer made it clear he would not tell more.

''Oh, Robert.'' Rose hugged him, her arms about his waist. She was saddened to feel the too-thin flatness of his belly under his clothes. "I have worried long for you all. Must you continue resisting the Normans?"

"Must I continue?" He released her, stepping back. "How may I not? If I sit back and accept these Normans as the masters they claim to be, I can have no self-respect. What would give me the right to call myself a man?"

Rose drew herself up, her chin trembling with hurt at his stinging words. "A man who accepts what can not be changed is just as brave as the man who decides to fight." She turned her back to him.

Robert moved forward and swung her around to face him. "I meant no slander to you, little cousin. You are only a woman and must do the best you can with no man to care for you. You have no way to resist these barbarians."

"Is resisting them really the best way, Robert?" she asked, studying his hauntingly thin features. Once Robert had been so handsome, with his golden hair and bright eyes. Many a young woman around the countryside had sighed with sad longing at the sight of him. Now he burned with a fierce hatred she feared would consume him.

He answered her with sadness. "Edmund would have fought at my side, would have shared my rage."

Rose felt a wave of intense anger and frustration. Did men really believe they were the only ones who suffered through the loss of honor? Words poured from a deep well of anguish inside her. "Must I ever be compared to Edmund and found lacking? I have given my very honor to protect my people. Edmund could not have done more. Father could never see that I, too, had inherited his sense of duty and honor." So surprised was his expression that she would have laughed had the situation been less serious.

"Rose, your father loved you dearly."

She pleaded with him to understand. "But I wanted his respect. I have done all I can for Carlisle."

"But you chose to yield." His eyes grew distant as he stared at something far beyond her. "I can not. It is something that, being a woman, you can't understand."

Was it really easier for her, as a woman, to accept the Norman domination? Rose could not acknowledge this as truth. She only knew she had done what she must to keep her people safe.

Rose's thoughts came back to Elspith. She would hold her tongue, her cousin would never meet her point. Once again, she must yield for the good of another. "Robert, I have something to ask you. I know it will be difficult for you to answer yes, but I want you to think carefully before you tell me nay."

His expression was guarded, as though he were preparing to reject her suggestion.

"I want you to allow Elspith to come to me at Carlisle," she blurted out. She clamped her lips shut and held her breath as she waited for him to answer.

Robert began to laugh, the sound filling the small clearing and rising up into the branches over their heads. Backing up, he leaned against a tree trunk, his mirth leaving him weak.

"What is so funny?" Rose asked, putting her hands on her hips and glaring at him.

"You are," Robert gasped, "and I am. The reason I asked you to meet me here tonight was that I was hoping I could convince you to let Elspith come to you." His face grew grim as his laughter faded, leaving his voice hollow. "It is no life for her. I should not have taken her or Mother with me into the forest. But what was I to do?" He lifted a hand in entreaty for Rose to understand. "I could not leave them to face the Normans alone, and there was not time to send them to you."

Rose could bear it no longer, happiness coursed through her. "Oh, I am so glad." She jumped up, throwing her arms around his neck. "I had thought I might have to beg you."

Robert hugged her close once more. "How will you explain her presence at Carlisle? Questions will be asked."

"I have thought of a way. You needn't worry," she told him confidently, her eyes shining like bright stars. "When

will she come?'' She squirmed around in his arms like a
child in her excitement.

''I am not certain,'' Robert answered slowly, scowling.
''De Thorne's camp lies between here and our own. We will
need to pick a night when he is occupied, possibly chasing
outlaws.'' He laughed, but it was a bitter sound.

''You have seen Lord de Thorne then?'' Rose questioned. ''He is very dangerous. You must be careful.''

''Don't worry,'' he soothed. ''Fortunately, so far, we have
only seen him from a distance. He thinks to squash our puny
resistance without much effort on his part. But he is in for
quite a surprise.'' He went on as if thinking aloud, ''I have
discovered we are not alone in our efforts to plague Hubert
de Thorne. The murderous devils . . .'' he muttered.

''Tell me.'' Rose knew he spoke of the attack on the farm.

His expression became guarded again. ''I would rather
not say. The less you know, the better. Suffice it to say there
are others besides my own men who wish the Normans ill,
and they will stop at nothing to accomplish this.''

He smiled and was transfigured into the old Robert. ''I
must go now.'' He pulled her close to him and, turning her
face up to his, he kissed her forehead gently. When she clung
to the safe haven of his presence with all her strength he told
her, ''Be brave, little one, and mayhap one day we will live
in peace as we once did.'' The small spark of hope that rose
in her was drowned when he went on. ''As soon as we have
chased the oppressors from our land.'' He released her then
and turned away, fading into the shadows of the forest, as
silent as a shadow himself.

Rose wanted to call out after him, to tell him that things
would never be as he envisioned them. The sooner he faced
the fact that the Normans had come to stay, the better it
would be for him.

But she did not wish to part on such a note. Besides, she
hugged herself with joy, soon she would have Elspith with
her, and nothing was worth jeopardizing that.

She had even more reason for happiness; Robert's words had convinced her he'd had nothing to do with killing Nigel and his family.

Some other evil was afoot and Rose meant to find out who was behind it.

Deciding it was high time she returned to Carlisle, Rose swung around—which brought her directly in contact with the rock-hard length of a male body. Her heart stopped, then started again with a lurch, sending her blood racing with fear. She closed her eyes with a groan of absolute despair. Gaston.

Her mind reeled with shock. How much had he seen? And if he had seen Robert, why had he not taken him while he had the chance?

Her limbs were shaking so badly she could barely move them, but by sheer force of will she made her legs obey, stepping back from him. She had to stand her ground.

His strong fingers closed over the fragile bones of her shoulders. She swallowed, waiting for him to speak, to denounce her as a rebel.

Finally, after what seemed an eternity, he said, "Well, damsel?"

"Sir—Sir Gaston," she stuttered idiotically, unable to think of how she should answer him.

His voice was rough as he prodded her. "Would you care to explain what I just saw here?"

Rose stalled for time. "What is it you think you saw, sir?" She knew she must think of something. There was no way she could possibly tell him why she was here.

"You know very well what I saw." His voice, raw and ragged, broke at the same time as his control. The strong arms that held her gave her a jarring shake. "That man is your lover. There's no good denying it. I saw him kissing you."

Her head was muddled with worry over her cousin, and it took a moment before she realized Gaston had totally misjudged what he had seen. "My lover?" Rose looked down at the ground. Would it not be better for Gaston to believe she was meeting a lover than have him asking questions about Robert? Their parting was still too fresh and the real sorrow in her voice added to the illusion that Robert was indeed her lover. "We were saying goodbye."

Gaston's tone was hard as the steel of his sword. "It is wrong for you to meet another man here, when you are shortly to marry my brother."

"I came only to say goodbye," Rose lied, her words coming in a rush. "He begged me to meet him. I had to say yes. I was afraid he would put himself in danger by coming to Carlisle if I did not meet with him."

He stood stiff and unyielding in the moonlight. "You have known this man for a time?"

"Oh, yes," she answered, warming to her subject. For some reason the edge in Gaston's tone no longer frightened her, for she caught a hint of the same green demon that had caused her such discomfort when Gaston had spoken with Evelyn. "I must make you believe," she continued, raising her clasped hands to her bosom, "I came only to tell him all was past between us. He had heard of my marriage to Hubert, you see, and sent word I should come to him. What else was I to do?" She looked up at him in the moonlight, her eyes dark and pleading for him to understand.

"If it was goodbye," Gaston grated, "then why did you allow him to kiss you?"

"What is a kiss?" she prattled, unthinking of her words, too relieved that he was believing her tale. "It was such a small gift to him. You yourself—" she turned on him "—are not above offering a kiss of peace."

"What is a kiss?" Gaston groaned, unheeding of anything that followed her first statement. "I'll show you . . ."

Before Rose knew what was happening, she was pulled into the circle of his strong arms. His dark head bent to hers.

Gaston's lips were hard and cool.

Rose was too startled to react with anything but surprise. Then his mouth began to move on hers, to caress and nibble with undeniable sensitivity. Her own lips moved against his, responding automatically to the stimulation. His first kisses had prepared her for this more passionate assault and she held nothing back. Her reaction was sheer desire, undiluted in its innocence.

Gaston groaned and pulled her closer against the warm hard length of his body, and she snuggled into him, her hands trailing up to the strong column of his throat to pull his head even closer to hers.

She strained up on the tips of her toes as her fingers tangled in the thick dark curls at his nape. Her head began to spin as she was swept into a swirling vortex of heat and flame, where nothing existed beyond the hardness of the man and the softness of the woman.

This was why she had been born, Rose told herself, to be held by this man. She moaned, sucking in her breath as he shifted and she felt him, firm against her belly. ''My love.'' It was a whisper against his lips.

At her whispered words, Gaston raised his head. Her face was alight with passion. But it was not for him. She was only thinking of the other man, their parting still sweet in her memory.

His desire cooled as quickly as it had risen. He stepped back, his hands dropping to his sides. His voice was devoid of emotion. ''We must return to Carlisle.''

His abrupt change of mood wilted her like frost on spring flowers. Her declaration of love seemed to have sickened him.

She raised her chin. Never would she let him see how his rejection had hurt her.

On the way back to Carlisle neither of them spoke. Silently he led her the long way around through the gate. Only as they entered the courtyard did he turn to her.

But Rose pretended she didn't see, stalking toward her bower.

She did not see the pain in Gaston's grey eyes as he watched her walk away, her back stiff with anger.

He held out his hand, wanting to call her back. He was sorry for having hurt her. Her love for the man in the forest was not wrong. She must have cared for him long before Hubert had come and claimed her.

It was Gaston who was unclean in this matter. He knew Rose was promised to his brother and that her heart was given to another man.

And still he wanted her—wanted her more than life or honor.

Chapter Seven

The following evening, the rain began. Water poured from the sky with a vengeance. Rose felt as though nature were trying to somehow wash away the stain that had come to their land in the form of the Normans.

The occupants of the keep had been driven inside the Great Hall.

When Rose joined the other women, Gaston made no move to check her. He sat conversing with the other knights around the huge fire burning in the pit. He seemed totally oblivious to her. And that was what she wanted, wasn't it?

Her mind flashed for the thousandth time to the previous night. She felt again the strength of his masterful male lips moving over hers; remembered the way her body had responded with all the pent-up longing in her. She heard her own voice calling out huskily, "My love."

Rose's face flushed hot with shame, and she looked down at her hands. What must he think of her? Could she really believe she would go straight from the arms of one man into those of another? And, believing as he did that Robert was her love, would Gaston tell Hubert of their meeting?

Rose was silent as the talk and laughter of the other women flowed around her. Her eyes strayed again and again to the man across the room. She did not want him to believe she was so hot for just any man. But she would rather die than have him know how much she cared.

Gaston threw back his head as he laughed at some jest.
Firelight gleamed on the bronze column of his throat and
her teeth caught at the fullness of her lower lip. Her gaze
followed his hand as he pushed at the stubborn curl on his
forehead. How she longed to touch that lock of hair, to feel
the thickness of it in her fingers. With a silent groan of anguish, Rose turned away.

There was no sense in torturing herself this way. In her
own bower she would be alone with her misery. She stood
and made her way out, having to pass close by the leaping
flames in the pit as she left.

Rose didn't see the way Gaston watched her every move,
nor the hunger in his eyes as he took in the way the firelight
turned her hair to molten flame against the pale yellow of
her tunic. Her own self-derision blinded her.

Stepping out into the pouring rain, Rose pulled the hood
of her mantle up to cover her head, though it offered little
protection against the downpour. Her best hope of remaining even nominally dry was to make a quick dash through
the muddied courtyard.

Rose jumped as a hand touched her shoulder. "Lady."

Turning, Rose found Maida standing there. The cook's
wet hair clung to her round cheeks and her teeth were chat-
tering loudly. "Come with me," Maida said, motioning for
Rose to follow as she began walking away.

Saying nothing about the abruptness of the request, Rose
followed. Something must be wrong to make Maida behave
so strangely.

To Rose's surprise, Maida led her to the storage cellar.
Still she didn't comment, simply waiting as she watched the
cook lower her bulk slowly to the bottom of the ladder. A
soft light came from inside the cellar, making it easy for
Rose to see the way as she too descended.

She stepped down onto the earthen floor and swung
around. Her gaze came to rest upon a slight figure huddled
in the corner across from her. It appeared to be a young
woman in a cloak and mantle soaked black from the rain.

Rose's gaze flew to Maida, who only nodded toward the crouched figure.

Rose looked at the maid more closely. The angle at which her head was held and the unmistakable grace of the posture were familiar to her.

Then she was flying across the short space that separated them to envelope the slender frame in her arms.

"Elspith, Elspith!" she cried. "I can't believe you've come."

Elspith sobbed loudly. "Oh, Rose, how I have longed to see you again." Her hood fell back and her hair spilled across her narrow shoulders. Even wet with rain and in such poor light, the silky mass shone a pale silver blond.

The two girls hugged and cried and laughed. It had only been a few months since they last met, but for all that had changed it could have been an eternity. Rose's father and brother were both dead. Elspith's mother had died and her brother had turned outlaw in his own land. And there was the ever-present threat of their enemies, the Normans, to remind them that life would never be the same.

"I had not thought Robert would let you come to me so soon." Rose pulled back. Even though her eyes shone with tears, her smile was genuine for the first time in months.

Elspith answered in her soft voice. "Robert believed the rain might keep Lord de Thorne and his men close to their fires this night. We saw no one as we came here."

Studying her cousin closely, Rose could see Elspith had changed. There was a new strength in her gentle golden eyes.

Elspith studied Rose, as well. Hesitantly she said, "You are the same, and yet I feel you are different."

Regretfully Maida interrupted them. "We must get this child into some dry clothing before she catches her death."

Realizing how icy cold the fingers in hers were, Rose had to agree, "Maida is right. Come, we will see you warm and dry."

For a moment, Elspith's face was uncertain. "Robert told me you have some plan to explain my arrival here."

"Yes, and to carry it out I will need Maida's assistance. Her forethought in bringing you to the cellar tonight will help us."

"I did not bring Lady Elspith here," Maida said, her round cheeks turning a bright pink. "I had come for a bottle of wine, you know how my bones ache when it rains. That was when I found the Lady Elspith here."

The wine stored in this cellar was the very finest, purchased from the nearby monastery at great cost. But Rose had no thought for that now. "How you found Elspith doesn't matter. We must agree on a story to explain her presence here at Carlisle." In answer to their expectant expressions, Rose went on; "Maida, I want you to pretend Elspith is your niece. You will say she has come from your sister near Mayhill."

Maida looked at Rose with some trepidation. Anyone with two eyes could see Elspith was not some simple farmer's daughter. "Lady Elspith is too fine a lady for anyone to believe that, Lady Rose."

Rose turned to Elspith. It was true Elspith did not look like a crofter's daughter. Her head was held at a proud angle and her hands were too slender and delicate for one who would have done much hard work. Her underdress was dirty and torn at the hem, but the cloth was of the finest blue samite.

Rose had never owned a gown of samite. Her father had not traded for such costly fabrics. Carlisle provided its own fine woolens.

Elspith saw Rose looking at her once-fine gown and shrugged. "It is all I have. We left the very night Robert returned from the war." Her offhanded shrug told Rose of her hopelessness in a way that no words could.

Rose knew how hard it must have been for Elspith living the life of an outlaw in the forest. She had never worked among the people, as Rose had.

Elspith had been groomed for marriage to a man of high position. There was even some talk of her alliance with the younger son of an earl. But the war had come and now things were very different. For what Rose had in mind, Elspith would need to use every bit of her will to survive.

"We must disguise Elspith as a servant. If Hubert discovers Elspith is a gentlewoman, he will not rest until he knows her true identity. If Robert's relationship to her is to be kept secret, this must be avoided at all costs. Should Hubert find out the truth, he would use Elspith to lure his enemy out of the protection of the forest." Rose faced the other two directly. "There is no other way."

Elspith looked down at her soft hands, which were pale in the candlelight. "I will be found out."

"These Normans will only see what is obvious. Luckily Hubert is gone and we will have only his brother to convince," Rose said in an attempt to sound reassuring.

Elspith's eyes were dark with uncertainty.

"How long must you keep Lady Elspith hidden?" Maida asked.

Rose could not be less than honest. "I do not know." She held out her hands, palms turned upward. "Gradually I will try to improve your situation until it is more tolerable for you. I know you can not want to live as a servant, but for Robert's sake it is the only way. At least for the moment. It is for you to decide. If you do not want to stay, I can have someone take you back tonight, before your presence here is known."

Those few weeks in the forest had been the most difficult of Elspith's life. She shook her head, her golden eyes wide and trusting. "I will stay with you."

Rose felt yet another burden descend on her too-slight shoulders. "I will see that you share my bower with me. That much, at least, I can do."

The next day Hubert returned to Carlisle. He and his men were soaked to the skin and more than eager for Maida's cooking.

Gaston saw his brother ride through the gate with relief. Since that night in the forest when he had kissed Rose, he had been able to think of little else. His only hope of avoiding another such incident had been to keep a distance between them. It had not been as easy as he would have hoped. Even though he knew she loved another man, he watched her wherever she went, listened for the sweet sound of her voice.

His long strides took him quickly to where the men were dismounting from their tired steeds. "Kyle!" Gaston beckoned a serf who stood nearby. "Take Lord de Thorne's horse to the stables. See that he is fed and rubbed down."

Accustomed to following Gaston's orders without delay, Kyle hurried to obey.

Hubert raised his brows but made no comment.

Taking no notice of this, Gaston drew his brother toward the Great Hall. "Come, you must have something warm to drink. I was just going to the hall myself. Tell me the news. Have you had any success in capturing these rebels?"

"You seem to have settled in quite well," Hubert commented dryly.

Surprised, Gaston looked up, then began to laugh. "I am sorry if I have usurped your authority. I grow accustomed to giving orders."

"As I see." Hubert grinned back. "It is evident you will soon be petitioning King William for your own lands. It is my hope—" he frowned "—that you are luckier in your portion than I have been."

They entered the great hall and Gaston raised his hand to beckon a serving woman, whom he told to bring mulled wine for himself and Hubert. "So you have been less than successful in finding these outlaws?"

Hubert shook his head. "I can not understand it." He threw his gauntlets onto the table. "It is almost as if the demons know what we do before it is done. And stranger still—" he leaned on the table "—there seems to be no reasoning behind what they do. One night they burn an empty grain bin. A deed done more to irritate than to cause real harm. Then only hours later, they beat a man to death when he refuses them his cattle."

With a grim expression, Gaston told Hubert of the events at Nigel's farm, concluding that he had had no more luck in capturing the perpetrators than Hubert.

Hubert banged his fist down in anger. "I have gone to Brentwood and questioned everyone, threatened most, even beaten a few, but no one will talk. It is almost as if the people are protecting someone. But why would they shield those who would do them such harm?" Hubert scowled.

"What of the old lord's family?" Gaston asked, trying to make sense of this riddle.

"There was a son and a daughter at Brentwood," Hubert said with a shrug, "but from what I have been able to learn they were little more than children."

"What has become of them?"

"I know not, and I do not care. It would take more than a half-grown boy to carry out the deeds these men do."

The serving woman brought their warmed wine and placed it before them. Hubert picked up his drinking horn and drank thirstily. The bright red liquid dribbled from the corners of his mouth. Setting the horn down, he wiped his mouth on his sleeve, which was beginning to steam in the heat from the fire, and sighed loudly in appreciation.

"Do you really believe you should rule out the lord's own family?" Gaston prodded after taking a sip of his own wine.

"I tell you I have questioned the people on this tract. The boy is too young. As their stories did not change, even under torture, I can only believe them. The children may even be hidden somewhere in the village, but no matter, they can do me no harm." He refilled his horn from the pitcher on the table.

Gaston raised his cup to his lips, thinking as he did so that Hubert's methods of securing information could be very persuasive. If the villagers continued to swear it could not be the lord's son, then very likely it was not. Who the per-

petrator was mattered little. The guilty party must be caught
and punished. "If the villeins can not identify these men,"
he said finally, "it is very likely they are not locals. Our enemy is likely a troop of soldiers without allegiance to anyone. Their methods of torture are quite professional."

"I had come to the same conclusion—" Hubert nodded
"—which could make them more difficult to capture. I can
see now that William may have been overgenerous in his
gifts to me." His grin was forced. "If matters do not improve soon, I shall have to send to Normandy for more
mercenaries, and that is always very expensive."

Gaston looked into the dark liquid in his cup. He felt as
though his stomach were tied in knots. It sickened him to
know Hubert was growing dissatisfied with his lot. Gaston
would have given everything he possessed to have the responsibilities Hubert so easily defamed. He enjoyed knowing he had been the one to make the right decision and
readily accepted the consequences when he was wrong. But
it was Rose who made Carlisle special, who changed it from
being a strange land, with faceless people, to a place of
welcome.

When Gaston did not comment, Hubert said, "I am
thankful you were here at Carlisle. Your presence leaves my
own mind clear to see to this."

Gaston could only nod. He was unable to look at Hubert.
Hubert would not be so grateful if he but knew how his own
brother lusted after his intended bride.

Guilt descended upon him like a poisonous vapor. If he
were a man of honor, he would refuse to go on with the
charade. But how could he tell his brother the truth without hurting him? He could not.

It was then Gaston knew what he must do.

When Hubert had managed to get his holdings under
control Gaston must leave Carlisle posthaste. It was the only
action he could take and retain his self-respect.

Hubert leaned back, unaware of Gaston's tormented
thoughts. "I have been well pleased with your stewardship.

Your letters have kept me well informed. I was most happy with your decision to marry the Saxon wench to one of my soldiers. The two peoples will learn to live in harmony."

With pride, Gaston told of how Rose labored so tirelessly to save Claude.

Hubert smiled. "The woman needs nothing so much as a firm hand to guide her. When the Lady Rose and I are united it will go further to seal the bonds between our peoples."

A muscle worked in Gaston's jaw. He needed no reminder that Hubert and Rose would be wed.

Hubert rubbed his hands together in anticipation. "I knew I could leave my bride in your capable hands. I only hope the Lady Rose proves to be as skilled in bed as she is at healing."

Gaston clenched his teeth to keep from uttering a retort. "You speak of the woman as if she were little more than a mare."

"Oh ho, what's this?" Hubert quirked a brow. "Why are you suddenly interested in my mode of speech? You, dear brother, are the one to be giving pretty speeches to women. As well you know I am not."

Gaston turned away, a foul taste coming to his mouth as he lied. "I only sought to remind you that she is the lady here and the people will accept you all the better should you treat her with honor."

"Right you are, Gaston," Hubert answered. "I would do well to remember that. Have you any other news for me?"

Gaston hesitated. Should he tell Hubert of Rose's meeting with the man in the forest? Hubert would not take such a thing lightly. As Gaston hesitated, the moment was lost, for Hubert took his silence as answer.

Hubert began to talk of a letter Sir Gerard had received from his brother at court. According to Gerard's brother, King William was having his own problems with a Saxon earl, some distance to the north of Carlisle.

Gaston only listened with half an ear.

Rose had said that she would not see the man again. If Gaston was allowed to keep his desire of her secret, then was Rose not entitled to a secret of her own?

The tray Elspith carried was heavily laden with meats, and she staggered under the burden. Rose spoke sharply to a young man who rushed to take the tray.

Rose then told Elspith to serve wine to the seated soldiers. With a look of thanks, Elspith went about her duties.

As Rose watched her cousin move away, she felt sorry she could not do more, though the ease with which Elspith had been accepted was heartening. Gaston had spared little attention for the young serving woman. And Hubert did not know the servants well enough to mark her presence.

With Elspith safely ensconced at Carlisle, Rose had more time for other worries. Would Gaston tell Hubert about her meeting with Robert?

Although Hubert had returned from Brentwood early in the day, Rose had not seen him. This gave her cause to hope Gaston had held his tongue. She was sure if Hubert knew, he would waste no time in confronting her.

Wishing to give her intended husband no cause for displeasure, Rose attired herself with more than her usual care. Hubert insisted she dress as befitted her station. He could be very difficult if he felt she slighted him or his position as lord. Her underdress of deepest salmon and her pale green tunic could offer no insult. Ribbons of each color were braided through her hair, which hung over her shoulders to her hips.

That Gaston would see her looking her best was of no consequence.

As she came close to the high table, Rose saw that Hubert had taken the seat next to hers.

Gaston sat to his left. She could feel the heat of his appreciative gaze and was warmed by it. When she glanced toward him, his eyes darkened to ash and her knees grew weak.

She took the seat next to Hubert. Once again, Rose was left to wonder how Gaston could affect her so with neither word nor touch.

Her would-be husband leaned forward, unintentionally blocking her view of his brother. "Lady, you are grown more beautiful in my absence."

Hubert's compliment left her unmoved, and her answer was stiff. "Thank you, my lord." Rose made an attempt to smile.

"Gaston tells me you have done well in my absence."

She looked up into his eyes, so much like Gaston's and yet so very different. Where Gaston's eyes were warm and intelligent, his brother's were hard and cunning.

Hubert was watching her with a mixture of benevolence and lust. Turning away, Rose wondered if she had made an error in grooming herself for his return; Hubert might well mistake her intentions. Realizing he was still waiting, Rose replied, "I have attempted to do my duty, my lord."

Hubert reached over and took one of her small hands in his massive, callused palm. "I am pleased with you, damsel. I look forward to our marriage, which grows closer as the days pass."

Rose's gaze darted to Hubert and away. Whatever was she to do now? As gently as she could, she pulled her hand from his, not daring to look upon her would-be lover.

Hubert frowned, drawing back on the seat. "I see you have not warmed to me yet."

Her voice was no more than a whisper. "I am sorry, my lord."

"You run hot and cold, lady." He grunted. "When you came to the meal garbed so finely, I thought you meant to please."

"I sought only to honor my lord's position," she said.

"And well you should," Hubert answered, his voice cold as December winds.

Rose forced herself to look up at him. She did not wish to cause Hubert anger. The well-being of her people depended upon his goodwill.

He stood up, leaning over her menacingly. "At the moment, I choose not to press the matter, damsel. But remember your fate is determined." His voice had risen to a growl. "I will have you. Will you or no."

"Yes, my lord," Rose looked down, barely repressing a shudder of revulsion. "I did not mean to offend you."

He placed his hand under her chin, his hard fingers digging into her jaw, forcing her to turn to him. "What you meant matters little to me. Make your mind sure on that. You are only a woman."

Tears sprang to her eyes as he increased the pressure, and Rose gulped back the retort that sprang to her mind.

With a disgusted snort, Hubert released her, pushing her away. He sat down, turning his back to her.

Resisting the urge to rub her chin where Hubert had held it so tightly, Rose tried to eat. The food tasted like nothing more than sand, but she made herself go through the motions. Her humiliation at having everyone see how Hubert had treated her was great.

Gaston felt an anger against his brother that was almost palpable. Was Hubert such a fool? He would never win the girl this way. Rose was a woman who must be wooed with love and tenderness. To treat her so badly would only force her away from him. When he spoke, his tone was frigid. "Hubert, must you behave this way before the woman's own people?"

Rose was horrified. What did Gaston hope to gain by challenging his older brother? Hubert held the power of life and death for her and her vassals.

Surprise made Hubert slow to answer, but when he did his voice held a warning. "What right have you to question me?"

Gaston realized he should have spoken with more care. He gave away too much of himself in defending Rose so vehemently. If he were to do her more good than harm, he must curb his anger. "The right of a brother. You do not further your cause by treating the lady with cruelty."

Hubert gave his brother a long look, his expression dark with speculation.

Gaston forced himself to return the stare. For Rose's sake, Hubert must not suspect how much Gaston cared.

The older man quirked a dark brow. "Methinks you protest overmuch, brother. 'Tis the second time you have called me to account this day. Remember these lands are mine, you but hold them in trust when I am away."

Knowing he had to steer Hubert from the truth, Gaston forced a smile. "A fact that never deserts me. I have no wish to play the country lordling. My loyalty to you and King William are what keep me here. When all is settled, the fortress built, and your lands intact, I shall be free to go where I might. It is in your best interest to treat the woman kindly."

The words seemed to mollify Hubert, but he had one last note of caution. "Mayhap you are right, but mind you, do not upbraid me again."

Gaston nodded. "Your point is well-taken."

His humor restored, Hubert shrugged, then picked up his glass, taking a long drink. Wiping his mouth on the back of his hand, he glanced around the room. "Perhaps, I may get what I desire from another source."

Elspith was serving wine at the long tables. As she moved around the room, she slowly worked her way toward their table. The time for her to pass Hubert's scrutiny had come.

Though Rose did not think such a thickheaded ass as Hubert could see past his nose, she knew a moment of tension as Elspith came to their table.

Elspith leaned close to the table as she checked to see if the pitcher between Gaston and Hubert needed filling. As she did so her silvery hair fell forward over her shoulders in a silky curtain. She reached up to push it back, and the thin fabric of her gown pulled tight over her bosom.

Hubert's gaze went to the gentle swell of her breasts and lingered. His tongue darted out to wet full lips, and Rose was reminded of a fox about to pounce on a rabbit.

Rose felt her heart sink with dread. Of all the things she had considered, she had not foreseen that Hubert would turn his lustful attentions on her cousin. Never had she thought he would be attracted to Elspith's subtle grace and beauty.

As the evening progressed, Rose's fears were not eased. Hubert's gaze followed the tall girl as she moved about the room, his eyes warm with appreciation. Finally, nodding as if some decision had been made, Hubert drained his drinking horn and beckoned to her.

Elspith approached slowly, like a frightened deer in the forest. She bent close to Hubert as she poured more wine into his glass. As her head came close to his, Hubert raised his mouth to her ear and whispered to her.

Rose could not hear what had been said, but she did see the way Elspith jumped in startled surprise. Unfortunately, as Elspith stumbled back she hit Gaston's shoulder with her elbow. This made her start again, and she dropped the pitcher she carried, spilling wine across the tabletop.

Before Elspith could move to clean the wine with her apron, it had begun to drip onto Hubert's lap. Bending hurriedly, she began to mop at the spreading pool.

To the revulsion of Rose—and the amusement of the men seated at the high table—Hubert took her hand and brought it to his groin.

Elspith leaped back as if burned. Crimson color stained her pale cheeks and she turned, running from the jeering laughter, tears bursting from her eyes.

Hubert whooped loudly in amusement and many of his soldiers followed suit.

Rose knew she must do something to protect her cousin. If Hubert decided he would have her, he would not rest until his desire was fulfilled.

Gathering her courage, Rose turned to her lord and future husband. "Lord de Thorne."

Hubert looked down at her with indifference, his eyes still glistening with laughter. "Yes, lady?"

She swallowed. "That woman is my servant. She is not to be used for your pleasure." To her surprise her voice was even.

Hubert's eyes became hooded and his brows rose with disdain. He spoke clearly and distinctly. "You are mistaken, madam. Nothing here is yours. All you see—" he made a sweeping motion with his arm "—is mine."

Inwardly Rose cringed, knowing she had gone too far. Only her fear for her cousin gave her the courage to continue. She stuck out her firm chin, and her eyes flashed bright with defiance. "You have decreed that no woman is to be taken against her will. Would you break your own law?" Her lips widened into a confident smile as she waited for his expression to turn to chagrin.

To Rose's amazement, Hubert's own mouth widened to a grin and a loud burst of laughter issued forth. He leaned close to her and his voice lowered to a conspiratorial tone. "Have no fear, damsel. Not all women find me as distasteful as you seem to. I shall have no need of force. In a very short time the girl will come to me of her own free will. She will see the honor I do her."

Rose shrank away from him, her mind reeling. How could he be so ridiculous as to believe Elspith would willingly go to him? He was repulsive.

She looked to Gaston. He had spoken for her earlier. Why did he keep his own counsel now, when Elspith's honor hung in the balance?

But she received no help from that quarter. His eyes were unreadable as he returned her gaze.

Rose forced herself to reason calmly. What if Elspith did not find Hubert as disgusting as she herself did? He was not an ill-favored man, and could even be pleasant—if he believed his ends might be gained.

No, she told herself, rejecting the thought. Elspith would not respond to his thin veneer of charm.

But Rose could not help wondering.

With only short respites from the rain over the next week, Hubert was able to concentrate on his pursuit of Elspith.

And try though Rose might to deny Elspith could ever succumb to the brute, she could see her cousin was indeed wavering.

Finally Rose knew she must speak out. She called Elspith to her bower to help with some sewing. The two women worked in strained silence for a time.

Now the opportunity was at hand, Rose was having a difficult time broaching the subject plaguing them both. In the end there was no other way but to speak her mind. "Elspith."

As if sensing her cousin's thoughts, the older girl rose and went to the window, her back to the room. The shutters were opened wide and Elspith watched the torrent of rain that poured from the sky. Her voice was low and strained. "I know not what to say. I know you are promised to him."

Rose swallowed past the lump in her throat. "Do you think I care for that? He is nothing to me. It is you I wish to protect." Her eyes narrowed with resolve. "He can not force you."

"He does not try." Elspith turned to her cousin, her wondrously golden eyes filled with sadness.

Unhappily Rose knew this was true. Even though Hubert continued his pursuit with dogged determination, he was careful to follow his own law.

Elspith went on, "When I reject his advances, he only smiles and pays me pretty compliments."

"You must continue to refuse him," Rose told her. "He wants only to use you. Hubert has no idea you are a gentlewoman. He would take you, then throw you away like a worn saddle."

"Do you think I have not told myself those very same things?" She turned back to her perusal of the rain. "I am little or nothing to him, only something he wants at this moment. When I no longer please him, he will forget me."

Elspith swung around, going to the warmth of the fire. "And yet," she said, holding her hands out to the flames, "there is something about him I find very hard to resist. He is so strong, so sure of himself and all that is his. I would not mind so very much to be cared for by one who is so sure of his own merit. I would feel I was more worthy for being his."

Her eyes met her cousin's. "I have ever been little more than a pretty child to my family and friends." She smiled at Rose's quick intake of breath, knowing she had struck a nerve.

There was no answer Rose could give to this. None of them had ever treated Elspith as an adult. But that did not change the fact that Hubert was the wrong man for her. "He will only use you," Rose reiterated desperately.

Elspith answered with a sigh. "This I know."

"You must continue to deny him," Rose said more forcefully.

"Yes," Elspith answered softly, looking down at her hands.

That night Elspith did not return to Rose's bower to sleep.

Chapter Eight

Gaston rested his elbows on the desk, steepling his fingers, and pressing them to his lips. He took a deep breath and let it out slowly.

Across from him, Alfred fidgeted on his seat.

Gaston fought the desire to tell him to be still. It was hard enough to work with the reeve. He seemed to have lost none of his fear of the Normans, even after so much time had passed.

Knowing his ill humor had little to do with Alfred did not alleviate it. Hubert was the true object of his displeasure, and in recent days, the man had been unavailable for discussion.

Hubert seemed disinclined to attend to business. For days, he had thought of nothing but the serving girl who had become his mistress.

Then, this evening, he had asked Gaston to meet him so they might go over harvest records. Gaston had been pleased to think Hubert meant to resume his neglected duties. Knowing the amounts of previous harvests gave them some idea of what to expect from the lands.

Hubert had not deigned to put in an appearance.

So here Gaston sat with Alfred while Hubert dallied with his doxy.

For the third time, Gaston asked, "Where could these ledgers be kept?" He tried but failed to keep the irritation out of his voice.

Alfred's nose twitched with alarm and he scooted as far from Gaston as he could without getting up. "I don't understand it, my lord. I know they were here. The Lady Rose and I—" He stopped his thin hand covering his mouth.

"Come on, man, what about the Lady Rose?" Gaston prodded. He felt as though he were spending his evening uselessly. If he could not accomplish anything, he might just as well seek his bed, as everyone else in the fief had apparently done.

"Lady Rose and I were examining the records together, when I was called away. She must have placed them somewhere." His eyes darted about, as if he were trying to find some clue of what she had done with them.

"Then I suggest," Gaston's voice grew louder as he spoke, "we ask her where they might be." His lips quirked in a thin smile. Rose would not thank him for disturbing her. Since the night Hubert had first met his woman, she had barely spoken to Gaston. Her reasoning was difficult to fathom. He had known she wished him to speak out against Hubert's actions, but her purpose escaped him. The lady had no love for her intended. If he chose to press his needs on some other woman, Rose should be pleased.

Alfred stood nervously, looking relieved. "I will see what I can do in the morning." He obviously felt the meeting had come to an end.

"Tonight," Gaston stated. "I want the matter settled immediately." He knew he should not summon her right now. He was tired and alone on a chilly night; the hour was late. He ignored the voice of warning in his head. Surely there could be no harm in talking about the stores....

He just wanted to see Rose, to hear her sweet voice.

"Now, my lord?" Alfred's eyes bulged.

"Now!" Gaston affirmed, little realizing how furious he sounded, intent on convincing himself he was not behaving foolishly.

Alfred started to go, then stopped, his mouth working convulsively.

"What is it?" Gaston demanded.

He wrung his thin, bony fingers. "It is late, my lord."

"I know that well, man, so make haste."

With an expression that clearly showed his reluctance, Alfred hurried out, his spindly legs bowed.

Gaston waited for what seemed a very long time before Rose appeared.

As she came toward him across the rush-strewn floor of the hall, he realized he had indeed erred.

Lady Rose of Carlisle had been summoned from her bath. Her auburn hair, which was freshly washed and already beginning to dry, clung to the dampness of her throat in fine wisps.

Gaston's eyes feasted on the unbound glory of her hair where it fanned out around the bed fur she wore as a covering. His fingers itched to touch it, feel its softness. His gaze fell lower to where he caught a glimpse of creamy thigh as she moved forward.

Intellectually he knew it was wrong to expect her to stay, garbed as she was in only a fur. But inside where his deepest desires lay hidden, he knew he could not send her away; not before he sipped his fill of her beauty.

Even if Rose was as enraged as her stiff movements told him she was, he wanted, needed to be near her.

Gaston closed his eyes and swallowed, his imagination dwelling on the delights her covering might shield from his view.

When she came to a halt before him, he knew. His body was attuned to her every movement, every breath. The ire she radiated was so real he felt he could almost reach out and touch it.

Her fury helped him to regain his composure. He could react to her anger without dishonoring himself and her.

As he opened his eyes, his attention went immediately to the small white foot that tapped the ground so insistently.

He stifled a grin. She had not even delayed to put on her shoes. His tone was overly polite as he said, "Thank you for coming so quickly."

A small gasp of outrage escaped her. He was acting as if he summoned her from her bath on a regular basis. "You are most welcome," she answered through stiff lips. "How may I be of assistance?"

Gaston motioned toward the seat Alfred had vacated. "Please, sit down. This may take some time."

The impossible gall of the man. His assumption, that she would calmly sit down and discuss some trivial matter with him, in nothing but a bed fur, was what snapped her control.

"How dare you treat me as if I were some servant to be beckoned hither and yon? Am I not even allowed the privacy of my bath, that you should send someone to order me here in the dead of night?"

He stiffened, barely keeping the tight rein he held over his emotions. Oh, but she could rile him so easily. "It is hardly the dead of night, damsel," Gaston told her.

"Would you quibble over the time of day, Sir Knight?" Rose began to pace before him. "What is of the utmost importance is that I am stripped of my dignity to bolster your ego."

This last remark was one that under other circumstances would have gained a heated response from Gaston. But he allowed it to pass.

He could think of little beyond Rose's state of dress—or rather undress. In her anger, the fur had slipped down, revealing the soft white skin of her shoulders. As the covering slipped lower, the gap at the side also widened and he was treated to an almost unobstructed view of one long leg.

Gaston felt his pulse quicken at the sight. She was so beautiful, it was hard for him to concentrate on what she was saying.

Rose, oblivious to his regard, continued. "You are all of a kind, you Normans. You take what you want, using whomever gets in your path, and discarding them when they are no longer useful." Elspith's defection was a sore spot in her heart. She hated Hubert and all his fellows, including Gaston. He could have tried to help her protect her cousin.

Hearing the very real pain in her voice, Gaston forced his attention to what she was saying. "I had hoped you no longer believed the worst of us," he said softly. "I meant you no disrespect this night, my lady. It was only out of necessity that I asked for you to be brought here. If I had known you were otherwise occupied, I would gladly have waited until a more convenient moment." Even as he said this, Gaston knew he did not speak the truth. He would not have missed seeing her thus for any reason.

Rose had stopped her pacing and stood before him. The fur had slipped down so he could see the rounded tops of her breasts, which drew his eyes with each breath she took.

Rose rolled her eyes toward the ceiling, her foot beginning to tap once more.

It was then Gaston noticed Alfred, hovering just out of the glow of the candles. The skeletal man must have returned with his mistress. Gaston had been so occupied with looking at Rose he hadn't noticed.

Squaring his shoulders as if seeking courage, the little man came closer to where Rose was standing. His attention was fixed on the slender leg exposed at her side.

At first, Gaston thought Alfred too was enjoying the sight of her, and he knew a primal rush of possession.

Then, as the reeve reached out, waving a cautious hand, Gaston realized his intent. Alfred was trying, in his awkward way, to bring her attention to the fact that she was baring more than she would wish to the knight.

Something, some inner sense of self-preservation, must have alerted Alfred to Gaston's frown of disapproval. The reeve turned to the taller man, and his eyes widened with apprehension. His hand halted in midmotion, and he stared down at it as if it were some unfamiliar object.

Gaston's expression told him more clearly than words that he need only wave that hand if he did not mind losing it.

Alfred drew his arm down to his side, breathing a silent sigh of relief when he saw Gaston's slight nod of approval.

The exchange happened so quickly Rose did not even take note of it. Frowning, she took a deep breath to steady herself. "What do you require of me? As I am already here, I will try to assist you."

To Gaston's chagrin, she drew the fur more closely around her shoulders.

He answered moderately, despite his disappointment. "I need the records of the last two years' harvests."

"They are in my bower," she stated.

Gaston turned to the reeve. "Would you be so good as to fetch them, Alfred?"

Following Gaston's eyes, Rose took note of Alfred's presence. "They are in the large chest where I keep my medicines," she told him. As he backed away, Alfred's intent gaze never left Gaston's face. Then he was gone, but the sour quality of his disapproval remained.

Gaston simply shrugged. He would not let the reeve's censure provoke him. He knew the people of Carlisle valued Rose above all else.

Rose's expression was puzzled as she watched Alfred leave. Why was he wearing such a long face and behaving so strangely? It had been Rose who had been called from her bath. At times the reeve could be so exasperating. She turned back to Gaston, her intense silence saying more loudly than words how much she resented being summoned here.

Gaston stood and came toward her. He stopped just inches away and she had to lean her head back to see his face. This position left her feeling decidedly disadvantaged, but she refused to let Gaston think his height intimidated her. Uttering a soft growl of annoyance, she pulled her covering up on her shoulders.

He reached out to touch her hands where they held the edges of the fur together. "Don't."

Don't what? she thought, glancing up at him. Then she stopped still, her whole being centered on what she saw in his face.

Gaston's eyes were filled with a dark hungry need, making her catch her breath in answer. His hand on hers was warm, the fingers gentle yet strong. Rose became achingly aware of her nakedness under the bed cover. This awareness made her realize she should not be standing here like this; that the two of them were completely alone.

But she couldn't move. Some invisible force held her immobile, even as he took the last two steps that separated them.

He made no move to touch her, only grazing her forehead with his lips. The contact was so light, like the brush of butterfly wings. She felt the slight rasp of his cheek against her own. Rose closed her eyes, breathing in the warm male scent of him that hinted of leather and the outdoors.

Being near him was so good, so natural. Her heart was filled to overflowing with his presence.

His arm moved around her slowly and Rose melted into his embrace, basking in his warmth. She lifted her head, her mouth seeking his and finding it.

The recollection of his kisses had been strong, but now with his lips on hers, she knew the memories could not compare with this wondrous reality.

His lips were so firm and so supple at the same time. Her head spun, and her senses clamored for more.

Gaston's mouth opened and he began to nibble softly on her bottom lip. Rose grew weak with longing and she had to lean against him for support.

Raising his head, Gaston looked down at her. Her lids were heavy with desire and he leaned forward, whispering against her lips, "You are so beautiful, little Rose."

"Gaston," she breathed, raising her mouth to him. She was not disappointed.

He met her with hunger, kissing her as if he could not get enough.

She wanted to be closer, to feel the hard male length of him next to her. As she lifted her arms to draw him near, her hold on the fur was gone and it fell to the rush-strewn floor, forgotten.

Gaston moaned low in his throat when his hands met warm smooth flesh. He ran his palms down her back, slowly tracing the swell of her bottom. Her damp hair clung to his heated skin as if encouraging him in his exploration of her.

Rose arched against him, her body reacting automatically to the feel of his hands.

His voice was husky with need. "I want to see you."

Rose felt her face color as he held her from him, his eyes taking in the rounded perfection of her breasts, the smooth flatness of her belly and the gentle swell of her hips.

When his gaze came back to her face he pulled her close again, feeling her trembling with shyness.

"Gaston..." she began. But a loud gasping sound stopped her from continuing.

She turned in his arms to see Alfred standing in the doorway. His mouth was opened wide, and his eyes bulged as if they would fall from their sockets. Slowly the pages of parchment he held in his hands slid to the floor. He took no notice.

Rose felt as if she were standing in some nightmare from which she must surely awaken. But she remained where she was, her eyes fixed on Alfred's shocked face.

There was no way of recalling the moment. She had been foolish enough to let desire overtake her common sense. She and Gaston had been caught in a position neither of them would have wanted. Rose, because she was engaged to another man and Gaston, because that man was his brother.

Rose's concerns did not stop with Hubert. Would Alfred begin to wonder about her allegiance to him and the other people of Carlisle? She must make him see that her loyalty to her vassals had not changed. If he should not keep this incident to himself, both she and Gaston had much to lose.

Hurriedly Gaston reached down and gathered up her fur, wrapping it around her shoulders.

Still silent, he stepped back, running his hands over his face.

Rose called out to the reeve. "Alfred."

He came forward slowly, his eyes downcast, giving away nothing of his thoughts.

When Gaston found his tongue, his voice was harsh with warning. "What you have seen here tonight must never be repeated to anyone. Your lady would suffer greatly at the hands of my brother, should he find out."

With surprising courage, Alfred spoke up. "As would you, lord."

Gaston turned cold silvery eyes upon him. "Make no mistake, little man. It is not myself who need fear. Though I would do much to avoid hurting my brother, I do not fear him or any other mortal man."

Alfred studied Gaston for a long moment before he turned to Rose, his eyes filled with sadness. "I will keep your secret, but only because I can see that you love her."

Rose swung around, surprise evident on her face as she looked to Gaston.

He said nothing, only stood there watching the reeve, his expression unreadable.

With a small cry, Rose ran from the hall.

She had no illusions about what Gaston felt for her. Desire was simply a physical reaction; Gaston felt no more for her than Hubert did for Elspith.

It would be nothing short of insanity to believe otherwise.

* * *

Gaston thrust upward with his sword, blocking the downward stroke of his opponent. Leaning his weight into the swing, he knocked the other man's weapon to the muddy ground.

The rains had only just stopped the day before and their legacy was apparent in the muck that passed for a surface on the playing field.

He stepped back, lifted his visor and waited for another challenger to come forward. Gaston's expression was eager, even though he had spent the better part of the morning on the practice field. He was determined to relieve himself of some of his pent-up frustration.

Rose.

Her name was a litany in his mind. Would that he could rid himself of the aching need of her.

The night Alfred had guessed at his love for Rose had replayed over and over again in his thoughts. Gaston felt as though he would go mad with wondering what might have happened had the reeve not returned to the hall.

For her part, Rose behaved as if the incident had never occurred.

Glancing up to see Hubert entering the field, Gaston smiled. His brother played no small part in his chaotic state of unrest.

Gaston knew from the way Rose treated him with cold civility that she had not forgiven him for his failure to protect the serving woman, Elspith. In Gaston's mind, Rose's sympathy was sadly misplaced. The fair Elspith was clearly one lamb who ran to the slaughter. She hung on his brother's every word, and the way she looked at him was anything but virginal.

The knight's smile twisted into a scowl. Hubert could be more circumspect. Gaston cared little if his brother bedded the serf, but Rose seemed to be unduly upset by the fact.

After much thought, Gaston had decided Rose must fear that Hubert would set the girl above her.

Hubert could not see the possible consequences of his actions. If the vassals thought their lady was being treated without the honor that was her due, they might rebel.

Calling Rose an ice-hearted maiden, Hubert had said he would be tied to her soon enough without her interfering with his pleasure now.

Gaston had bitten back the retort that sprang to his lips, knowing Rose was far from being the ice maiden Hubert described. Who was he to question Hubert's actions? But for the interruption of the reeve, Gaston would have taken Rose upon the floor of the accounting chamber.

Whichever way he turned, Gaston could find no honorable solution.

Near to bursting with unvented frustration, Gaston had come to the field. Surprise had rippled through the assembled men when he offered to take on all challengers. Astonishment had deepened to admiration as Gaston had fought on through the morning, and won.

Hubert's armor gleaming from a recent polishing, he slipped, then righted himself as he came toward his brother.

All the men who had fought that day were covered in thick black mud. Gaston was no exception.

Hubert stopped before him, giving him a level stare. "I believe you wish to take on all comers."

Gaston nodded. "You believe rightly."

"Then stand ready." Hubert dropped his visor into place.

Gaston followed suit, taking up a fighting stance.

The contest was begun.

Gaston took up the offensive, his sword ringing as he slashed and hacked, forcing his heavier brother backward. With every stroke he poured out his anguish and resentment. Hubert held in his hands all that Gaston found most dear, but he cared for naught. To Hubert, Rose was simply a means to an end, a way of cementing his claim to her lands.

Hubert bellowed with excitement. Here was a test of his skill. Then it was he who pressed Gaston.

And so it went, the clash of their swords ringing as they circled and fought, first one and then the other on the defensive.

Finally, seeing an opening in his brother's guard, Gaston struck hard, knocking Hubert to the ground.

Gaston stood over him, his sword poised to strike.

Hubert emitted a laugh of sheer exhilaration. "A good contest!" he pronounced. "I yield!"

The younger man made no move to drop his sword, simply raising his visor, his breath coming in ragged gasps.

For one long moment, brother faced brother.

Shame made Gaston look away. He was wrong to blame his brother for his troubles. Hubert had accepted him readily when he left the monastery; had taken him to his first battle; protected his back in time of danger; offered him a place of equal worth at his side.

Gaston lowered his weapon to his side and held out his hand. Clasping the offered hand with a hearty shout, Hubert stood.

At that moment, a cry went up at the side of the field, making them all look up.

Carl, one of Hubert's soldiers, was dragging a young boy onto the field. The small fellow was thrashing about, trying to escape. Gaston watched Carl as he led the boy directly to Hubert, who pushed his helmet back and wiped the mud from his eyes. "What is going on here?" he asked as he eyed the burly soldier and the squirming boy.

"This, my lord," Carl answered, holding up a well-wrought silver buckle so it could be seen by all. "I found this buckle in the child's possession. He is a thief."

"No, please!" the accused screamed with renewed energy. His mousy brown hair was long and flew about his head wildly as he struggled to free himself. "I only wanted to look at it."

Gaston had started toward them as soon as the buckle appeared. As he reached the group, he could see that the culprit was only a child, no more than ten or eleven. The knight took note of the fact that the boy's appearance was a bit wild. But his clothes, though of poor quality, were clean and well mended.

"Things started disappearing as soon as this boy began skulking around the barracks," Carl explained. "Today I decided to search him and I found the proof." He looked up to see many of the men nodding in agreement.

"What were you doing with this, boy?" Hubert asked, his voice frigid as he studied the buckle.

"I was looking at it." The child pointed to Carl. "When I saw him, I hid it in my shirt so he wouldn't see."

"He lies," Carl growled, giving the accused thief a shake. "If someone were to search his belongings, I'm sure they would find many missing items."

"No!" the boy screeched, sobbing.

Calmly Hubert asked a question. "You are Wes, the serf Rob's boy, are you not?" The answer was apparent in the child's eyes. Hubert turned to one of the other knights. "Sir Simon, you will find Rob and together you will search his possessions."

Wes redoubled his frantic efforts to pull his arm out of Carl's grasp. But the boy's puny strength was no match for the battled-hardened warrior.

The child cried out piteously. "Please Lord de Thorne! It is a mistake."

"Cease that caterwauling," Hubert bellowed.

Wes obeyed, growing instantly still, his eyes wide with fear.

Grimly Gaston awaited Sir Simon's return. Stealing was a very serious crime. Living so closely together, it was easy for one man to know what another possessed. A soldier had to trust his fellows implicitly.

If the boy was indeed a thief, the penalty would be stiff.

The silence seemed to stretch on forever.

There was a combined exhalation of relief when Sir Simon finally appeared at the edge of the field. Behind him came

Rob and his wife, Athelgard. Their faces were white with fear for their son.

Approaching Hubert, Sir Simon held out his hand. In it was a small woolen pouch.

Hubert took the pouch and opened it. Deep lines appeared at either side of his mouth as he looked inside. With solemn gravity, Hubert withdrew a bronze shoulder brooch.

In the crowd of soldiers that had gathered, someone called out. Hubert beckoned him forward and handed the brooch over to him. Other objects were taken from the bag, and these too were claimed by their owners. When the pouch was empty, Hubert let it slip to the ground as he turned to the silent thief.

Deliberately Hubert pronounced the punishment. "You are guilty as accused, boy. The penalty for this crime is twenty lashes."

Athelgard cried aloud and fell into her husband's arms.

Hubert motioned to two burly soldiers, who came forward and took the dull-eyed Wes between them. Only as they began to lead the boy away were those assembled able to take a breath. They surged toward the stock.

Hubert moved to stand behind Wes, whose woolen shirt was removed before he was tied to the post.

Assisted by one of his men, Hubert took off his armor and tunic. He held out his hand, and one of the men placed a strap with long vicious ends across his palm.

Athelgard leaned on her husband's shoulder, which was stained dark from her tears.

Gaston stood back, battling with his conscience. The boy was guilty. But his sense of justice told him twenty lashes were far too many. The child would never withstand the punishment. Yet Hubert had a duty to see that Wes was punished. He could not expect his men to live by the rules he set if he did not make the people on his lands live by them, also.

Though Gaston would have given the boy a lesser sentence, he must keep his own counsel. He had to accept

Hubert's decision. His brother was lord here and had the right.

The whip whistled as it flew through the air to bite into soft flesh. Wes cried out in a piteous screech.

Hubert's face was grey with the repugnance he felt at having to carry out this punishment, but he drew back his arm and struck again. The boy's small body jerked against the thongs that held him to the post and he screamed anew.

Suddenly a tall form interposed itself between the boy and the whip.

Gaston did not know why he was interfering, only that he must. His sense of responsibility would not allow him to be silent another moment. What he had told Rose the day of the fire was true. Her people had become his.

Hubert faced his brother, his voice gruff. "What are you doing?"

Gaston spoke quietly. "He has taken enough." He turned to Rob. "Cut the ropes." The serf hurried to do as he had been told. His knife quickly slashed through the leather.

Bending, Gaston caught Wes in his arms as he fell.

Hubert stepped closer to his brother, his eyes hard, his tone accusing. "They have made you soft."

Gaston lifted the boy higher in his arms so Hubert could see the vicious red welts on his back. "He is only a child, Hubert. Can you not forgive this first offense when he knew nothing of the law?"

For a moment, Hubert said nothing as all eyes turned to him. Gaston could see the revulsion on the faces of the men. They had no more love for this situation than he. These men, who had seen so much that was evil in battle, could not accept such cruelty toward a child.

Finally the whip fell to the ground. "Take him." Hubert stepped back stiffly. "Take him away." He turned and strode off the field.

Athelgard went to Gaston, her gratitude shining in her eyes. "Thank you, my lord, thank you."

Gaston said nothing, simply handing the boy over to his father. As he watched them leave the field, Hubert's words echoed in his mind.

Had he grown soft?

Somehow Gaston did not believe this. He felt strong, stronger than he had ever been. And he knew what had given him strength.

Rose.

Her own courage and sense of justice had fortified his, making him a better man. She did not punish those who had wronged her, she took them in, healed their hurts and accepted them, each man according to his own merit.

Gaston had yet to meet anyone who possessed more strength than the Lady of Carlisle. There was no room for cruelty in her heart.

Hubert had never been more wrong.

Chapter Nine

Since the night when Gaston had held her naked in his arms, Rose had been deeply troubled.

It would have been so easy for her to give herself to Gaston—too easy. She tried to believe she would have found the fortitude to say no, but the belief held little conviction.

Gaston seemed to want her, no matter how fleeting that desire might be. Clearly Hubert did not want her, and Elspith had turned her back on their friendship since she'd become Hubert's mistress.

Gaston had proved himself worthy of her love as no other before him. Her people spoke of him with the highest regard since the day he had saved the boy, Wes, from Hubert's whip. He treated Rose with kindness, respecting her opinions. He worked diligently to improve Carlisle, while Hubert dallied with her cousin.

Rose did not know which way to turn.

Thinking Father Liam might be able to offer advice, she set out to speak with him.

Behind her, she heard the sound of hooves on the soft turf. Turning her head, she saw three mounted men coming across the hill toward her.

Immediately she recognized the white stallion in the center of the group. It was Pegasus.

Rose swung around, hoping the men would go on without stopping. Chagrined, she heard the horses slow as they drew near.

She ran a shaky hand over the skirt of her worn lilac gown and smoothed the hair around her face.

As Gaston reined in beside her, he smiled at the sheer pleasure of seeing her. She wore her glorious hair loose, and the sunlight turned it to flame. Her creamy cheeks pinkened under his appreciative regard.

He was so handsome, and when he smiled her heart did funny things in her chest. Rose felt her blood begin to pump just a bit faster.

"Where do you go, lady?" he asked.

Guilt assaulted her at feeling so much joy in being with him. She countered it by allowing irritation to creep into her voice. "Am I not allowed to walk to the village?"

"Of course." He sat aback, obviously disappointed at her tone. "I sought only to offer you a ride to wherever you might want to go."

Rose looked down at her hands. "Forgive me, I should not have spoken so hastily. I fear—" she looked up at him with a shy smile "—the wagging of my tongue is often too quick."

He leaned closer to her. "Then, might I understand that you accept my offer?"

Rose looked up, seeing the other men shifting restlessly in their saddles. They looked impatient to be off. She bit her lower lip. "I would not wish to keep you from whatever you were bound to do."

Gaston quirked a brow. "Wither do you go?"

"To see Father Liam," Rose said.

Gaston grinned and reached down for her hand. "We ride by there on our way."

The other men nodded. The easy smiles on their faces told Rose the church was not out of their way.

There was little she could do but accept. Taking his hand, she allowed Gaston to pull her up before him. The ground seemed a long way down, and the narrow saddle forced her into close contact with the man behind her.

When Gaston nudged his sides, the giant stallion started forward. Rose grasped Gaston's arm with both hands.

With a deep chuckle, he leaned close to her ear and whispered. "Don't be afraid. I won't let you fall. Lean back on me."

Rose wasn't sure this was a very good idea, her pulse was already racing too quickly. But when Pegasus sidestepped around a rabbit hole and she swayed, Rose did as Gaston had suggested.

The warmth of his powerful body radiated through her clothes. Seductive visions filled her mind as she watched his supple hands on the reins. What would it be like to again feel his hands upon her flesh? Would her body respond with the same shameless compliance?

Rose closed her eyes with a silent moan. She must do something to turn her thoughts to less carnal matters.

The other two knights rode a small distance behind them and were of no assistance in diverting the wayward path of her thoughts.

The weather, she thought with relief. It seemed a safe enough topic of conversation. "It is a lovely day."

"Yes, it is a lovely day." Gaston's voice was deep and caressing, his breath stirring her hair. He rested a possessive hand on her hip.

How safe and protected she felt in his arms. Though he was a Norman, this man had proved himself of great worth.

"I want to tell you how grateful I am that you rescued Wes," she said.

"Wes?" Gaston mused. "Oh yes, the little thief. How is he?"

"His wounds are healing," she answered. "But you have changed the subject. I want you to know how much it means to me that you stopped his punishment."

Gaston smiled wryly. "I did only what I felt I must. Hubert is not as pleased with my actions. He thinks the Saxons will believe they need not obey his laws."

"That is not true," Rose assured, turning to look up at him. "My people will think carefully before acting in future. They have now seen what an unjust man Hubert really is."

Gaston frowned, his gaze holding hers for a long moment. "Hubert is not unjust. A man must be strong to lead people."

Rose gave him a haughty look and turned her back on him, answering with certainty, "It is strength to be wise, and Hubert is not a wise man."

To some extent, Gaston agreed with Rose, but he could not tell her. He did not wish to encourage the streak of rebellion in her. Hubert would not accept such ideas in his wife, and Gaston could not bear to think of Hubert punishing her.

Just ahead of them, not far off the road, stood the church. It was a tall stone building at the edge of the village. At the same point, the road branched, taking travelers either to Brentwood or Mayhill. Directly behind the church was the glebe. Rose's father had set aside this small tract of land so Father Liam might raise some of his own food. A sturdy outbuilding housed a cow and a few hens.

Gaston rode his horse around the side of the church to the front entrance.

What met their eyes as they came around the building made Gaston stiffen in the saddle behind her.

A group of mounted men were gathered around the tall thin figure of the priest. They ringed him in a tight circle, and their manner appeared to be threatening.

Recognizing Robert's golden head amongst the group, Rose knew the men posed no real threat. Robert would never hurt the old priest.

Gaston saw the tableau from a different perspective. With a growl of outrage, he set Rose to the ground, then spurred his horse forward.

Knowing she had to do something to protect her cousin, Rose cried out. Her shout alerted the men to the knight's presence. There was a moment of turmoil as the rebels turned to ride. Inadvertently Father Liam fell and was almost trampled in the scuffle.

With her heart in her throat, Rose watched as Robert and his men galloped from the churchyard, with Gaston just behind them.

She caught back a gasp as the other knights rode past her in a flurry of flashing hooves.

It all happened so quickly that for a moment she was too stunned to move. Then she ran forward to assist Father Liam. Even as Rose helped the priest to stand, her eyes followed the mounted men as they disappeared into the trees.

All were riding too fast for safety, and fear dug its sharp talons into her belly. At such speeds, a clash with a limb or a stumble could be deadly.

"How could he be so foolish?" she asked, not sure which one of the men she was talking about, Robert or Gaston.

Believing she meant Robert, Father Liam said, "I was just telling the boy he shouldn't have come in broad daylight. It was far too dangerous a chance to take."

Her brow puckered in consternation, Rose asked, "In heaven's name, why did he?"

The priest's expression was grave. "He was inquiring about the Lady Elspith." He spread his hands helplessly. "I could not lie, but neither could I tell the boy the truth. It is a sad road the child has been forced to take."

Rose glanced away, hiding her dejection. "Elspith has chosen her own path."

Father Liam steepled his long fingers. "Circumstances can sometimes force us to take wrong paths. There is much in this life that is difficult."

Rose flushed. She had come here to speak of her own dilemma, but something kept her from it. Mayhap it was the wisdom and understanding in his blue eyes. She needed to be told black from white, right from wrong. This talk of human frailty did not give her the strength to withstand her own emotions. When Gaston touched her . . .

Gaston!

Rose clasped the priest's arm. "You must not be here when Sir Gaston returns. If he is not successful in capturing Robert or any of his men, he will want to question you about his presence here."

"I understand." Father Liam nodded in agreement. "I must have some time to think about what I will say. My God would not have me lie, but I can not betray Lord Robert, either."

"I will wait here for Sir Gaston," Rose told him. "If Robert is fool enough to get himself captured, there may be something I can do to help."

Father Liam studied her closely. "You will not put yourself in jeopardy?"

She smiled wryly. "Do not worry. I am in no danger from Sir Gaston." *At least not the kind you imagine.*

Father Liam studied her for a long moment. He looked as if he would speak but did not. Instead, he patted her shoulder gently. "I will return later just to be certain. Go with God, my daughter."

Watching as he started down the trail to the village, Rose sensed that the priest had guessed at her feelings for Gaston. First Alfred, and now Father Liam. Her secret seemed to be less of a secret than she had hoped.

But she had no time to worry about that now in the face of more pressing matters.

Gaston might be successful in capturing or killing her cousin.

Or worse yet, the knight could be injured or slain by Robert or his men. Thoughts of Gaston lying hurt somewhere in the forest crowded into her mind, almost crushing her with the pain they brought.

Seeking comfort from her tumultuous thoughts, Rose was drawn to the graveyard. She went directly to her mother's resting place and knelt to pray.

Rose had been fourteen when Wendolyn had died, old enough to remember her mother clearly. Wendolyn had been a good wife and mother, so much so that her husband had not remarried as most men would have.

But Rose could find no comfort there this day. Her mother's voice was too far in the past. She stood up slowly, her legs cramped from the long time she had been kneeling. She would have to search for her answers in the present.

She looked out across the greensward and saw a man on a white stallion riding toward her. Gaston.

She was filled with such joy she forgot all the obstacles that lay between them. Rose only knew he was the man she loved, and he was returned to her unscathed.

As the stallion halted beside her, Rose held out her arms. "You are safe!" she cried.

He reached down and drew her up before him. "Of course I am, little one."

Rose put her arms around his neck and held him, breathing in the salty warm scent of him. She murmured against his tanned throat, "I was so worried."

He held her close to him. "There was no need to be afraid. We did not catch more than a glimpse of them as they raced through the forest." He stroked her soft hair. "I'm sure they won't be coming back."

"I wasn't worried for myself," she admitted, turning her luminous emerald eyes up to his. "I thought those men who were talking to Father Liam might harm you."

Gaston gave a start as the name recalled his concern for the priest. "Father Liam," Gaston said. "I came to assure myself of his safety. Sir Hugh and Sir Gerard have gone to tell Hubert what has occurred."

"Father Liam is fine," Rose assured him. "Someone needed him in the village," she lied.

"Did he tell you what they wanted from him?"

"Only that they had not tried to harm him."

"Then why are you trembling so?" Gaston hugged her tightly. She felt so good in his arms.

"It was you I feared for," she told him, her eyes bright with love for him. "When I saw you ride after them I realized if you were killed, I would never see you again. That I could not bear." She put her hand to his cheek. "I . . ."

"Shh." He touched his finger to her lips. "Don't say it. Once the words are said, there will be no turning back. For myself, I would gladly hear you, but for you it is a different matter."

"But I want you." She drew his hand to her lips and kissed the callused palm. "I want you." Rose didn't care anymore what happened. All she knew was that she wanted Gaston, had wanted him from the first moment they met. He was, and always would be, the other half of her own being.

Gaston could not resist the guileless invitation in her gaze. He bent his head and touched her lips with his own.

What he had meant as a gentle caress turned to a melding of flesh. She offered her soul and he took it, his mouth moving over hers possessively, branding her as his.

Rose tried to snuggle closer to him, her hands going up to the nape of his neck. Her fingers twined in his thick curls. She groaned. There was not enough room on the horse's back for her to turn to him fully.

Feeling the same desperate need to get closer to her, Gaston put one hand under her knees and the other around her back, slipping to the ground with her in his arms.

A copse of apple trees grew a short distance from where they were standing. Its blossoms filled the air with a delicate sweetness. Gaston carried Rose into the orchard and lay her on the soft green grass that was dotted with the tiny white blossoms. Like warm snow, the petals drifted down to land in her bright auburn hair.

His hands cupping her face, he leaned forward and kissed her. "You are so beautiful, Rose."

She held his wide shoulders, kissing him fiercely, making the blood sing in his veins. "It is you who are beautiful," she whispered. Rose was aflame, her body heavy with a languid passion that left her aching for something she couldn't describe.

He was shaking with the effort it cost him to hold back the raging hunger that threatened to break free and consume him. "Are you sure this is what you want?" he asked.

She kissed him again, her teeth nipping at his lower lip. "Yes, oh yes. Don't you want it, too?" Rose didn't know where this woman had come from, this creature of desire, but she welcomed her, accepting her as a part of herself.

"I have never wanted anything more in my life." He kissed her back, opening her mouth with his. His tongue circled hers, and he groaned in rapture as her tongue followed his lead.

He lay down next to her, pulling her pliant body close to his. He arched against her stomach, letting her feel the rigid hardness of his need. "Do you understand what you are saying?" His grey eyes were dark with barely suppressed hunger.

Rose looked into his face for one long moment. "I know what I am saying. As I waited for you, fearing I might lose you—" she placed her hands over her heart "—I realized I had nothing of you to hold close to my heart. If I give myself to you, that, at least, can never be taken from me."

Gaston placed his hand over hers where they rested on her breast. "Would that you were mine."

Rose let her hands slip down, but Gaston's stayed at her breast. "For this moment, I am."

He bent his head slowly, tasting her lips, accepting what she offered. He knew he had no right to ask for more. That she desired him did not mean Rose would be willing to give up her people, her home, everything, for him.

His hand moved over her breast in a caress, and she felt it rise and swell under his fingers. "Gaston," she breathed his name. Her heart was full to bursting, and it showed in her glowing eyes.

He lowered his head to kiss the delicate line of her throat, and her heart began to beat so loudly she thought the sound would deafen her. His lips moved lower to nuzzle her bosom where it swelled over her bodice, and she sighed.

He raised himself up, frustrated at the barrier of their clothing. Lovingly he began to undress her.

Rose felt a little shy now, realizing they lay in the midst of a sunlit garden. Gaston would see her as no other man had. He drew her gown over her head, and she lowered her arms to cross them in front of herself.

"Rose." Gaston leaned over her, kissing her softly. "Don't ever hide yourself from me."

She moved her arms, not trying to obstruct him as he removed the last of her clothing. Rose cast down her gaze in shyness, not seeing the wonder and love on his face as he feasted on her supple beauty. After a long, indefinable minute, Gaston put his hand on her chin and turned her to look at him.

The heat of his gaze scorched her, touching a place deep inside her and awakening it to desire. Rose reached out her arms in surrender.

He held her as she trembled, his voice hoarse with wanting. "You are lovely, more exquisite than my awkward tongue can describe."

Rose suspected Gaston had loved many women, and so hesitated to put credit to his word, though she wished to. "You have no need of pretty speeches."

"And use none." He lowered his head, and she felt his breath hot on her flesh as he trailed a path of delight to her breast. "Lovely, lovely." His lips closed around the tip of her breast, and she gasped with shock at the pleasure.

Then there was no more time for thought as Gaston's hands began to caress her in a way that made her blood flow like warmed wine.

He pulled and nibbled at one nipple until she thought she would go mad, then turned to the other.

Rose was lost, her head spinning with the fire that raged in her body. When his hand moved lower to brush over the soft skin of her belly, she moaned. "Gaston, please."

He flicked his tongue over the tip of her breast, teasing. "You must be patient, my heart." But she could hear the rasp in his voice and knew that he wanted her urgently.

Then Gaston's palm moved down to cup the little mound covered in bright curls, and she arched against him, unable to control her body's response to his knowing caresses. When his fingers dipped into her, she thought she would faint, and her legs opened of their own accord.

"So wet," he murmured against her skin. "So warm."

"Oh, help me," she moaned, her head turning from side to side.

"Yes," he whispered. "I will help us both." He pulled away from her for a moment then, but when he came back there was nothing between his heated skin and hers.

Rose welcomed him, putting her hands up to his wide shoulders and pulling him down to her.

Gaston knelt over her, his body poised to enter hers. "Look at me," he told her huskily. "I want to know it is me you desire."

Rose opened her eyes to find her gaze captured by his. She could not have looked away had she wanted to.

Slowly Gaston entered her. There was a slight resistance as he broke through the barrier of her innocence and he felt her stiffen under him. It took every ounce of his will to lie above her, not moving, when every fiber of his body screamed out for release.

But he read the pain in her eyes and waited for it to pass. Only when he saw that the discomfort had faded did Gaston begin to move, carefully, willing his body to go slowly.

With infinite tenderness and mastery, Gaston moved above her. Rose's lids drooped then closed as her lips opened on a sigh. "Gaston."

Her pleasure made his all the more complete. Until this moment, Gaston had never known what it was to really love a woman, not just with his body but with his heart.

The flame in Rose's body had turned to a white-hot heat that drove her higher and higher on its flickering tip. She could feel him moving in her and thrust up to meet him, giving of herself until she lost all sense of their separateness. She was Gaston and he was her. Then, suddenly, when she thought there could be no greater joy in the universe, her soul touched the sky and exploded into ecstasy, washing her with light.

Gaston's eyes never left her face as she approached her peak, and when he felt the convulsions take her body, he gave himself up to the force of his desire. He too gasped, and with one final thrust he called out her name. "Rose."

Gaston lay still for a moment, loving the feel of her beneath him, wanting to stay this way forever. But he realized he was too heavy for her and moved to pull away.

Rose refused to let him go, wrapping her arms and legs around him tightly.

It was at that moment she heard a voice calling from the direction of the church. "Lady Rose." She refused to pay any attention. The mundane didn't matter anymore, all that existed was her love for Gaston. What had just happened was too shattering for life to go on as it had before.

The voice grew more insistent. "Lady Rose!"

She opened her eyes to find that the sky over her head was still blue, not the incandescent silver in her mind. Everything was different, and yet, everything was the same.

"It's Father Liam," Gaston said urgently, pulling away to reach for his clothing.

Rose gasped, her shaking hands searching for her own gown. "Oh, Lord, what will we do?" She couldn't make her fingers work properly as she tried to pull the underdress over her head. "No one must know of this."

Gaston stopped still for a moment, looking at her. He turned away. "You are right, no one must know of this. You stay here. I will go and tell him you have returned to Carlisle."

Rose held out her hand, not liking the way his face had turned to carved marble at her words. What had she said?

Only that no one must know they had been together. Why had that caused him to look at her as though he were drawing away from her?

Rose could only believe Gaston had realized what a mistake they had made. That neither of them could ever allow this to happen again.

If Father Liam had come upon them, there would be no explaining their actions.

Her hands shaking uncontrollably, Rose dressed and made her way around the glen. As she went, she resolved to stay away from Gaston. Though now she had experienced the joy to be found in his arms, that would be doubly difficult.

How could she have been ignorant enough to believe tasting his love would free her? All she had succeeded in doing was binding herself even more securely to him.

Several days later Rose came upon Elspith working in the courtyard. Rose had spent much of her time trying to forget what had happened between her and Gaston.

Her own pain made Rose want to make Elspith see what she was doing to herself. Her cousin's association with Hubert could only end in disaster.

Elspith was rubbing pungent sage on the chickens she had placed on a spit. Her once-white hands had tanned to a light gold.

"Elspith," Rose said softly.

The taller girl turned slowly, her face set. Elspith knew Rose disapproved of her relationship with Hubert, but

Elspith loved him and she refused to give him up, even to please her cousin.

A soldier passed close by and Elspith spoke out clearly. "How may I serve you, lady?"

"I wish to talk with you," Rose told her. "Can you not come with me to a more private place?" Her gaze moved over the busy courtyard.

Elspith turned back to what she was doing. "There is nothing to say."

Rose's voice grew angry. "There is much to say. Do you know Robert was almost captured because he had come to ask Father Liam how you were? What would he have done had the priest told him of your affair with Hubert de Thorne, the very man who wishes to hunt down and kill him?"

Elspith flinched, her hands stilled. Rose felt a stab of guilt for having hurt her cousin.

Elspith dropped the spit, putting her head in her hands. "Do you think I do not know he wishes my brother harm? How can I forget you will be his wife? That each night when he takes me in his arms it may be the last? Yet, knowing all this," Elspith said as she turned to face Rose, her eyes bright with some inner fire, "I would take all he will give me, until the day he sets me aside."

"You must tell him who you are," Rose burst out. "He has no right to treat you so."

Elspith's expression was without hope. "And have him learn of Robert? How could I explain my presence here without giving away my brother's secret? The very fact that we have created the lie to protect my identity would make Hubert ask questions. I can not sacrifice my own brother, even for Hubert." A single tear slipped down her alabaster cheek.

Rose laughed without humor. "Would that I could give him to you. I feel for your pain, yet I can not understand the reasons for your devotion to such a man. His whipping of

Wes was the last straw for me. Hubert is a man totally
without feelings for any but his own kind.''

Elspith bristled. ''You know him not. He only whipped
the boy because he feels any sign of leniency will be mistaken for weakness.''

Rose recalled Gaston saying much the same thing, but
these excuses would not serve. ''A man of true strength
knows when to bend,'' she said with absolute assurance.

Elspith just stared at her cousin for a long time, then
sighed. ''Oh, Rose, don't you see? Not all of us see the
world with as much clarity as you. For others the line between right and wrong is harder to judge. That does not
make us evil, only human, including Hubert.''

''Even if what you say is right—'' Rose put her hand to
her cheek ''—I could never love a man who did not see the
difference.'' Gaston had helped the boy, Wes, even though
he thought others saw him as weak.

Elspith stood up and patted Rose's arm wearily. ''It gives
me no pleasure to know you go to a loveless marriage.
Especially when I will never love another man as I do
Hubert de Thorne.''

''I hate him,'' Rose whispered vehemently, catching hold
of Elspith's hand. ''He has taken everything from me, including you. I had thought we two might help one another
in this reign of hell, but that was not to be.'' Rose stood, her
gaze directed out over the courtyard. She sucked in her
breath with shock, letting go of her cousin's hand.

Gaston stood only a few feet away, watching them intently.

God's blood! she thought. Was she not allowed one minute out from under his constant regard? This was just one
more thing for which she must hate Hubert, for surely it was
he who had set Gaston to watching her.

He had always seemed to be close by her, but since the
afternoon when they made love, there was a difference in his
gaze. His eyes seemed to sear her, branding her as his. It was
unsettling and at the same time compelling.

What would Hubert say if he knew?

Elspith stiffened as she saw the look on Rose's face. "What is...?" She swung around to see what Rose was looking at. "Oh no," she breathed as her attention centered on Gaston. Her voice lowered to a whisper. "He must not come to think I am anything but a servant."

Rose took a deep breath, willing herself to be calm. "Do not worry, I will think of something to tell him."

Elspith nodded, dipping Rose a respectful curtsy, and she sat down on the bench to return to her work.

Rose started across the courtyard, hoping Gaston would let her go on her way without comment. Her hopes were dashed when his long strides brought him to her side.

His voice was cool, polite. "Lady Rose."

Perversely, she was disappointed at his distant tone. Gaston's voice had been so different when they made love. His words had flowed like thick honey over her heightened senses.

She did not understand how it was so easy for him to disguise his feelings for her. Mayhap his desire did not run so very deeply. When she looked at him, her love seemed to rise up in a golden haze.

Rose was surprised when she sounded so cool and equally courteous. "Sir Gaston." She gave no hint of her inner turmoil but was unable to meet his gaze.

His voice, softening, became intimate. "Rose. You are being very kind to this servant...." It was a statement and a question.

Rose flushed, realizing Gaston was accrediting her with more compassion than she possessed. He thought she was being kind to Elspith in spite of the fact she was Hubert's mistress. He didn't know of the two women's relationship to each other. Rose shrugged, uncomfortable. "She is troubled."

"She is only a diversion," he said quietly, thinking to allay any fears Rose might have on the subject.

Rose stiffened, her back going rigid as she stared down at the ground. Gaston's sympathy for Rose was sorely misplaced. Except that the woman was Elspith, she cared nothing for the fact that Hubert had found a mistress. It kept him from pressing his attentions on her.

What riled her was Gaston's choice of words. They struck home all too surely. Gaston had no intent to marry Rose when he pursued her. He had not even made a move to be with her again. Had she too been a 'diversion,' nothing more than an afternoon's dalliance?

Her eyes flashed green lightning as she looked up at him. "Thank you very much for your concern, Sir Gaston," she said as she clenched her hands at her sides, "but I really don't need your pity. And now if you don't mind I have much work to do." She nodded stiffly and stalked away.

Gaston stood for a moment in stunned surprise. He had not anticipated her reaction. There wàs no way of guessing how the Saxon maid would behave at any given moment. He had only meant to comfort her, and she flounced away as if he had insulted her in some way. It was Rose, not Gaston, who was unduly concerned over the matter.

Elspith seemed in no way unwilling to accept Hubert's attentions. If anything her devotion had deepened. Gaston was still spending his nights in the barracks.

It was then Gaston remembered why he had come in search of Rose. "Lady Rose," he called out, his long strides making it easy for him to catch up to her.

Rose was so furious she didn't even slow her steps.

Gaston grasped her arm and pulled her up short. "I do not know why you have chosen to take offense at my words." He willed her to look at him. "Nor do I fool myself into believing you would tell me, should I ask. Unfortunately, the subject will have to wait until I am at leisure to use more persuasive methods of extracting the information than I can at this moment."

Unexpectedly Rose felt a shiver of anticipation at the threat. What methods of persuasion might he use to make her confide in him? Far from angering her further, the commanding tone of his voice thrilled her. It was clear in the way he looked at her, heat smoldering just below the surface, that he still desired her.

To Gaston's complete surprise, Rose smiled up at him meekly. "What may I do for you?"

As he had told himself before, she was completely unpredictable. It was hard to think with her emerald eyes shining up at him that way, but he managed to answer. "Hubert is leaving today."

"What has happened?" she asked, the light going out of her expression as her thoughts went to Robert.

"Nothing that need cause you worry," he reassured her. "A rider arrived from Mayhill a short time ago. He reports that a group of men rode in this morning and set the barracks to burning. Gerard is furious, as the building had just been completed."

She grasped his arm tightly. "Was anyone hurt?"

When she touched him it was no easy task to think clearly. "There were no injuries except a slight burn one of the men suffered while putting out the fire."

Rose frowned. How careless Robert was becoming. It was totally out of character for him to do anything that might endanger fellow Saxons.

"I must send some medications," Rose said, her thoughts running ahead of her.

Gaston's tone was strained as her touch reminded him of the feel of her hands on his naked flesh. "Hubert will need provisions for himself and his men."

Believing Hubert would want to remain at the keep with his mistress, Gaston had pressed his brother to send him to Brentwood in his place. Although taken with the servant girl, Hubert refused to shirk his duties. He was adamant in the belief he must track down the rebels himself.

Hubert felt Gaston was needed at Carlisle, having made himself familiar with all aspects of running the keep.

Looking down at Rose and seeing her smile warm as a summer sunset, Gaston found he was not as disturbed by remaining at Carlisle as he should be.

Chapter Ten

Rose dug into her bag for the little pouch of henbane. When she finally pulled it out, her mouth turned down in a frown. The packet was almost empty. There was barely enough for her purpose. Her nose wrinkled at the thought of gathering more of the odious plant.

She crossed the tiny floor and picked up the wooden bowl Ruth had given her. Pouring the powder into the bowl, she mixed it with a small amount of water.

Turning to Ruth, Rose said, "I will put this into your daughter's ear. It will ease the pain and help her to sleep."

Ruth's only reply was a nod as she watched the small form of her daughter tossing on the pallet. The little girl was so tiny and her sobs so heartrending Rose was hard-pressed to keep from crying herself.

Much of the liquid spilled, wetting the golden-blond curls and the pallet. But they managed to get some of the medi-cine inside the child's ear.

"Now hold her on her side so the medicine can work," Rose directed, stepping back.

Rose took another pouch from her bag and placed it on the rough-hewn table. "This is dried peony leaf. Make a tea from it and give the warm brew to her when she is thirsty. It will help the ear to heal. If she begins to cry from the pain again, use what is left in the bowl. Should you have need of more, just send your boy to me."

Ruth's face was filled with gratitude. ''Thank you so much, Lady Rose.''

''I only do what I can,'' Rose told her, gathering her belongings from the earthen floor. Away from the fire there was not much light, even though the rough leather hide had been thrown from the doorway to let in the sunshine.

On the walk back to Carlisle, Rose drew in a deep breath of the warm summer air. There was a restlessness stirring in her, a feeling that made her wish she could forget all her responsibilities, be free to do what she wished. Love whom she wished, as Elspith did.

Hubert had sent for Elspith to join him at his camp and she had gone, willing to brave the deprivations to be with her lover.

As Rose passed an old goat tethered on the hillside, she patted his rump. It would be best for her to keep her thoughts on the ground. Dreaming was for others.

She had made a vow. The thought of how her father would view the breaking of that vow bound her.

The goat turned and peered at her with watery eyes, its beard wobbling back and forth as it chewed. Obviously put out by her interruption, the billy presented his back to her, bending to take more of the bright green grass.

Rose stopped short as she entered the gateway and saw the activity in the courtyard. People were everywhere doing some job or another. Over their voices, she could hear the constant clash of swords on the practice field.

Surprisingly Rose was not questioned by the guard at the gate as she left a short time later, her collection bag over her arm.

He simply smiled and waved as she passed through. It was well-known among the men that Rose was a healer of some skill. Claude, who many had taken for dead, was up and about, though he had been assigned lighter tasks than before.

She smiled, really smiled, an occurrence that had become rare. She was free, even if it was for a short time. The only one who knew where she had gone was Maida and she would keep her own counsel.

At the midday meal, Gaston waited for Rose to join himself and Sir Gerard. When she did not come, they finally began without her, but Gaston kept his attention on the open door of the hall, alert for her entrance.

He knew he was foolish to put himself through this kind of agony over a woman he could not have. Though Hubert mentioned the marriage less and less, it was ever in Gaston's thoughts.

As yet, there had been no word on Hubert's return to Carlisle, only more news detailing his quest for the rebels.

Hubert seemed no nearer to seeing the matter finished than in the beginning. His letters read of chases through the forest that ended in his men getting lost; of mornings having awakened to find the horses had been set free or that the foodstuffs had been dumped out. He complained more and more of his lot.

When Gaston had received Hubert's letter, asking him to send the servant Elspith, he had reached a turning point. Hubert did not love Rose. Why then should Gaston keep himself from her? In honor, he could not be with her as a man, but he could take joy in her smiles, pleasure from her nimble mind.

He wondered if she still thought of the man she had met in the forest; his instincts told him she did. She would look off into the wood and an unmistakable sadness would come into her eyes.

Gaston closed his eyes, gulping back the nausea that burned his throat when he thought of Rose in connection with any other man.

When the meal had ended, and still she had not come, Gaston went in search of her.

Sometime later, he came to a halt in the courtyard, with a puzzled frown. The little Saxon maid was nowhere to be found.

At that moment, he saw Maida entering one of the cooking sheds. She might know where Rose could be.

Maida was alone in the cook house. She stood facing the narrow table with her back to him, a drinking horn raised to her mouth. "Maida?" he inquired.

She gave a start, spilling some of the dark red wine. She raised her apron, wiping the liquid from her chin and the folds of her neck. Putting the drinking horn on the table with studied care, she turned to face him. "Yes, my lord." Her round face was flushed and her blue eyes sparkled brightly.

"I was wondering if you knew . . ." He stopped, taking in her benign expression. "Are you well?" he asked with raised brows.

"Why yes . . . fine, my lord." Her smile widened and she blinked, swaying on her tiny feet.

Gaston took her arm, gently pushing her onto a bench, with a knowing grin. The cook was drunk if he didn't miss his guess. "Why don't you rest here for a moment?" he advised.

Maida looked up at him, her round face trusting as a child's. "Thank you," she hiccuped.

Gaston shook a finger at her. "You've been drinking."

"Only a little." Maida's plump hand fluttered in the air to reassure him, just as another hiccup escaped her cupid's bow mouth.

His eyes took in the bottle, which was tipped on its side. A wicked grin lit his eyes. "From the look of it, you've had more than a little."

"Aye, it may be that I have," she admitted. "It's not as if there hasn't been enough trouble to drive a woman to drink." She wiped a single tear from her eye.

"I'll call someone to help you to your bed," Gaston told her solicitously. Obviously she would be of no help to him in her present condition.

"No, no, my lord." Maida leaned toward him, one hand outstretched. "I'll be right as rain in a minute."

Gaston took the outstretched hand in his own. "Are you sure you wouldn't feel better lying down?"

She waved her other hand in the air. "Yes, don't worry about me." With surprising strength, Maida pulled him down onto the bench beside her.

Gaston was unable to think of a way to excuse himself from this situation. He had meant to spend some time with Rose, not the cook. But he settled himself next to the corpulent woman, his long legs stretched out in front of him on the low bench.

Those blue eyes turned on him with obvious favor. "You're a fine figure of a man if I do say so myself," she said, her gaze taking in the hard, muscled length of him. "Even if you are a Norman." She nodded to emphasize her words. "Would have been sore tested to keep from yearning after you myself. In the old days," she clarified. Her eyes were a little bleary as she attempted to focus on his face. Maida gave up, wiping the back of her hand over the tip of her nose with some difficulty.

"I..." Gaston began, uncomfortable with the way the conversation was going.

"No," she insisted firmly. "I can't blame my lady that. But it wasn't until you saved my Wes that I knew there was more to you than a pretty face. I should have known my lady could only moon after a man who deserved it."

"Wes?" Gaston asked aloud, though his thoughts were on the other things she had said. The cook must surely be mistaken to think that Rose would moon after him. He could make her desire him, but any experienced man would be capable of that.

She wagged a plump finger under his nose. "Aye, my Wes. He was my first grandson. There have been five since him, but the first, he's special. Could have kissed you myself when you stepped between him and that monster." Her scowl was fierce.

Realization dawned in Gaston's mind. The boy who had been whipped was Maida's grandson. The monster she referred to could only be Hubert. It appeared that, in saving the child, Gaston had earned this woman's loyalty.

"That evil devil," Maida went on. "He's taken our girl and used her up."

Gaston felt a twist of pain. Maida talked as if Rose and Hubert were already married.

Thinking of Rose brought back his desire to find her. "Do you know where your lady is?"

"Said she needed some time to herself. So many people about that she couldn't think. Made me promise to keep it to myself," she muttered.

"What are you talking about?" Gaston felt warning bells going off in his mind.

"She's gone to gather some plants, she said. Her and her plants." Maida chuckled.

Gaston spoke calmly, telling himself there was no need for alarm. "Can you tell me where?" Rose knew the forest around Carlisle as well as anyone could.

But why hadn't she returned for the meal? He thought of Nigel and his family who had been tortured and killed before their home was torched.

Maida made a sweeping gesture with her hand. "The West Wood."

Getting to his feet without another word, Gaston left. Anger at Rose churned in his belly like bubbles in boiling water. She wandered about with too little thought to her own safety.

Only minutes later, the dark knight spurred Pegasus forward, racing through the gate unhindered. Mud flew up behind him as the white stallion's sharp hooves tore at the soft turf.

Pegasus cantered lithely over the ground, sidestepping obstacles in his path, leaving his rider free to search for any sign of the lady. It was as if some of Gaston's inner anxiety transferred itself to the stallion, because he strained and pulled at the bridle in his mouth. Gaston leaned close and soothed the horse with a hand on his neck, checking the pace only slightly, even though the trees made such speed dangerous.

Suddenly the sound of a scream filled the air, rebounding off the trees and filling the forest with a frozen chill. Gaston's heart began to pound with dread.

He pulled up his mount, turning it around, trying to detect from which direction the sound had come.

He heard another scream coming from his right. He kicked with his heels. Pegasus reared straight up in the air, then landed at a gallop. Neither horse nor rider paid heed to the trees that reached out with sharp-clawed limbs to tear at clothing and flowing white mane. Each trusted to providence to keep them from stepping into a rabbit hole or running into some object that might block their path.

The two burst into a clearing and what Gaston saw there made his blood run cold. Rose lay on the ground. One man in ragged clothes held her arms, while another squatted at her side. The second man was busy trying to still the thrashing of her feet and legs as she fought to keep him from pulling up her skirts.

Another man stood at her feet, his hands working at the laces of his clothing.

The three men were so intent on what they were doing they took no notice of the horse and rider. The curses Rose flung at them also helped to cover the noise of her rescuer's arrival.

The man at her feet let out a grunt of pain as Rose's foot shot out and connected with his chin.

"Can't you hold her?" shouted the man who was standing.

The assailant at Rose's head gave her arms a vicious jerk, making her cry out. "Be still, bitch. It will all be over soon enough," he laughed rancorously, showing black rotting teeth.

All this Gaston observed in the split second it took him to leap from his horse. His hand went to the sword at his side, his mind a blinding hot well of fury.

A beam of sunlight coming through the trees caught on the sword and reflected off it in a bright shaft of silver. It was this that finally drew the attention of the three. They looked into Gaston's livid face and saw death staring back at them. The two men on the ground leapt to their feet and began to beg for mercy.

Gaston neither heard nor cared for their cry of quarter. His anger had taken him into a place from which he could not retreat.

Seeing that the pleading of the others had made no impression on the tall knight, the third man drew a pitted knife from his tunic. He crouched, ready to defend himself. Dimly Gaston's mind registered that this man was no stranger to fighting.

But this thought was only passing. Gaston was aware of nothing beyond the desire for their blood. He swung his arm high, the sword cut through the air and the first man fell. A steady pounding continued in Gaston's ears as he stepped over him and moved to the second assailant. He raised the sword again, and this man was dispatched as quickly as the first.

Gaston turned to the last of the trio. His clothing was slightly less ragged than the other two, but he was just as filthy. His greasy hair hung in jagged clumps, as if it had been cut with a knife. An ugly scar ran the length of his right cheek. The cur lunged with his knife, but Gaston knocked the weapon from his hand with the flat of his sword. He would not allow such vermin to die fighting. He would be slaughtered like the animal he was. The knight's sword struck true.

Gaston shook with the force of his anger. It burned like the heat of a forge inside him. He was only sorry they were dead. He wanted to make them suffer for touching Rose with their filthy hands.

A movement caught his eye and he turned his head.

Rose had crawled up beside a tree trunk and sat huddled against it. Her arms were wrapped around the base, and her lovely eyes were wide with fear as she watched him.

Gaston took a deep breath and his sword clattered to the ground. He covered his face with his hands as he bent over the fallen sword. He tried to still the shaking in his limbs as he worked to clear his thoughts.

Never before, even in battle, had he so lost control of himself. But the sight of them had driven him near to insanity. He could not endure those men manhandling her, hurting the woman he loved.

And love her he did, with all his heart and soul. She was as much a part of him as his belief in God and the hereafter; as much a part of him as his own flesh. He rose slowly, his feet leaden as he moved toward her.

He knelt at her side. Gaston's voice, when he spoke, was barely above a whisper. "Rose."

She looked into his eyes, smoky grey and dark with love for her. "I did not mean to frighten you. It's just that when I saw . . ." His voice broke and he reached out his hand.

Her heart constricted with love, and she took the outstretched hand. He enfolded her in the safe circle of his arms. As she drew on his strength she didn't know that he too was taking comfort from her.

When those men had come upon Rose as she was gathering henbane she thought there would be no hope of escape. Her pleas for mercy had been met by laughter so demoralizing she had cringed from its evil, knowing she would hear the sound in her nightmares as long as she lived. The man with the scar had smiled as he leaned over her, telling her of the vile things they would do to her.

The dirty, ragged men were symbols of all she had been through these past months: the death of her family; the loss of her freedom; her marriage to Hubert and the countless other things that had left her feeling as though she had no say 'in her own destiny. She had fought them with every ounce of her will, but they had overpowered her.

Rose had no way of knowing her struggles provided Gaston with enough time to reach her before the villains could fulfill their objective.

Feeling the tremors that shook his powerful body, Rose put her arms around Gaston and held him with all her strength.

"Forgive me," he whispered into the tangled silk of her hair, his voice husky.

"There is nothing to forgive," she told him softly. She pulled back to look up into his eyes. "You have saved me from a terrible fate. How could I feel anything but gratitude for what you have done?"

"But they begged for quarter."

"And deserved none," she said, refusing to look at the mutilated bodies. "I had done these men no harm and thus should have expected none from them."

He clutched her to him fiercely, nearly smothering her. "I would gladly kill them again." Gaston drew away, holding her so he could read her expression. "Even if you say you do not blame me, I saw the fear in your eyes for what I have done."

She faced him directly. "I can not deny that I was frightened by your anger." She smoothed the hair back from his brow. "You are a fierce warrior."

He turned away. "You have watched me killing Saxons. Now, more than ever, you will resent me for being a Norman."

"Those men were not my kind." She drew herself up straight, bringing his gaze back to her. "They were nothing but savages. They were cowards who would prey on someone of lesser strength than themselves." She closed her eyes and shuddered as she thought of their dirty hands and foul breath.

Groaning, Gaston pulled her close against the warm hardness of his chest. Gladly would he kill ten times their number to prevent them from harming one hair on her precious head. He ran his cheek over the auburn waves, breathing in her wildflower scent. She was his and his alone.

Gaston stood with her in his arms. Going to where Pegasus stood quietly, nibbling the tender lower branches of a tree, Gaston settled his lady upon the stallion's back. He retrieved his sword, wiping the blade clean. Then he swung into the saddle behind her. Gathering up the reins, Gaston kneed the destrier forward.

Rose snuggled back against him. She felt protected as she never had before, and completely whole. Even with her family she had thought of herself as a separate being, together and yet apart from them. It seemed as though his one strong heart pulsed for the two of them. As long as Gaston stood firm, she would, too.

Leaning back against his shoulder, Rose breathed deeply of the forest that smelled of living things, moss and the rich dark earth that constantly renewed itself. Gaston bent forward and kissed her temple. He did not speak, seeming to sense her need for silence.

It would go against everything she held holy for her to marry Hubert now, with this love for Gaston so great and real inside her.

It wasn't until they reached the palisade at Carlisle that Rose regained her senses.

Hubert and his men were just riding in on lathered horses. The foot soldiers moved off toward the barracks.

The reality of Hubert's presence penetrated the heavenly lethargy that had enfolded her. Rose sat up straighter in the saddle, very aware of the fact that her shoulder still touched Gaston's hard chest.

How could she have allowed herself to dream she and Gaston could be together? Hubert was the man she would marry. She was bound by her word to her people.

She turned in the saddle to look at Gaston. His handsome face was as emotionless as carved marble. His withdrawal was an empty pit in her chest, aching beyond measure. It was as if the past hour had never been.

Rose turned to Hubert, reminding herself that Gaston had not actually said he loved her. Now she truly doubted he had such feelings. Rose could not meet Hubert's gaze. Her pain was too intense to hide from his prying eyes.

Hubert dismounted and came toward them. It was then that Rose noticed Elspith was seated on a pretty chestnut mare behind Hubert's horse. The blond maid's expression was uneasy as she looked toward her cousin. One of the knights moved forward to help her to the ground. With a last glance at Rose, she hurried away.

Chiding herself for feeling betrayed, Rose clasped her hands tightly together. It was not as if she hadn't known Elspith was with Hubert, but it was awkward to be confronted so blatantly with the relationship.

She was unable to face the embarrassment in the knights' expressions as they looked from her to the retreating Elspith. Rose closed her eyes and swayed, leaning into Gaston's arms. She did not care that he didn't want her. She only knew he offered the first protection she had known since her father and brother died.

Gaston caught her in his arms as she lost consciousness, his quick actions preventing her from falling.

Hubert took the last few steps toward them at a run. "What is wrong? Has she taken ill?"

Gaston answered without looking at his brother. "Rose was set upon by ruffians."

"The same men we have been trying to catch?"

"From the look of them, I would say yes."

"Where are they?" Hubert growled.

"Dead." Gaston moved to dismount.

Hubert reached up to take Rose. "Let me..."

But Gaston wasn't listening. He slid from his horse, the limp girl clasped tightly in his arms. He strode toward her bower, Hubert falling into step beside him.

"How was it that you found her?" Hubert asked.

"When she did not return for the meal I began to worry." Gaston glanced over at his brother. "I kept thinking of how the farmer's family had been tortured. From talking with the cook, I found out where the lady had gone. After that it was just a question of finding her." Gaston went on to explain what had happened, not telling his brother how crazed he had become, only that the men had died fighting.

Hubert shook his head. "This little maid has been almost more trouble than good." He scowled down at her.

Under the guise of settling her more comfortably in his arms, Gaston cradled Rose's head more closely against his shoulder.

Hubert slapped his gauntlets against his thigh. "As soon as the criminals are caught, and my estate settled, the marriage must go forward. I will soon teach the damsel to stay out of trouble."

The knife twisted in Gaston's guts.

Chapter Eleven

Rose awoke to find herself in bed, with Maida hovering over her. For a moment she was disoriented. The last thing she remembered was sitting atop Pegasus with Hubert glaring up at her.

Rose rubbed her forehead in confusion. "How did I come to be here?"

Maida folded her hands over her ample girth. "When you fainted, Sir Gaston carried you. He would not relinquish you to Lord Hubert."

Flushing, Rose could not meet the cook's gaze. "He was concerned for my well-being. I was set upon by miscreants in the forest and he rescued me."

Maida's blue eyes were damp with concern and she reached out to smooth the hair back from Rose's brow. "Sir Gaston told us what happened. You . . . you are certain you are well?"

Rose sat up, fussing with the bed fur, unwilling to let Maida see her pain. "Ga . . . Sir Gaston arrived before they could do me any real harm." She gave a shaky laugh, running her hand through her hair. "I feel very silly to have fainted. I must have been more disturbed by what happened than I thought."

Maida looked down at her hands. "Did Sir Gaston mention that we had talked?"

"No." Rose frowned. "Why would he? I am sure you've conversed on many occasions."

Maida picked at her nails. "This conversation was of particular note. At least what I remember of it."

Rose's brow puckered as she wonder what Maida could be getting at. "Why wouldn't you…" Realization dawned. "You had been drinking." Her tone was accusing.

"Only a little." Maida hunched her rounded shoulders.

Rose covered her face with her hands. "What have you told him?"

"Nothing, really." Maida shrugged, her palms turned up. "I believe I did say something about Lady Elspith, but I do not believe he understood," Maida amended when Rose glared at her.

"How do you know he did not understand?" Rose asked.

"Has Sir Hubert come bellowing at the top of his lungs for an explanation?" Maida reasoned. "That one would not waste any time had he learned of Elspith's true identity."

"You are right." Rose bent forward, massaging the back of her neck. "But you must be more careful to guard your tongue."

The cook's expression was earnest. "I know, my lady, but Sir Gaston is such a good man, I forget he is a Norman. I believe even your father and brother would have thought well of him."

Rose swallowed down the knot in her throat. In all honesty, she had to admit the truth of this. Both of them would have liked Gaston, for there was much good in him. She also knew they would not have forgotten he was a Norman. Nor would they want her to.

Turning to Maida, she forced a note of determination to her voice. "And so we must be doubly careful to think of what we say, before we say it. Gaston's foremost allegiance is to Hubert."

There was no way for Maida to deny this, though she did not believe Gaston would say anything that might harm Rose.

Maida knew what had happened the night Gaston had
summoned Rose from her bath. The reeve had confided in
the cook, after first swearing her to secrecy. He was troubled by Rose's engagement to Lord Hubert, believing his
lady and Sir Gaston were in love. Maida agreed, but there
was nothing she or Alfred could do. Rose seemed bent on
going through with the marriage.

Thinking to put Sir Gaston in a favorable light, Maida
said, "He was so very worried about you when you did not
come for the meal. Sir Gaston feared you would be set upon
by the very bandits Lord Hubert pursues."

Rose turned to Maida in consternation. "You know as
well as I that Robert would more likely fly to the moon than
harm me."

"And well I know that." Peevishly Maida put her hands
on her ample hips. "But would you have me telling Sir
Gaston this? Oh," she minced, batting her lashes at an
imaginary knight, "Sir Gaston, have no fear for my lady.
Her own cousin is the leader of the rebels and will see her
protected from any hurt."

Rose almost laughed at the comic picture presented by the
cook. But she restrained herself. Maida must accept the
gravity of the situation. "I think you have managed to say
enough," she answered.

Maida was kept from making a reply when the door
opened and Elspith hesitantly stepped into the room.

Rose looked at her cousin for a long moment, then turned
away, her chin set at a stubborn angle.

Elspith stood still, her face draining of color. She put her
hand up to stifle the cry that rose to her lips. Her golden eyes
filled with pain, and she spun on her heel, closing the door
behind herself.

"Lady Rose!" Maida turned to her mistress, her eyes
wide with shock. "How could you treat her so?"

Rose gasped. "How can I treat her so? I warned her of
Hubert's ways, but she would not hear me." She turned on
her side, facing the wall, fighting back tears. "I thought if

we had one another...that together we might...please, might I be alone now. I am very tired.''

She heard Maida go to the door, keeping a tight hold on her emotions until she heard it shut. The dam broke and hot tears poured down her cheeks. Gaston, Maida, Robert and Elspith. They expected too much of her, wanting her to be strong and understanding. But she was so tired, so lonely.

Elspith, at least, would have some memories of her lover, whispered words in the night, fond embraces to relive.

Things had been better between the two girls before Elspith had gone to Hubert. But it was too hurtful for Rose to compare herself to the other girl, who had, if for a short time, been able to have her love.

For Rose there would only be that one glorious afternoon, lying beneath a summer sky dotted with apple blossoms.

By the next day, the attack on Rose was still uppermost in the men's thoughts.

As they waited for the meal to be served, Hubert said, ''Would that you could have taken one of them alive. The whore's sons were the only ones we have even gotten close to.''

Gaston nodded. He could not but agree. The three men who attacked Rose had to be part of the same band creating so much havoc for Hubert.

Hubert's hand tightened on the stem of his cup. ''I am only sorry I could not kill them myself. Rose is mine, and what I have I hold.''

Gaston bristled. Hubert spoke as if Rose were no more important that a tapestry, or a horse; in point of fact, Hubert would likely place more value on his destrier. His lips were tight as he replied, ''I assure you, I would not have given up the pleasure of seeing those three dead. Even for you, brother.''

Hubert banged his cup down on the table, causing the wine to slosh over the side. ''The scum. If only I knew how they manage to stay one step ahead of us. It is uncanny, the way these thieves know our every move before it is made.''

''How much damage have they actually done?''

''It is very odd,'' Hubert answered slowly. ''They strike hard at the storage bins, and many buildings have been burned to the ground, such as the barrack at Mayhill. Even though we rode with all possible haste the day of the fire, there was not a sign of the men who had done it. The people come to me with many complaints, such as stolen cattle and pigs. We find not a trace of either animals or thieves.'' Hubert shrugged. ''Lack of evidence makes it hard to know how much ill the raiders have been able to accomplish.'' He grimaced, taking a sip of his wine.

Gaston could see why Hubert had not been able to catch these criminals. It would have been better if he could have brought one of Rose's attackers back to Carlisle; still, he was not sorry he had killed them. He would not allow himself to think about what would have happened had he not arrived to rescue her.

These marauders struck like poisonous snakes, then disappeared into the forests.

Hubert's scowl was dark. ''Just last week a party of men rode into the village at Mayhill and killed a young woman who withheld her favors. Then later that same afternoon, they struck at a barn not far from Brentwood. They made off with the farmer's bull and several chickens.''

''But that is impossible.'' Gaston's brows arched over puzzled eyes. ''Brentwood is a day and a half of hard riding from Mayhill.''

''I know that as well as anyone. I have spent most of the last three months in traveling the distance repeatedly.'' Hubert squeezed the stem of his cup as if he wished it were the throat of one of his antagonists.

After a moment of contemplation, Gaston said, ''Do you believe that they may have enough men to try to confuse you by splitting their forces?''

"I have asked myself that very question many times. I have no answer. The only way to tell is to locate their camp, and that has proved most difficult." His expression grew thoughtful. "If it weren't for the holder's lost property, I would almost believe they are protecting someone. Or at least I was beginning to think so. Since the girl was killed at Mayhill, the people have made every effort to assist my men." He rubbed the back of his neck. "My head aches with trying to make sense of it all. When I find them, these men will die slowly and painfully, and by my hand."

With a world-weary sigh, Hubert looked up then smiled, his features going soft with love.

Gaston followed the path of his gaze and saw Elspith. He did not know when she had come, but he did notice her fair cheeks were paler than usual. She seemed to sway where she stood.

Hubert jumped up, taking her in his arms. "Are you all right, my dove?" He cupped her chin, turning her face up to his.

While Hubert and Gaston had talked, the hall had filled as people gathered for their evening meal. Complete attention was focused on Hubert and his mistress. Then, as if connected by a single consciousness, all eyes swiveled around to stare at the entrance to the hall.

Without looking, Gaston knew Rose would be standing there. Slowly he too turned to watch her. With the same unconscious grace that had so deeply impressed him on the day they first met, Rose walked toward the high table. She held her head at a regal angle, and her carriage was that of a queen. Gaston wanted to shout of his love for her to them all.

Hubert, meanwhile, was totally oblivious to Rose's presence. With tender care he seated Elspith next to him at the table.

Rose hesitated, so slightly Gaston was sure no one else had even seen the uncertainly in her eyes.

Acting purely on instinct, Gaston rose from his place and went to stand before her. He offered his arm with courtly grace.

Looking up into his clear grey eyes, Rose knew with Gaston at her side she could withstand any difficulty. With a slight inclination of her head, she accepted the proffered arm and fell into step beside him.

As the couple crossed the hall, the people at the tables could not help being moved by them. The lady was so lovely in a gown of midnight blue and pale blue tunic, her hair a bright flame against the cloth. The knight, so tall and powerful, made a perfect foil for her, dressed in a scarlet shirt and black tunic. They seemed to glide across the room until they reached the high table, where Gaston settled the lady in his own place, on Hubert's right, then took the seat on her other side.

Looking out over the crowd of onlookers, Rose's eyes flashed emerald fire as she dared them to stare.

Most onlookers flushed and turned away. Self-consciously the people began to eat. Only surreptitiously did they peek up to study the tableau at the head table.

Casting a nervous glance toward Hubert, Rose saw he was frowning. She felt her heartbeat quicken, fearful that Gaston's courtesy toward her had given away their feelings for each other.

She needn't have worried. Hubert had noticed Gaston going forward to offer Rose his arm. But his only reaction was relief. He was pleased that Gaston had helped him through a difficult moment.

Hubert had thought of nothing beyond his physical needs when he first took Elspith to his bed. He had only meant to enjoy her, then marry her off to some soldier or well-to-do farmer when he had finished with her.

Somewhere his plans had gone awry. The more he knew of Elspith, the more he cared. The nights he spent away from her gentle love were long and empty. His love for

Elspith went beyond practicalities. Women were nothing but a nuisance in the field. And still, he sent for her.

Hubert did not want a confrontation with Rose about Elspith. From what the interfering Gaston told him, he gathered that Rose was disapproving of his open relationship with his mistress. Gaston seemed to think it reasonable for Rose to feel that way. Hubert could not understand why, when the woman had made it clear she did not want him.

Rose would have to learn her place. Hubert had come to realize he could not give up Elspith. He would be forced to get sons on Rose to carry on his name, but Elspith would be his true wife in all else.

Watching Elspith and Hubert, Gaston felt a deep well of contempt for his brother. It was one thing for him to enjoy his mistress in private, and another to dally with her here before the whole fief.

Hubert should be doing everything in his power to win Rose to him. She was a prize beyond price and Gaston would have gladly laid down his life to have her. Hubert did not deserve a woman of such noble character as Rose.

Should the opportunity present itself, Gaston meant to win her to him, not just for now but for always. If Rose could be persuaded, they would go away together, somewhere that they would be free to love each other. He knew it would mean her giving up Carlisle, but Gaston had served his king well. William would be generous in rewarding him.

Unaware of Gaston's intentions, Rose watched as Hubert toyed with a strand of Elspith's pale silky hair. Elspith looked nervous and unhappy.

When Gaston put his hand on her arm, Rose started, turning to face him. He tried to tell her with his eyes how much her suffering affected him.

"You have suffered no ill effect from your ordeal yesterday?" Gaston's deep voice soothed her, low and intimate, creating a velvet bond between them.

She met his eyes and looked away, made breathless by the intensity of his smoky gaze. "I...I have all but forgotten the incident."

Automatically, she took food from the trencher he formed for them.

Gaston brushed the backs of his fingers over hers, and a shaft of piercing sweet sensation shot through her.

"For that I am thankful," he murmured. "I would not have been able to bear it had anything happened to you." He leaned closer, his breath caressing her cheek. "Do not allow what he does to hurt you. He does not know what he has lost."

"I thank you for your care," she whispered, all the while wondering what Gaston could mean. The phrase, "he does not know what he has lost" repeated over and over in her mind.

"Rose..." Gaston began.

His voice was stilled by the sound of Elspith's soft laughter.

Rose turned to see Hubert bending over the girl, his mouth bare inches from hers.

Rose blanched, seeing the way the people had turned to look. She was hurt anew to see how Elspith could display her defection so openly. It did not help that Hubert and Elspith were so wrapped up in each other they didn't even notice the stares.

Suddenly there was a commotion from outside the hall, and all turned to the open doorway. Through it stepped a man wearing King William's colors. He moved purposely across the room to stop before Hubert.

Rose saw that this occurrence was enough to take Hubert's and Elspith's attention away from each other.

Hubert rose, his smile showing his pleasure. "Sir Walter, you are well come."

Gaston also smiled—a bit stiffly—and rose to greet the newcomer. "Sir Walter."

"You must sit and dine with us." Hubert motioned for a seat to be brought.

A servant ran forward, placing a bench across the table from the brothers so their guest would face them.

Hubert himself poured the dusty man a drink and handed it to him. With forced patience, he waited for Sir Walter to take a long draught. "You bring word of His Majesty?"

There was a barely restrained tension in the hall. Normans and Saxons alike could not help being interested in the doings of a king.

Sir Walter wiped his lips on his sleeve. "I do." He held out his cup for more wine. "The wine is good, and more than welcome after a long dusty ride."

There was a long pause as food was placed before Sir Walter and he began to eat the good brown bread and roasted meat with unrestrained enthusiasm. Rose studied the visitor with interest. He was an older man, but handsome still. His hair was grey and thick; his beard of the same color was neatly trimmed, as was his mustache. His eyes were a deep brown, intelligent and keen-looking. "The king is but a few hours behind me. He will arrive here sometime tomorrow."

Over the hum of excitement, Hubert asked, "William is on his way to Carlisle?"

Sir Walter swallowed a mouthful of venison. "His Majesty is on his way north. He will call upon a number of his trusted subjects." Sir Walter's gaze moved over Elspith, where she sat at Hubert's side, her hand in his.

Hubert motioned for more wine. "We are honored."

Sir Walter smiled at Elspith, his tone courteous. "May I be introduced to your lady?"

There was a strained silence, during which even Hubert had the grace to blush. He let go of Elspith's hand, answering, "No, my lord, this is my lady." He turned to Rose on his other side. "Perhaps His Majesty will be able to attend our wedding. We have not set a date as yet, but the marriage will certainly take place before long."

After a short silence of his own, Sir Walter managed to drag his eyes from the two beautiful women and face Hubert. "I believe that will be impossible as His Majesty still has many obstacles to eradicate before his kingdom is in order."

The awkward moment had passed without complicated questions from the king's man. Hubert breathed deeply with relief. William was known to set great honor by his wife, Mathilda of Flanders. When he left Normandy, he named her along with Rodger of Beaumont, as regent over his son and heir, Duke Robert.

Sir Walter's sharp gaze flicked from Hubert to Elspith, then to Gaston to Rose and back again.

Rose made every effort not to touch or even speak with the man at her side, little realizing that this in itself was enough to give her away.

What a pickle these men had gotten themselves into, Sir Walter thought. But they would have to sort it out for themselves. The king had more pressing matters to attend. Not all the Saxons were ready to accept his rule. Which brought Sir Walter to the true reason for the king's visit. "I must tell you, Hubert, that His Majesty wishes to call upon your knight's fee. We travel north to subdue a Saxon earl who is holed up in his castle. His fortress is strong, having been built by the Romans. The siege may well be long and tiresome." He sat back to observe Hubert's reaction.

Hubert shifted uncomfortably in his seat. "I would be honored to provide His Majesty with a portion of my knights. But I would be hard-pressed to leave Carlisle at this time. We have been having our own problems with a band of renegade Saxons."

Sir Walter scowled, his heavy grey brows meeting over his nose. "How long has this been going on?"

"Since shortly after we arrived here," Gaston answered.

"And you have not been able to stop them?"

Hubert colored. "Gaston and I believe these men must have been soldiers at one time. They operate with more skill and cunning than any of us would have thought possible."

Sir Walter's brow puckered in thought. "William may wish to assist you after this other matter has been dealt with, but of course I can not speak for the king." He lifted his hands and shrugged. "These pockets of rebellion must be routed out lest they incite others to rise up against us."

Hubert answered stiffly. "I would be grateful for any assistance His Majesty might be willing to offer." Then he smiled coldly. "Though I believe it will only be a short time before the devils make a mistake and fall into one of the traps I have set for them."

Elspith drew in a sharp breath.

Rose's feelings echoed her cousin's. With William's resources behind him, Hubert would be assured of capturing Robert. But something else troubled Rose. Hubert seemed too smug. What traps did he speak of?

Rose had to force herself to attend what Sir Walter was saying. "None the less, I shall mention the matter to His Majesty. That much can do no harm." He leaned back, pressing his long fingers together like a priest offering a blessing.

Sir Walter's gaze lingered upon Elspith with appreciation, making her blush.

Rose watched as Hubert scowled, putting a possessive hand on Elspith's shoulders. Hubert's tone was oversolicitous. "The hour grows late."

Looking up, Rose saw that Hubert spoke the truth; the sky outside the open door was dark and filled with twinkling stars. Taking their cue from Hubert, the people began to file out of the hall.

She stood, intent on making her way to her bower. She must devise a plan to warn Robert, firstly as to Hubert's veiled threats. And more importantly, her cousin must be told the Bastard himself might raise arms against him. Robert must realize the gravity of the situation.

Behind her she could hear Hubert talking to his guest. His voice was low and suggestive. "I'm certain we will be able to accommodate you. There is a woman in the village who..." Hubert's words faded away.

Rose felt her face flame.

Sir Walter gave a lurid laugh. "Is this true, Gaston?"

Before Gaston could make a reply, Hubert interjected, "Do not ask him. I am afraid my brother has no taste for Saxon flesh. To my knowledge he had not taken a woman since our arrival here."

Sir Walter's brows rose in surprise. "No taste for Saxon flesh?"

Rose glanced toward the men from the corner of her eye. Sir Walter was standing, stroking his beard, amusement lighting his gaze as it met hers.

Chapter Twelve

William the Conqueror's arrival was awaited with all the tension of an encroaching electrical storm. The serfs kept glancing up from their work, nervous and uneasy at what the king's visit might bring. Word of the Bastard's keen intellect and fierceness as a warrior had spread far and wide.

Even the Normans were not immune to these feelings of unrest. Tempers were short, and Rose noticed an unusual number of men heading for the practice field to vent their energies in combat.

The whole courtyard was alive with activity as a feast was prepared for William and his entourage. The men had slaughtered cattle, sheep, pigs and fowl. From the roasting meats and savory dishes rose the piquant scents of cloves and cinnamon.

It would take an enormous amount of food to feed William's army. Rose resented the added burden on her vassals, but she wisely kept her own counsel. Hubert did as he wished.

It was Gaston who suggested a hunt. If the king and his knights took wild game from the forest, it would reduce the demand on her people. How different things would be if Gaston were Lord of Carlisle.

Leaving the men at their breakfast, Rose went out to oversee the digging of another fire pit.

Elspith had not made an appearance this day. Rose wondered if Hubert had told his mistress to remain out of sight. She hoped he would not humiliate them in front of his king, as he had before Sir Walter.

She remembered the way Sir Walter had looked at her the night before. The expression in his eyes told her he was not blind to the attraction between her and Gaston. Her only hope was that he would keep his thoughts to himself, for he had no proof of wrongdoing by either of them.

With the pit dug, and a fat cow on the spit, Rose went in search of Maida. She found her overseeing the baking of the sweet pasties. The pies were filled with apples and spices that made her close her eyes and breathe deeply of their heavenly scent.

Glancing about the room, Rose saw Elspith sitting on a bench, removed from the other women who chatted and teased amongst themselves. Elspith's dejected pose and listless attitude made Rose look at her, really look at her, for the first time in weeks. Her face was pale and drawn. Elspith had always been very slender, but now her arms and throat were so thin they made her appear incredibly fragile.

Rose had to stifle a wave of sympathy. Elspith would not welcome her interference. The fair maid had gotten what she wanted—Hubert.

With a final word to Maida, Rose turned to walk away.

She felt a touch on her shoulder and stopped. Elspith stood behind her. Her expression was contrite, pleading for forgiveness. Even though Elspith had taken the first step, Rose did not know what to say.

Seeing her cousin's silence as condemnation, Elspith flushed, looking at the ground.

Feeling an overwhelming sorrow for the older girl, Rose viewed the room through a sheen of moisture. When she spoke, her voice was a whisper. "I am sorry, Elspith, but I can not pretend things are as they once were between us."

Elspith swallowed back her tears, trying to make her voice sound cheerful as she answered. "Do not feel badly. I know

I have hurt you. My sorrow is of my own making. You, at least, do not treat me cruelly. I have received much worse treatment from the other women.''

Rose bristled, her back going rigid. ''How dare they treat you so? You are still my cousin, and a gentlewoman. They have no right.''

Heads turned at the sound of Rose's raised voice, but when they heard her words, the women quickly looked away. None of them had wanted to call down their lady's wrath.

Elspith clutched at Rose's arm. ''Do not berate them. To them I am less than nothing for having turned my back on you.''

''That is no excuse—'' Rose began.

''I have to work among them, Rose, please, do not continue. Now that the women have seen you disapprove, they will not torment me further. I had not meant to stir your ire.''

Rose moved close to her cousin. ''Elspith, I . . .''

Elspith stopped her from going on with a touch on her arm. ''I must explain about last eve. I know how difficult it must have been for you. I did not mean to take your place at table,'' she whispered, putting her hands to her cheeks. ''When I went to the hall, I heard Hubert telling Gaston what he would do to Robert when he caught him. It frightened me so that I became dizzy.'' Elspith began to cry silently, her eyes dark with guilt. ''Robert is my brother, yet I love the man who seeks his death.''

''Elspith . . .'' Rose began, only to halt as the fair woman swayed and crumpled.

As Rose reached out to her cousin, her arms passed through empty air. She looked down to see Elspith, so pale she could have been dead, lying at her feet.

''A baby!'' Elspith gasped, her golden eyes round with surprise. She looked so young lying there on Rose's bed.

"Yes," Rose told her, her voice empty of expression. This was too much. How could Hubert have done this to Elspith?

Elspith spread her hand over the flat line of her stomach. Her eyes shone with the brilliance of stars as she looked up at Rose. "When?"

Rose could not fathom her joy. "The babe will come in winter; Christmas. Your lover lost no time in filling your belly."

"Modra nect." Elspith smiled.

Rose frowned. "You should not talk of such things. The old religion is best forgotten."

"I do not follow the old way, but I grew up with tales of the ancient beliefs, just as you have." Elspith cradled her belly with her hands. "Mayhap our child will be born on the Night of the Mothers, when the old sun passes away and the new sun is born."

"Do not speak so in front of the others," Rose warned, turning away. "How silly of me to question your mode of speech. You with your belly full and no husband."

Elspith flushed, her hands twisting nervously. "I am so very sorry, Rose. Please, can you not forgive me? You will be marrying my love. At least with the babe, I will have something of him." Her eyes pleaded for understanding.

A voice in Rose's head screamed out in silent anguish, *And what am I to hold of my love?*

Then Rose's stiff shoulders slumped, and she turned back to her cousin. "Forgive you?" Rose leaned down and put her arms around the too-thin shoulders of the older girl. "It is not your doing that Hubert takes what he wants. It is I who should ask for forgiveness. I am consumed by my jealousy of you."

Elspith's expression was incredulous. "Jealousy?"

"Yes." Wearily Rose sank down onto the edge of the bed. "I am consumed by my envy. You will have a child to keep the memory of your love fresh within you. I will have nothing to bolster me."

"Who...?" Elspith stopped, her eyes going round. "You love him. I have seen the way he cares for you, but..."

Rose drew away. "What are you saying?"

"Why, that you love Sir Gaston." At Rose's stricken expression, Elspith shook her head slowly. "I don't know why I did not see that you cared for him, too."

"You saw that he cared for me?" Rose rested her forehead on her hands. There was no point in explaining that Elspith had mistaken passion for a deeper emotion. "Does Hubert know?"

"No, I am sure he does not. My love is not the kind of man who would easily see another's pain." There was so much loving indulgence in her voice Rose was shocked anew that Elspith knew the man's weaknesses and still cared for him.

Rose's lips tightened with determination. Hubert must never know of her love for Gaston. He would set her aside, and her vow to her people would be broken. She gave a hopeless sigh. "What a muddle we have made of our lives."

"It is not we who have made a muddle," Elspith spoke up with surprising strength. "It is fate, destiny, whatever you will. It was your fate to love Gaston just as was mine to love Hubert. To rail against one's destiny is foolish. We must only wait to see what else might come."

"But there is no chance of happiness for either of us," Rose interjected. She was astounded at the core of resilience that Elspith displayed.

Elspith looked at some point far away. "We can only hope for happiness."

In late afternoon, a call went up from the watchman at the gate.

Preceded by a rider bearing the king's standard, the army came out of the forest. And they continued to come, pouring out over the hillside in a seemingly unending stream, like an army of large menacing ants. The smooth gleaming surfaces of their helmets only heightened the illusion.

Watching from the palisade, Rose clenched her jaw so tightly it ached. There must have been hundreds of them, she told herself with morbid fascination. The sight of William's army reaffirmed her decision to accept the Norman rule. Carlisle could not have withstood such an onslaught.

Her fear for Robert intensified as she imagined this army at Hubert's disposal. She shivered.

Both Hubert and Gaston had been waiting for this moment. Their horses had been saddled and ready for quite some time. The brothers were riding down the hill within minutes of the guard's shout.

With an unconsciously possessive smile, Rose watched as Pegasus easily outdistanced Hubert's mount. The white stallion fairly flew across the bright green turf. The two men rode into the large body of mounted knights at the front of the army.

Smoothing her hair back as it blew into her eyes, Rose tucked the strands into her thick braid. She checked the green ribbon to make sure it was secure. Self-consciously, she smoothed the front of the white tunic she wore over her dark green underdress. She took a deep breath to calm her frayed nerves.

Maida and Elspith had insisted she prepare herself for William's arrival just as if he weren't the greedy usurper she knew him to be.

Since their talk, much of the tension had dissipated between the cousins. They were simply two women trapped by circumstance.

Rose had been surprised when Elspith insisted that she, Maida and Rose were to be the only ones to know of her pregnancy. Elspith was sure the child was a boy, but she did not mean to tell Hubert of his son. Rose's children would be his heirs.

Rose argued that Hubert would know of the child soon enough.

Elspith was adamant. By that time Rose might have found a place in Hubert's heart. Rose could have told her cousin she neither expected nor wanted ever to have a place in Hubert's heart. That place was already filled by Elspith. Rose realized more and more that Hubert had not been acting out of spite for her, but out of love for Elspith.

A group of five men, including Gaston and Hubert, separated from the retinue of knights and rode up the hill. One of the other men appeared to be Sir Walter, who had ridden out early that morning to meet the king. The other two she did not know. She wondered if one of them might be William himself.

Rose climbed down the ladder. Her knees felt weak as she moved across the courtyard to where the knights were dismounting.

She folded her hands together to still their trembling. William the Conqueror might be nothing more than a bloodthirsty savage, but he had led his men to conquer a country against all odds. This made him a man to be reckoned with.

Tilting her head at a proud angle, she drew herself up as the men turned to watch her. She would not let them see her apprehension.

Hubert motioned her forward. "Your Majesty, may I present, the Lady Rose of Carlisle."

The remark was addressed to a tall, thick-set man in hauberk and helmet. His nose plate covered most of his face so all that could be seen was a set of determined lips. He lifted his battle-hardened hand and took off his helmet. His face was darkly handsome, his hair black as pitch. His eyes were dark and piercing as he regarded Rose and her home with solemn intensity, missing nothing as he appraised the value of the prize he had bestowed on his loyal knight.

The hairs rose on the back of her neck, and she understood in that moment how he had crossed a sea to take a kingdom. Nothing and no one could keep this man from fulfilling his destiny.

William turned to Hubert. "I see you have done well for yourself."

Rose saw Gaston stiffen where he stood beside Hubert. Unintentionally she took a step away from her future bridegroom. It sickened her to be thought of as nothing more than a prize of war.

"Yes, your grace." Hubert nodded, but Rose could feel the displeasure in his eyes as they momentarily rested on her. "I have much to thank you for."

William raised his hand to prevent Hubert from continuing. "Nonsense. You have earned all."

The king turned to Hubert's brother. "And you, Gaston. How do you find this land? As I remember, you were not eager to end your fighting days and settle down."

Gaston's smile was tight. "Hubert has been gone from Carlisle so oft, chasing after a band of renegade Saxons, that I have grown accustomed to running the estate."

William threw back his head and laughed. "I fully understand your problem. Hubert is not a man who would willingly miss any fighting. But I am surprised, knowing you, Gaston, that you have stayed to protect the women." The king quirked a mischievous brow. "Or rather should I not be surprised?"

William did not miss the quick glance Gaston cast toward Lady Rose. He could see what Sir Walter had told him could well be true. He gave a mental shrug. As long as there was no fighting between his knights, he did not care which of them took the girl, or for that matter the estate.

He had been watching Hubert very carefully since his arrival, and he sensed the unease in the older brother. If Hubert were as dissatisfied with domestic life as it appeared, he would welcome any excuse to be rid of the responsibilities he had taken on.

Watching Gaston carefully, the king put his arm around Hubert's shoulders. "I am sorry, my friend, that I can not be here for your wedding, but it will be some time before this land is fully taken. I must stamp out each revolt with all possible haste.''

As Gaston stiffened at his mention of the marriage, William smiled, allowing Hubert to lead him to the hall.

Though William had not spoken directly to her, Rose was glad to see him leave with Hubert. Her knees were shaking so badly she felt as though she must sit down. William was a man who observed too shrewdly. And she had the feeling he might well be as relentless, if angered, as he seemed generous when pleased.

The next evening, Rose stood on the palisade, her eyes drawn to the encampment on the hillside. The light of the fires shone brightly in the darkness and she could see an occasional spark rise up to float away on the same breath of breeze that ruffled the wisps of auburn hair at her temples.

Below her, a man and a woman strolled hand in hand. As they drew closer to the wall, she could see it was Evelyn and her Norman husband, Jacques. They paused and kissed, their silhouettes outlined against one of the fires.

Rose sighed, looking away from them.

At least these two had found some happiness. Their marriage had accomplished just what Gaston had hoped; even though Evelyn's parents had not totally accepted Jacques yet, they were beginning to.

Inevitably the gentleness of the warm summer night brought thoughts of Gaston. How she wished there could be more for them. But she was without hope. Rose had almost resigned herself to her marriage to Hubert.

It was only the night, and the loneliness she felt seeing others who need not hide their love, that made her sad.

Rose felt the rough wood of the palisade. It was good and solid beneath her fingers, protecting them all from harm.

She too must be good and solid, acting as a protector to her people.

Turning from the scene, she made her way to the ladder that led down to the courtyard. There was no use in daydreaming, she told herself as she descended, unheeding of the slivers of wood that caught at her gown and unbound hair. Her underdress was an old one, once blue but now faded to grey.

The night was warm and she had not bothered with a tunic. No one was about to see her. She could clearly hear the sounds of Hubert and his guest coming from the Great Hall.

She had only taken two steps from the base of the ladder, when she stopped, crying out sharply, her hands going to her hair. Looking behind her, she realized her hair had caught in the joining of one of the lower ladder rungs.

She turned around, tugging at the thick strand, wincing as she pulled her scalp.

"May I be of assistance?" asked a low masculine voice that tickled along her senses.

Rose rolled her eyes heavenward. She did not want him here now, when her resistance had been lowered by her loneliness and the beauty of the night. She was too susceptible to the way he made her feel, the things he made her want. "No..." she began.

But Gaston had already stepped forward. He worked carefully, his long supple fingers gentle, to release the auburn tresses.

Meanwhile, Rose stood tapping her foot, her arms folded over her chest in agitation. Her instincts told her anger would be her best defense. If she could maintain a distance between them, she could keep from falling into his arms and telling him how much she hated what she had to do; that she would give anything for it to be him she wed instead of Hubert.

"Must you always spy upon me?"

His expression was incredulous, his black brows arching. "Spy on you?"

"Yes, spy upon me," she affirmed, tugging at her hair.

He spoke slowly, continuing to work at the long silky strands. "I do not spy on you. Why would you believe such a thing?"

Her green eyes widened. "Why would I believe such a thing? Do you take me for a fool? I know Hubert has set you to watch my every move."

Gaston scowled as if he were confused by what she was saying. "Hubert?" Her hair came free in his hand and he gave a little half smile of accomplishment. But he did not release the thick mane. He stood there with the ends of her hair in his hands as he looked over at her with genuine surprise in his clear grey eyes.

Her voice was less certain now, but she could not stop herself. "Is that not why you follow me about? I can not breathe without looking up to find you there." All the pent-up longing she felt for him was emerging as anger that, at least, gave her an outlet for her feelings.

Without answering, he rubbed the ends of her bright hair between his fingers. He closed his eyes and enjoyed the soft texture, then raised a silky lock to his cheek. Her hair smelled of wildflowers, heady and intoxicating.

Rose gasped and felt her body grow weak at the totally sensuous gesture, her anger forgotten in an instant. She glanced away, trying to regain her control. Why was it like this between them? The fire was always so close to the surface, ready to flare up and consume her. Why had the Lord in his heaven sent her a love like this, if she were not to be allowed to have him?

Gaston opened his eyes and looked at her with such longing her breath caught in her throat. "I do not follow you because Hubert has asked me to." His voice was husky, intimate, caressing. "I watch you because I can not help myself. I am tied to you by some unexplainable force over which I have no control. I am little better than a helpless moon, bound to you but unable to get any closer."

She was incapable of speech or movement, her gaze captive as he went on.

"Do you think I have not told myself you are not mine? That though he does not deserve you, you are bound to Hubert? When I see him touch your hand, I feel a twisting in my heart that almost makes me want to kill him—my own brother.''

"Gaston . . .'' she whispered.

"You are a fever in my blood, and I wish for no cure. My soul is on fire with longing for you and I would gladly betray my brother to have you again, even once. But I know—'' his eyes burned into hers ''—that having you, I would only cry for more.''

She held out her hands in appeal. "Can you not see, it is the same for me? I dream only of you, and when I look at you there is nothing else, only you and I. My heart is so full that I feel I will die with joy when you hold me in your arms.''

She pulled her hair free of his grasp and turned her back to him. "But what we feel is wrong. I am bound to Hubert.'' Going to stand against the wall under the walkway, she put her hands against the palisade. Only a short time ago she had told herself she must remain firm as this very wall; that she must not forget who she was and that her duty to her people came before anything else.

Feeling the warmth of his body as Gaston moved close behind her, Rose stifled a cry of longing. They were secluded here in the darkness beneath the walkway, with only the night to witness their love. She could feel her resistance draining away. The rough logs were not powerful enough to compete with the potent lure of the man she loved.

His hands trailed over the fiery length of her hair to her hips. She wore nothing beneath the threadbare gown, and his knowing fingers seared her flesh.

Then he was close against her back. His rock-hard body pressed against the swell of her bottom as he bent and breathed her in. He loved the way she smelled—of the outdoors and wildflowers and growing things, and the warm scent of woman.

Gaston had dreamed of this moment so many times that the feel of her soft feminine body so close to his made his head spin with the force of his need for her.

Rose gasped as she felt the hot brush of his breath against her ear and throat. Her heart began to thud in her breast and she felt as though she would faint. "Please," she whimpered, not knowing what she wanted, for him to stop or go on. She was too confused by his nearness to think. Feelings she had tried to bury rose up in her.

He whispered, his voice so low and rich it made her shiver. "Please, what?" His hands came up to clasp her waist, kneading the flesh gently. "Please, do this?" He put one hand on her stomach, making her suck in her breath. "I am so filled with desire for you that the heat of it scorches me."

His touch was a brand on her, binding her to him in such a way that she knew there would never be any escape. And right now, she wanted no escape.

She sobbed aloud when he held her hips and drew her to him, molding her lower back to the fierce readiness of his desire.

Her lids drooped as he pushed her hair aside and nibbled softly at the back of her neck. She was lost in a swirling mist of delight, unwilling to do anything that might break the spell.

Slowly his hands traced her ribs, then paused, his thumbs rubbing the delicate undersides of her breasts. As his hands moved up to close over each of the full globes, he felt the way they heaved with the panting breaths she took. The nipples hardened under his palms and her head fell back against his shoulder. "I want you as I have never wanted anything," he breathed. "You have bewitched me until no other woman can awaken my desire."

Rose started and tried to pull away at his mention of other women, but he held her firm, a husky laugh escaping him.

"Have no fear, little Saxon beauty. I will never find comfort in the arms of any other woman. You have taken my heart and my soul into your keeping."

"Gaston," she begged, not knowing what she wanted him to do, only that he would understand. She pivoted to face him, turning her face up to his, her lids heavy.

With a groan of hunger, Gaston took her lips. His kiss was fiercely possessive, drawing out her soul and making it his. When his lips nipped softly at hers, Rose opened her mouth to him like a flower to the rain. She drank him in and made herself whole.

His mouth left hers to place velvet kisses on her cheeks and closed lids, her delicate nose. "Rose." Her name was an endearment.

"Gaston," she answered, her breath mingling with his. Opening her eyes, she saw his face above hers. So many times she had wanted to touch his hair, but she had stopped herself. She reached up, running her fingers through the wavy mass. It was not soft as she had imagined, but heavy and thick, so undeniably male, so undeniably Gaston.

Her hand trembled. This was too wonderful, too perfect to be happening. "Are you real," she asked him softly, "or will I wake to find I was only dreaming again?"

He chuckled, kissing her white throat. "I am real." His hands were again on her hips, pulling her close.

She strained up against him, her lips parted for his kiss. He met her with a passion so demanding she could not doubt the reality of him.

Liquid heat filled her body with an ache only he could assuage. Rose pressed her cheek to his heart. "How can what we feel for one another be wrong? I have thought of little else besides that day in the glebe."

With a deep shudder of longing, Gaston picked her up and laid her in the soft grass.

She made no protest, knowing this moment was inevitable as time. That he should make love to her, on this night created for lovers, was right.

With gentle hands, he drew off her gown. When she lay naked before him, she shied away from the heat in his eyes. His gaze was so possessive it almost unnerved her. She wondered if any woman could withstand so much love and not be consumed.

But the fierce heat inside her told Rose that her own love burned as hotly as his.

Putting her arms around his neck, Rose drew him down to her. The fire became a blazing inferno that threatened to set her aflame as Gaston lowered his dark head and put his mouth to her breast. His lips trailed a path of ecstasy over the sensitive flesh, then he took one hard nipple in his mouth as she arched toward him, catching back a cry of delight. When she thought she might faint with the pleasure of it, Gaston turned to the other breast.

All the while, his hands made their own magic on her heated flesh. He smoothed the flat plane of her belly and he moaned. "How I long to fill you with my sons." He kissed the soft skin.

Her eyes flew open and a strangled little cry escaped her lips as he cupped the mound covered with auburn curls.

"Shh." He kissed her lips.

He began to massage her with his palm, laughing huskily when she moaned and arched against his hand. When his fingers slid into her, Rose was beyond thought. Her legs opened in invitation as she moaned again.

Gaston did not resist. He moved to position himself between her silky legs. His manhood found her. He thrust forward as she raised her hips, and he was sheathed deep in her velvety warmth.

She rose up to meet each thrust of his powerful body, giving herself to him without restraint. She opened her eyes and saw his face above her, his eyes closed and his lips parted. He was totally lost in her, driven by a need that was all-consuming.

Seeing the expression on his face, Rose was overcome with the force of her own passion. She ran her hands down his sides to his lean hips, pulling him even closer to her.

And then she was like a flame, so hot that the heat scorched her to her soul and she burst into shards of light, teetering at the brink of heaven. She arched against him with a cry that Gaston silenced with his lips as he shuddered with his own release.

He slumped above her, taking his weight on his arms. It was a moment before his breathing slowed and he was able to smile at her.

Rose studied her lover's face, drinking him in, a gentle smile playing about her lips. Her eyes were the color of luminous jade. She could not remember ever feeling so content.

He put his hands on either side of her face and leaned down to kiss the tip of her nose, then her lips. "You are so beautiful."

She lifted her hand and touched his face. "As are you."

"I adore you." He kissed her again. "And this moment has been too long in coming. I never thought I could feel such desire."

He rolled to the side, drawing her with him so she lay in the circle of his arms against his side. "When we are wed, I will love you like this each and every night for the rest of your life. For the rest of our lives."

Sated as Rose was, it was a moment before Gaston's words penetrated her conscious mind. She stiffened in his arms, pulling away.

Her voice was a whisper, her eyes pleading for him to understand. "I can not marry you."

"Do not jest." Gaston made an attempt to draw her back to him. "You want me as I want you. Hubert will forgive us in time." He sat up, reaching for her hand. "He does not love you."

She was unable to look at him. "It is not Hubert I would care about," Rose said. "I can not leave Carlisle."

Gaston stood up, towering above her, his body magnificent in the moonlight. "Is it because I am a landless knight, that you will not go?" It was a question, but his tone told her he knew the answer.

Rose leapt up to stand beside him, unheeding of her nakedness. "It is not true. I have made a solemn vow to my people, and I must live by that vow, no matter how much pain it might bring." Her voice broke with trying to hold back her tears.

"This is your final word?" he spat. "You would give yourself to my brother, knowing I want you, that I would betray my own brother to have you?"

She turned away. "I have no choice." Reaching down, she picked up her discarded gown from the grass. Her cheeks flamed with the memory of how she had reveled in its removal only a short time ago.

"Then I must leave Carlisle," he said through clenched teeth as she turned back to him, pulling the bliaut over her head. "You leave me no choice. I would only end in killing Hubert to prevent him from bedding you."

"But Hubert needs you," Rose cried in desperation, using the first excuse that sprang to her mind. She could not go with him, but neither could she bear for Gaston to leave her.

His tone was rough with bitterness as he pulled on his clothes. "I will stay until the raiders have been caught." He turned his back on her, striding away into the shadows of the night.

Rose put her hands to her face and felt the tears that streamed down her cheeks. She made no move to wipe them away. Her misery was too great. With limbs that felt as though they were molded from lead, Rose turned to the lonely solitude of her bower.

The prospect of facing life without Gaston was so painful she ached with the force of her grief. And he had not even gone.

Chapter Thirteen

William and his army left with the same fanfare with which they had arrived at Carlisle. The men swarmed from the hillside just as quickly as they had come, following their leader.

Hubert had sent five of his own knights and ten foot soldiers. He had not been pleased by such a heavy demand from the king, but he had little choice as he owed the men as his knight's fee. Hubert could have used gold as part of his debt to William, but his store of funds had been sorely drained already.

The lost manpower would make the task of settling his own lands more difficult, but Hubert must make do with the remaining force. After all, William had offered his assistance if the raiders were not caught by the time he returned.

Just what form William's assistance might take, Rose could only wonder. Surely she would think of some way to help Robert before the king's next appearance.

Her heart grew heavy as she remembered that no matter what might happen Gaston would soon be going away. It was even possible that he might rejoin William's own troops. The thought was almost too painful to bear.

Her face burned anew as she remembered the way she had responded to him. The soft moans of pleasure she had uttered. What must Gaston think of her; she accepted his caresses so freely, only to reject him.

Though Gaston had not spoken to her, he made his feelings known to her every time their glances crossed. His gaze was so filled with heat it fairly scorched her. It was hard for Rose to imagine she had ever thought of those molten grey orbs as cool and distant. His eyes branded her as his, with a possession that left her breathless.

Knowing it was she who had rejected Gaston was no comfort when she ached for him. It was a cold destiny she had taken onto herself. She tried to remember what Elspith had said about accepting one's lot. But Rose could find no comfort in the words today.

As if thoughts of Elspith had made her appear, Rose heard her cousin's voice speak her name. "Rose."

Rose turned to her cousin. Her pale blond hair was tousled and her lovely golden eyes were rimmed in pink, as if she had been weeping.

"Good morrow," Rose returned, though her manner was reserved. She was not in the mood for Elspith's confidences after her fight with Gaston. If Elspith and Hubert had had a disagreement, Elspith would do well to keep the matter to herself.

Furtively Elspith peered about the courtyard. "I must speak with you."

"You need not fear Hubert will overhear," Rose said. "He and Gaston have gone to escort the king to the boundary of Carlisle."

"I know this." Elspith leaned closer. "What I would tell you is very important." Her eyes, looking down at Rose, were dark and her too-thin frame swayed like a reed in a breeze.

Shamed by her lack of compassion, Rose took her cousin's arm to support her. "You are tired. We will talk after you have rested."

Elspith pulled her arm away, her voice surprisingly firm. "No. You must hear me now."

Surprised by Elspith's insistence, Rose began to know a moment of disquiet. "Let us go to my bower. I was going there even as you hailed me."

When the two girls were inside Rose's bower, with the door securely closed, Rose turned to her cousin with a look of concern. "What is it you would tell me?"

"Last night, after Hubert and I..." She blushed, looking down at the floor.

Rose flushed, too, Elspith's shyness bringing thoughts of Gaston. Rose could understand how Elspith felt. Things that were so right in the heat of passion seemed very different when viewed in the cool light of reason.

Pushing these thoughts from her mind, Rose focused her attention on her cousin. "Yes," she prodded, urging Elspith to go on.

"Well, Hubert was talking," Elspith's hands twisted together in her lap, "and he brought up the subject of the Saxon rebels. He spoke at length about how he would punish them when they were captured." She turned to Rose, her eyes round with pain. "I must tell you, Rose, my blood ran cold at some of the things he said he would do."

Elspith went on. "I have always told myself Robert was too clever to be caught, that he was safe in the forest he knows so well."

She hugged herself, shivering. "But last night, Hubert told me of his plan. Hubert has found a young man at Mayhill who hated his former lord, Athel, the greedy. You know, as well as I, how Athel drained his properties of all he could take. I had even heard talk, before the war, that his villeins planned to send a delegation to the earl asking for his removal."

"Yes, of course I remember," Rose answered impatiently. "We, being his closest neighbors, heard of all Athel's evil deeds."

"It seems as if Hubert has found a young boy who was...uh...assaulted by Athel." Elspith blushed deeply. "His experience has soured the boy. He hates all and everything, and is willing to do anything that will further his own personal gain.''

Rose was growing impatient. ''Yes, yes.''

''This boy has told Hubert he will seek out the rebels and infiltrate their camp. Hubert is to pay him a large sum of money.''

Rose sucked in her breath. For one of their own kind to do such a thing was unthinkable. Even if he had been sorely used by his former lord, the boy had no justification for betraying his own people. ''You are certain of this?''

Elspith held out her hands in appeal. ''Would I bring such a tale to you were I not sure?''

Rose thought for a moment, then shook her head, looking at Elspith. ''This boy will not know who Robert is, being from Mayhill. He will not know where to find him.''

''But this boy is just the kind Robert is looking for. He is young, strong, and espouses his hatred of the Normans. He need only ask a few questions at Brentwood, and Robert would find him. The boy being a Saxon—'' Elspith shrugged ''—Robert will believe what he says to be true.''

Rose sat down on the bed slowly, her knees weak. Elspith was right. Robert's own belief that the Saxons represented good and Normans evil would be his undoing.

Elspith clasped her hands together, trying to control their shaking. ''What will we do?'' she asked.

There was another long silence as Rose tried to make sense from her chaotic thoughts. She had to calm herself in order to devise a solution.

Suddenly Rose stood. ''We must warn him.'' She brought her closed fist down against her palm with a smack.

''How can we possibly reach Robert in time?'' Elspith cried. ''It would take days to get a message to him. Then he would have to send a messenger telling when he could meet us. Speed is of the essence, this boy may already have infiltrated my brother's force.''

Rose gave her cousin a determined look. ''We will go to him. You know where the camp is located.''

Elspith's expression was lit with hope. "Yes." She nodded with enthusiasm. "We could go to Robert."

Rose considered Elspith's hollow eyes and thought of the coming child. She shook her head negatively. "No, we could not go. You must stay here. There is the well-being of your child to consider."

"But..."

"There is no but," Rose insisted firmly. "I would not forgive myself if something were to happen to you or the babe. You have not been well of late."

Elspith stared down at her hands. There was no way she could argue with this logic, no matter how much she would like to see her brother.

"I will go alone," Rose said then, making Elspith raise her head with renewed hope.

Then Elspith's shoulders slumped down. "You would be missed, you can not be gone from here for a long enough period of time."

"We will simply think of some illness for me to catch." Rose tapped her chin, concentrating. "I will not go to the Great Hall today. You," she said, turning to Elspith, "will spread the word that I am not feeling well. Now let me see," Rose went on, "it must not be anything too serious and yet something that would keep people from trying to see me."

Elspith spread her hands. "What will I say?"

"You must give me time to think," Rose told her. She started to turn away but stopped. "There is one whom you must definitely keep away, though you will have to be very careful not to arouse his suspicions."

"Do you mean Sir Gaston?" Elspith questioned.

"Yes, Sir Gaston," Rose frowned. "He, if anyone, is most likely to foil our plans. He sees too much for my liking."

Elspith looked at her cousin with determination. "If others can be fooled then he too can be fooled."

"You do not know him as I do." Rose's eyes focused on some distant thing that only she could see. "Too often he knows what I do before it is done."

Rose didn't speak her next thoughts aloud. The previous night, Gaston had not only been able to read her mind but also her body. He had led her to the brink of paradise.

Gaston was in the stables, grooming Pegasus. The pace the king's army had set that morning was slow, and the stallion had become restive. On their return to the keep, Gaston had given the animal his head. He ran his hand over the heavy mane of the white stallion. The horse accepted his presence, even welcomed him, nudging his shoulder with a velvet muzzle.

How he wished a certain little Saxon beauty could be gentled to his touch so readily. Last eve, she had been so responsive, so eager for his caresses and the love he offered.

He cursed his body's reaction to the memory, wishing there were some way he could ease the ache. Only with Rose could he find relief from the fires that drove him. Only in the sweetness of her body could he find peace.

But that was not to be. She had refused him, his love, his soul. And all because of some ridiculous sense of duty. A muscle flexed in his jaw.

Gaston stopped the path his thoughts were taking. He knew he loved Rose for all she was. If he were to take away her sense of honor, she would not be the same woman. It was one of the things that had drawn him to her from the very beginning.

Patting the horse's powerful neck, Gaston gave a humorless laugh. Knowing he loved her for all she was did nothing to ease the chill of loneliness in his heart.

Claude came into the stable, giving a start of surprise when he saw Gaston. A strained smile appeared on his lips. "Sir Gaston." He nodded quickly, then turned away.

"Claude." Gaston nodded in return. He was glad of the interruption to his melancholy thoughts, though he was a bit put off by Claude's reception. "How are you faring?" he asked, attempting to make conversation.

Claude put down the bucket he carried in his good hand and flexed the injured arm slowly. "Very stiff." Then an adoring smile lit his craggy face. "But thanks to the Lady Rose, I will learn to use a sword again in time."

He looked away so Claude would not see the longing that came with a simple mention of her name. "She is very skilled as a healer."

"Yes," said Claude with complete conviction. "I owe her my life. What use is a soldier who can not hold a weapon?"

"Yes," Gaston agreed. A soldier without the use of his arm was of little value.

Claude bent and picked up the bucket. He carried it over to a stall, where the head of a delicate chestnut filly appeared. Giving a whinny of welcome, Hera dipped her head as Claude raised the bucket.

Claude spoke as though to a child. "Now, beauty, have a little more patience."

The mare snorted and tossed her mane. Claude chuckled and poured the grain into a trough just inside the stall door. "I suppose you can't help yourself now that you'll be eating for two." Claude laughed again as the filly bent immediately to the trough.

"Am I to understand that Pegasus made good of his time, when he escaped from his stall a few weeks ago?" Gaston smiled on the white stallion with parental indulgence.

"Aye, my lord," Claude nodded, a fond expression on his own face. "It shouldn't be long before we have at least one colt with his father's white coat."

Gaston chuckled as the stallion turned his great gleaming eyes to his master with a look that seemed to say, *of course*.

Watching the exchange between horse and rider, Claude too joined in. The sounds startled the other horses, and their heads appeared as they came to investigate.

A short time later, Gaston turned to leave. There was other work that needed his attention. He planned to continue on the wall outside the palisade. William had been very clear in his desire to see it finished as soon as possible.

Breaking the comfortable silence that had developed between himself and Claude, Gaston brought up the subject that was uppermost in his thoughts. "Have you see the Lady Rose today?"

Claude gave a visible start, glancing at Gaston and wetting his lips.

Gaston viewed this odd reaction with some puzzlement. A frown appeared at his brow.

Claude cleared his throat and shuffled his feet without turning to face the knight. "Why do you ask, Sir Gaston?"

He made his tone light. "I had not seen her today. And I fear she is too fond of going off without an escort." Gaston watched as Claude's shoulders slumped in relief.

"Aye, I have seen the lady, my lord, early this very morning." He cleared his throat again. "But she said she wasn't feeling well, and was going to lie down."

Gaston took a step toward the man, his eyes dark with anxiety. "Why wasn't I informed of this illness? I should go to her," he added, realizing Claude had reacted so strangely because of worry for Rose. It was well-known that Claude was devoted to the lady since she had cared for him.

Urgently Claude raised his good hand. "No, my lord. I mean..." He lowered his arm, his eyes directed to the floor. "I mean, I don't believe it is serious, my lord." He colored and hesitated again. "I think she has some form of woman's malady."

Gaston took a long breath of relief. "I see." There was not much to be said on such a subject. His own sister, Marguerite, had spent many days in her room with just such a complaint. Though the particulars of the affliction were vague, her illness was not questioned by the male members of the household. He turned to go.

It was surprising that Rose would fall victim to such an infirmity. Not since their coming to Carlisle had she been indisposed, even for a few hours. He halted, swinging around to face Claude once more. "Are you..."

Claude was in the act of leading a gelding from his stall. "What are you doing?" Gaston asked curiously.

Claude stopped still, without turning to face the knight. "I thought I would take some of the horses out and tie them on the hillside to graze."

"A good idea." Gaston nodded, then went on to ask his question. "Are you sure the lady's illness is not serious?"

"No, sir." Claude turned around, his voice light. "I overheard the cook, Maida, talking about it. She didn't seem at all worried and you know how that one is." Claude rolled his eyes heavenward.

Gaston chuckled as he stepped out the door, knowing exactly what Claude meant about Maida's overprotective attitude toward Rose. She was ever swelling her plump chest and flapping her wings over her chick.

But even as Gaston walked away from the stable, something about the way Claude had behaved disturbed him. Unable to define the problem, Gaston dismissed it for the time being. He had much to do.

It was late the same evening, when only darkness watched, that Claude tapped at the door of Rose's bower. The portal opened immediately, and he was bid to enter.

Rose stood facing the devoted soldier, her hands twisting in nervous anticipation. "Is all as it should be?"

"Yes, everything is ready." Claude opened his mouth, then closed it again, fidgeting nervously.

"What is it?" Rose asked, pulling on her long cape and mantle, which she fastened at the shoulders with intricately wrought buckles.

"Must you do this thing?"

"Yes," she told him. "There is no one I can trust with delivering my message."

He held up his hands in a gesture that pleaded for her to see sense. "But there will be danger from the raiders."

"I will be in no danger," she insisted. How could she tell him that Robert would never harm her in any way?

He groaned in frustration. "At least, take me with you."

She put her hand on his arm. "That I could not do, Claude. My friends would not know you are a man they could trust. You are, after all, a Norman."

"But..."

She held up her hand to stop him from going on. "I have told you I wish your master no harm. This you must believe. I go only to save a life that is dear to me."

He answered her fiercely. "Norman or no, I will be your man, until death, my lady."

Rose's smile was gentle, but her tone was adamant. "You are a good man, Claude, and I thank you for your loyalty. But the less you know the better. If I am found out, you can plead innocence of my actions."

"But, Sir Gaston—"

Rose interrupted, demanding, "What of Sir Gaston?"

Claude stepped back in surprise at the vehemence in her voice. "He was asking after you."

Her nails bit into her palms. "You didn't tell him anything?"

"No, lady, only that you were not well."

Rose relaxed with a deep-felt sigh. She would not have Gaston spoil her plans. "That is good." She led him to the door. "And now, you must go, as I will be leaving shortly."

"Be careful, my lady," Claude warned just before he slipped out, leaving her alone.

Carefully Rose went over her plans once more. She would need more than luck to guide her through this night safely. Elspith had told her where Robert's camp was located in the Pitted Wood. Rose shuddered, thinking of the danger involved in traveling there.

The forest floor was riddled with deep holes that could swallow an unsuspecting traveler. When they were children, Rose, Edmund, Elspith and Robert had played in the wood. At one point, they were caught by Elspith's father,

Hugh. He had explained to the children that an underground stream had eaten away the ground in places. The trees, which were thick through the area, could disguise these holes by retaining the surface earth around their roots.

Even after his warning, the children had continued to play there as often as they could slip away. The danger seemed to draw them as moths are drawn to light.

Robert had been very clever to think of hiding there. Even the local residents shunned the Pitted Wood.

Only a short time later, Rose emerged from her bower. She surveyed the courtyard carefully. It was a quiet night and she could hear nothing above the faint sigh of the breeze. Slowly she moved out into the courtyard, pulling up the hood of her midnight-blue mantle.

Her footsteps on the path sounded loud in her own ears so she moved to the grass, which muffled the faint sounds. She did not want to take any chances now.

As she made her way toward the tunnel, she saw the guard on the walkway, outlined against the light of the moon. For one long moment her heart stood still as he stopped in his endless pacing to peer in her direction. She stood still as death, waiting for him to call out, but he said nothing, and finally Rose knew what had drawn his attention.

A few steps behind her, stood an old nanny goat. She was staggering along, her belly heavy with young, the moonlight shining on her white, spotted hide.

The guard went on.

Her fear drained away. In its place came a strange elation that filled her and left her giddy. Nothing could stop her now.

Rose's anxiety returned for only a moment when she realized she must close the door to the tunnel behind her. She would not be returning for two days. The entrance could not be left open.

As the door fell behind her, blocking out the light from the moon, Rose took a deep gasping breath, then choked on the musty air. Turning, she ran through the tunnel, guided by her hands on the walls on either side of her. She blocked out the scuffling sound that preceded her, knowing she had come through the tunnel before and she could do it again.

When she emerged from the tunnel, she spent none of her precious time reveling in her freedom. She must get to Robert. As Rose ran across the side of the hill, she realized her decision to warn Robert was not solely for his sake. She needed to take action. For too long, she had let others control what she did and said. Making the choice to go to Robert had freed her, put her in charge of her own destiny.

When she was directly below the tall staff that flew Hubert's colors of black and red, she ran down the slope to the trees. This is where Claude had told her a mount would be waiting.

He was true to his word. Rose had only gone a few steps into the trees when she heard the soft whinny of the horse.

Cautiously she moved forward on the balls of her feet. She must take care to make sure the horse had not been discovered and a trap laid for her.

She grinned with heady relief when she saw the gelding standing under a tree, quietly munching the lower branches.

"Hello, my fine fellow," Rose said, going up to the horse with her hand extended, as Claude had shown her. Rose was not an experienced rider, but Claude had assured her he would bring her the gentlest of mounts.

To Rose's relief, the gelding turned and placed his soft muzzle in her outstretched palm, sniffing delicately. How difficult could this be? she thought with bravado.

Unfortunately, Claude had not been able to bring the gelding equipped for riding. It had been obvious to both him and Rose that the horse would draw attention should it be put out to munch grass with a saddle upon its back.

The task of mounting was made doubly hard by the fact that she must mount with only the aid of the bridle.

Rose wished she had spent more time learning to ride with Edmund, and less time with her books. Oh, well, there was nothing for it now but to go on with getting atop the beast.

Looking around, Rose spied a stump not far away. If she could step up onto the stump while holding on to the reins, she might be able to climb on.

The horse followed docilely enough as Rose led him to the stump. She was beginning to feel fairly confident as she stepped up onto the stump. Her face set with concentration, Rose drew the horse close, guiding him with the reins.

Lifting her leg, Rose muttered a curse. Her skirts had tangled around her as she positioned the gelding. By the time she had untangled them, the animal had moved away.

The gelding only blinked, his large brown eyes baleful.

Rose led him back to the stump once again. And this time she was able to climb onto his back.

Her tailbone soon became sore from the jarring motion of riding bareback. But she did not stop. She could not. Robert must be warned before it was too late.

Chapter Fourteen

Silent as a shadow, Gaston sat atop the huge white stallion. His muscles rebelled from being so long in one position, but he ignored the discomfort. His experience in battle had stood him in good stead tonight, having taught him patience.

Looking up through the leafy canopy over his head, Gaston could see the moon was well up in the sky. It cast a soft luminous glow upon everything around him.

As he had countless times over the course of the evening, Gaston wondered if the gelding's presence here could have been nothing more than a simple oversight by Claude. But he stayed put, his instincts telling him he was not wrong.

He went back over this afternoon's conversation with Claude and the odd way he had behaved when Rose was mentioned. The soldier had been too nervous, too agitated.

This evening, when he had gone back to the stable to give Pegasus an apple, Gaston had noticed the black gelding was not in its stall, though all the other horses were now stabled. Wanting to make sure no horses were left out as easy marks for the brigands, Gaston had made a point of mentioning the stall was empty. The way Claude had pulled at his collar and assured Gaston the horse would be brought in had raised more suspicions.

His evasive answers about Rose, coupled with Claude's odd behavior over the horse, made Gaston wonder.

What was afoot?

Unable to quite put his finger on the reason for his uneasiness, Gaston had decided to bide his time.

After the evening meal, he returned to the stable and saw the gelding was not in his stall.

A quick search of the woods had turned up the missing equine. After that it was simply a question of waiting to find out what Rose was up to. For he was sure she was behind the soldier's mysterious actions.

It was then that he saw the horse shift his feet restlessly and raise his head.

A moment later, Gaston heard the sound that had alerted the gelding. Someone was approaching, and making a great effort to be quiet, stopping often.

Gaston nudged Pegasus with his knees, and the horse moved back, further out of sight behind a clump of brush.

A figure in a long, hooded cloak appeared on the other side of the clearing. The cloaked figure stopped, peering around carefully, then moved forward, going directly to the tethered mount.

Gaston quirked a brow as Rose spoke in hushed tones to the horse, gingerly holding out her hand.

He sensed her uncertainty as she glanced around the tiny clearing. Clicking her tongue, she untied the horse and led him over to a stump.

After much grunting and lip biting, she managed to get herself atop the animal.

Gaston waited for a moment, then started after her.

For Rose, the next few hours passed in a blur. She was sore, tired and hungry. The elation she'd felt earlier had evaporated like morning dew from rose petals.

She had little realized how difficult it would be to make the journey after a whole day spent preparing for it. But she was determined to reach the woods before she stopped to rest.

Much of her way was through forest, so Rose did not notice how the deep rich blue of the night sky had turned grey. Nor did she note the coolness of moisture in the air, concentrating as she was on her goal.

It was only as the first drops of rain began to fall that Rose realized her mistake in not paying more attention to the weather.

But the rain could not deter her. She had to reach the Pitted Wood before morning. With dogged determination, Rose went on. After a time the rain soaked her so thoroughly she could tell little difference between herself and the puddles the stupid beast she rode seemed to find with unerring regularity.

At last, when she was afraid she might fall from her mount with numbing exhaustion, Rose entered the Pitted Wood. There was no outward sign that this place was any different from the other forest she had ridden through. But Rose knew the danger.

Reluctantly she realized she would have to seek shelter until daylight. For in this weather, even Rose, who knew the copse well, could easily make a wrong step and fall into one of the holes in the dark.

As children, she, Elspith, Edmund and Robert had come upon an abandoned hut, which had become a secret place of their very own. In it, they had kept the materials to start a fire, a blanket, and enough stores to prepare a simple meal.

Certainly, the food would be gone after so much time had passed. But if fortune was with her, there might still be the makings of a fire.

The cottage had become so overgrown with blackberry vines that she nearly missed it in the dark. Relief washed through her when she finally drew the gelding to halt before it.

Rose swung to the ground. For a moment it was hard to stand erect, her legs and buttocks were so stiff, but she

managed to do so. She took a deep breath, then let it out
slowly as the cramps began to ease.

First, Rose tethered the horse beneath a tree where he
would at least be somewhat sheltered from the elements.

Inside the hut, she found everything she would require to
build a small fire. After clearing the fire pit of excess dirt
and debris, she quickly had a tiny flame burning. It flickered, then licked greedily at the wood she fed it.

Rubbing her hands over her wet sleeves, Rose looked
about her. The foodstuffs were indeed gone. It appeared as
if the hut had been inhabited by furry creatures at some
point. Their scent and droppings were in evidence, though,
thankfully, they seemed to have vacated the premises.

Then, with a cry of triumph, she pulled a blanket from
the corner. Though it was musty and worn, the wool cloth
would offer her a dry covering.

A short time later, Rose knelt and held out her hands to
the warmth of the fire. Quickly she unbraided her hair,
combing it with her fingers to speed its drying. In a few
short hours, it would be daylight. By then, her clothes would
be dry and she would be able to make her way to Robert's
camp. She would be able to warn Robert in time.

As the hours had passed Gaston had become more and
more uneasy.

What could be so important that the Saxon maid would
be willing to press on through such miserable weather and
uncertain terrain?

Unbidden, the truth had come to him.

Rose was going to her lover. The same man who had met
her in the forest that day. The one she was unable to forget.

A jealousy such as he had never felt gnawed at his insides
till he thought the pain might unman him. Gaston would do
anything if only Rose would forget.

He was puzzled when she stopped before a great heap of
tangled vines and brush. Then he realized it was some sort
of dwelling. Was this where the lovers' tryst would be?

When Rose entered the hut, Gaston waited out of sight in the forest. It took every measure of his will to sit quietly, knowing Rose could be in another man's arms at that very moment.

Finally he could bear no more.

After securing Pegasus beneath the shelter of the tree alongside Rose's mount, Gaston crept close to the cottage.

The silence from inside was almost worse than hearing them together. His imagination painted sickeningly vivid pictures across his mind.

He would know the truth. Gaston ducked through the opening.

At that moment, Rose heard a soft scraping sound from outside the hut. Her eyes riveted on the low entrance as Gaston appeared in the opening.

She gave a gasp of despair as he straightened, seeming to tower above her.

She sensed a change in him. In his eyes was the stark, hungry aggression of a hunting wolf. This was a Gaston she did not know, unpredictable and volatile.

Slowly Rose stood, her gaze never leaving his face.

She watched him warily as she stood. Her tone was stiff with self-control. "Why have you come? Why can you not leave me in peace?"

Gaston's relief at seeing her there, alone, was almost overwhelming. But he did not let down his guard. The other's arrival must be imminent, else why would Rose have traveled to this unlikely place? Gaston held his rage before him like a shield.

For too long he had loved and desired this woman. At every turn she had thwarted his attempts to show her that love, though she seemed eager enough to accept his passion. He wanted—needed—more; needed to rest by her fire; lay his head on the bed next to hers. Without her, he could find no surcease to his torment.

His gaze took in her pale face, the play of firelight on her bare shoulders and unbound hair. Gaston remembered the times they had made love. She had welcomed his most intimate caresses on every part of her body, had cried her joy aloud.

Now she seemed remote, as if those moments had been erased from her mind. Gaston made no effort to disguise his aggression and frustration. "There can be no peace in this for either of us."

Her back stiffened with the pride that was so much a part of her. "I will not shirk my responsibilities. I will not risk the well-being of my people, even for you."

His reply exploded in a torrent of rage. "And yet you would risk all for this?" His cutting gesture swept the room. "You ride through half the night, uncaring of the rain and danger to meet your lover in this hovel!"

He raised his hands to his head. If only he could squeeze her from his heart. But she was inside him, down to the deepest, darkest regions of his soul. This woman had become his reason to draw breath.

Rose could only gape at him. Meet her lover! Could he really believe that of her, after all that had passed between them?

She would not allow herself to recall that it had been she who had encouraged his belief that she had a lover.

Her anger burned like a bright hot flame inside her. How dared Gaston? And to accuse her of selfishness. It was the worst insult he could offer. Rage flattened the soles of her feet against the floor and raised the hair at her nape. "You accuse me of coming here for my own pleasure? What do you know of me and the things I hold dear? I have tried to do what was right at every turn. Given up my own happiness to see to the needs of others."

She shook her fist under his nose. "Until you Normans came I knew nothing of running this fief. I have done my utmost to look after my villeins. I swore a solemn oath to protect them. Though my pride called for us to fight, I feared for their lives and the future of Carlisle. I counseled peace and the people listened. When I doubted myself, I had no one to turn to for answers. I could only pray that I had made the right decision. I even agreed to marry Hubert, the revolting toad, though I detest him with every fiber of my being. Do you think I have never questioned my choices? That I have not wished to change my mind?''

He leaned over her, his jaw hard. "Then why do you not? The villeins would survive. Hubert is not the best of leaders, but he is not deliberately cruel. If what you say is true, then why do you force this upon yourself? How could the people expect you, a woman, to keep such an oath?''

She beat her fist against her breast. "It is not what they think. It is what I think. You do not understand. My father and brother were men such as you can not know. I try to live up to the example they set, and ever find myself lacking.''

"But you are only a woman. They would not expect so much of you.''

"How dare you say that? I am more than a woman. I am all that is left of my family. I am Carlisle. Don't you understand?'' she cried. "It is not what they would think, but myself. I need to believe I have acted with honor.'' Rose choked back a sob. "But I fail at every turn.''

"Fail!'' he exclaimed, incredulous. "You are the strongest, most honorable individual I have ever known, man or woman.''

The words would have meant more had she been less angry and had Gaston not followed her here. If he believed what he said, then why did he accuse her of coming here to meet her lover? Did he not know that she would never put her position as protector of her people at risk for such a selfish reason?

She turned her back to him. "Your actions decry your words.''

Gaston clenched his hands to keep himself from forcing her to face him and listen. He spoke, his voice deceptively quiet. "Tell me then what I am supposed to think. Why indeed are you here?"

His more reasonable tone gave Rose cause to think he might heed her. "I can not tell you."

His voice grew louder. "Do you expect me to simply get back on my horse and leave you here with no more explanation than that? How am I to know you are not putting yourself in danger?"

Desperately she tried to think of some way of making him trust her, but she could not. In frustration, Rose swung around to face him again, stamping her foot. "Do you think I am nothing more than a child that I should require your assistance at every turn? Can you not accept that I am a grown woman, capable of looking after my own interests?"

Gaston crossed his arms over his wide chest to keep from shaking her. "If you would but tell me what you are about, I might feel more inclined to allow you your way."

Rose clenched her teeth, rolling her eyes heavenward. His condescending manner rankled, but she did her utmost to keep from screaming. She had to make him see reason. "I will tell you I can come to no harm here. I know the forest and need none of your help. As soon as the rain stops, I must be on my way."

Quickly he leapt to interrogate her. "So this hut is not your destination?"

"No."

"Are you to meet someone?"

She crossed her own arms, glaring up at him. "I will not answer."

His reply was low, menacing. "Then I was correct. This does have something to do with that man, doesn't it?"

Rose took a step backward. For a moment, she was frightened by the intensity of his gaze. Then she remembered that this was Gaston; however furious he might become, he would never harm her.

She raised haughty brows. "What man?"

"Let us not play games. You know of whom I speak. The one you were with that night in the forest. The very same man who I rode after that day in the village." He watched her closely.

Rose closed her eyes. Sweet Jesus, he knows, she thought. Then she calmed herself, fighting down the waves of panic that threatened to take away her breath. He could not know Robert was her cousin. He had only just accused them of being lovers. She looked up at him, unblinking and defiant. She refused to answer any further questions. "I will only tell you that I mean no harm to you or any of your kind. What I do, I do to protect someone I love."

Gaston's face paled and he felt as if he had been kicked in the chest. Though he had known she loved this mystery man, to hear her say the words aloud was a torment beyond measure. Now it was he who turned his back. "Then you admit you care for this man."

Why did he continue to prod her so? She tried, time upon time, to make him see that she would never betray him, and still he accused her of loving another. Mayhap if she told him the truth he would believe her. "Yes, if admitting it will make you listen to me, yes, I do love him, but not in the way you believe."

But Gaston wasn't listening. He couldn't hear anything past the throb of his aching heart. His eyes darkened with pain. "I offered you my life and my honor by asking you to marry me. You rejected my love."

He took a ragged breath. "Yet you are willing to risk all for this man. Not more than minutes ago, you told me you stayed at Carlisle because of your sense of duty to your father's and brother's memories. Your honor and duty to your fief mean everything to you. But you have come here, knowing Hubert could become aware of your actions. What of your responsibilities to Carlisle then?"

Rose's chin jutted out stubbornly. She had been honest and he refused to believe. Nothing would make her try again. Short of telling the knight Robert was a member of her family, she had no explanation that would satisfy.

Had Gaston been facing her so she could see his face, Rose might have been ready for what came next.

Her rejection of him burned in Gaston like a torch. In his pain, all he knew was that he loved her beyond measure and she dismissed that love as if it had no value.

With a groan of anguish, Gaston swung around, crushing her to him as his lips found hers.

As always when he touched her, Rose was incapable of resisting. Desire replaced anger with blinding intensity. She raised her arms, holding his head to her as she gave him back passion for passion.

His knowing hand found her breast. The rough wool of the blanket rasped her tender flesh, causing it to swell enticingly. She could no more stop the hardening of her nipple against his palm than she could stop the tides that called to the moon. And had no desire to do so.

Too many times she had acted against her own needs. Now for this one instant she would please herself, and the devil take the consequences.

"I want you," she gasped against Gaston's mouth. Rose broke away from him, her hands working furiously at the knot that bound the blanket.

Seeing her intent, he reached out, ripping the fragile cloth from top to hem in one quick motion. Mayhap with his body he could show her how very much he loved her, that he had been born to love her.

Then she was in his arms again, her head thrown back, hands reaching beneath his tunic. She found his hard, muscled flesh as he rained kisses on her vulnerable neck and shoulders. But Rose wanted more; she could not get close enough with the boundary of his clothing between them.

Hoarsely she whispered, "Help me," as she tugged at the heavy garment.

"Let me," he told her, pulling away only long enough to drag it over his head. Then came his shirt.

Rose, impatient to see all of him, knelt to remove his leggings. He groaned as his manhood sprang free, and he looked down to see her hand close over the hot aching flesh. His wide chest gleamed bronze in the glow of the flames. She pressed her lips to his hard thighs. "I love you... love you," she told him.

Her hair was a glorious curtain about her. He reached out to smooth it back from her brow, and she looked up at him, her luminous eyes dark with hunger. "Rose?" He moved to pull her up beside him. He wanted to touch her, kiss every inch of her smooth skin, but she resisted.

She gave a husky laugh, her voice low and seductive. "Let me."

Surrender was not enough for Rose this time. She wanted to remember this night in Gaston's arms; to close her eyes and know the feel and taste and scent of him.

Her warm lips closed around him and he could no longer think as she took him to the brink of madness.

When he knew he could withstand no more, he pulled away, kneeling to take her in his arms. Rose returned his kiss with unbridled enthusiasm, holding nothing back. She was destined to be his woman, and had been since the beginning of time.

Her love for him was like a surging river that thundered through her in an unstoppable current. This moment when she would offer herself to him without restraint had been preordained.

Gaston's chest rose and fell with each wrenching breath as she pushed him onto his back.

His hands caught in her luxurious hair that fell across his body in a glorious curtain of fire. Her mouth warmed him and made the blood sing in his veins. "Rose, my lovely Rose," he breathed, as she lowered her head to trace the hard muscles of his chest. Her tongue flicked out to taste the salty perspiration on his skin, and she smiled at his gasp of pleasure.

A powerful elation came over her, brought on by the fact that she could give Gaston the same kind of exquisite enjoyment he was so adept at giving her.

That sense of power was a strange aphrodisiac that made her own belly quiver with wanting. God, how she loved him; loved him with the very quintessence of her being.

Rose lifted her head to look at him, and a jagged bolt of heat sliced through her at the naked hunger in his eyes. The orbs had darkened to deepest twilight, the lids half-covering them. Breathing raggedly, he reached down with his powerful arms and pulled her up beside him. With a growl he buried his face in her throat, his teeth nipping at her.

He groaned. "I want you, witch. You set me on fire with your touch."

"Then let me love you more." She raised her arms to pull his head down to hers, drawing out his essence with her lips, her tongue circling his.

She left his mouth, her hair a trickle of silk on his sweat-dampened skin as she moved to ply him with her tongue. Gaston groaned and arched upward, unable to control his body's reaction to her.

"No more," he demanded, dragging her along the length of his hard body. "You will unman me, and I will not be denied the pleasure of loving you." Holding her in the circle of his arms, he rolled over her, his hands and mouth creating streaks of lightning on her heated flesh.

He bent his head and flicked his tongue over the taut peak of her breast. Rose put her hands on his head and clasped him to her. She felt as though he took her very will and made it his as he suckled first one breast, then the other. She writhed beneath him, glad of that taking; joyous that he wanted and loved her as no other.

Her body cried out for fulfillment. "Oh Gaston, I can stand no more."

Gaston moved to position himself over her, but Rose was not willing to act the supplicant. This time she wanted to give, and in that giving to show him how very much she loved him.

Insistently Rose pushed him onto his back. Her breath coming in ragged bursts, her body shaking with desire, she straddled him. She paused above him, willing him to see only her, her dark eyes in the flickering firelight. Her voice was husky with wanting. "I love you."

And in that moment, he knew, no matter what had come before or might come after, she did love him.

With one swift plunge of her hips, Gaston's longing found its home. A deep groan of ecstasy escaped his lips as he rose up to meet her with a powerful thrust. His hands found her hips, pulling her to him with masterful urgency.

Rose could neither speak nor think, only feel, giving more of herself with each thrust.

His name became a chant of desire, "Gaston, Gaston, Gaston." She felt the heat build until she thought she would surely explode. And then she did, with a white-hot heat that burst and crashed in upon itself with incredible sweetness.

At that moment he cried out. "I love you. You are mine." Then Rose felt the shudders take him as he too was lifted beyond himself and into the flames.

She held him fiercely, not yet ready to surrender the moment to reality.

Nothing had been solved between them. Gaston still believed she had come to save her lover. And Rose could not trust him enough to tell him the truth.

But for this instant, at least, she could indeed be his, as she would never be any other man's.

Chapter Fifteen

A soft rustling sound woke her, but Rose didn't open her
eyes, just snuggled closer against Gaston's side.

Then she remembered—Robert! She had to warn her
cousin. Her eyes flew open, and she sucked in her breath in
shock.

For there, standing above her, was Robert.

His face was dark with hatred, and when he saw she was
awake, he laughed cruelly.

Rose turned to Gaston. Clearly he had been awakened
before her, because one of Robert's men held the point of
Gaston's own sword to his throat.

"Get up," Robert growled, backing away from her.

"But—"

He turned his back on her, not even making an effort to
listen. "Remove her from my sight."

Two men came forward to take her. Rose barely had time
to pull the woolen blanket around herself before they raised
her by the arms and started to drag her out.

She turned to see Gaston, who had risen now, facing
Robert with disdain. To her eyes he was glorious, standing
there without benefit of clothing. His well-muscled form
was covered with smooth golden skin, and he stood a head
above the tallest of them. The Norman knight made no
move to cover himself, his expression mockingly calm. This
was the way the ancient Saxons had gone to battle, with no

covering to shield them from the power of the gods. She raised her head high, proud to be the woman of such a man.

The warning in Gaston's eyes belied his casual stance as he looked to Robert. "What will you do to her?"

Robert turned to face the Norman, his anger burning bright with the hatred inside him. "I think I will leave you to wonder at the fate of your whore."

Gaston smiled without humor. "I know the woman is no stranger to you. I have seen you together and I believe you will not harm her because of the love you bear her."

"How I feel about Rose is none of your concern." Robert moved closer to Gaston. "Norman." He spat the last word as if it were a curse. Then he backed away, not liking to be looked down upon by the warrior who seemed so fierce, even with his own sword pointed at his belly.

Robert's voice grew quiet. "You should not have touched her. I must make you pay for that."

Gaston stated his case without apology. "I love her."

"Why were the two of you here?" Robert asked, unwilling to listen to the Norman's protestations of devotion.

Gaston shrugged. "That you will have to ask the lady. I only followed her to protect her from harm." He did not wish to rile this young Saxon who he believed had once been Rose's beloved. The thought brought less pain than in the past. Now that Gaston knew Rose loved him, he could almost pity his enemy.

Gaston knew Rose had been on her way to meet this man, yet the Saxon seemed unaware of the fact or he would have behaved differently. What could have brought her here? With Rose separated from him, there was no way of knowing at this point.

When he had awakened to find the point of his sword at his throat, Gaston had hesitated to fight, for fear of Rose's safety.

The way the Saxon, Robert, had looked down on the sleeping Rose had made Gaston's blood run cold. Even if the opportunity should present itself, he knew he could not

escape without her. He must allow these men to take him
without a struggle, then he could devise a plan by which he
could take Rose when he made his escape.

The Saxon studied Gaston with a hatred that was fierce
in its intensity. "I will get the answers to my question from
you, one way or another."

"Take him back to the camp." Robert gestured violently
and, turning, left the hut.

Gaston allowed himself to be led from the hut. There was
no sign of Pegasus. His captors, all three very young men,
bound his hands behind him. They seemed almost frightened by the knight and Gaston knew his freedom could
easily be secured.

Feeling the light rain cool on his bare flesh, Gaston reminded himself he must go to the camp so he could find
Rose. He would have to bide his time.

Rose arrived at the camp, seated before one of Robert's
men. The horse they rode had an uneven gait that jarred her
until her teeth ached. She was more than glad to slide down
to the solid ground. The man, whom she recognized as a
former resident of Brentwood, turned and rode away. He
seemed to have no fear that she would try to escape.

Glancing about, Rose recognized many of the men who
moved about the camp. Off to her right, Edgar, who had
once been captain of the guard at Brentwood, talked with a
group of men. Among them she saw many more young faces
that were familiar to her.

She shook her head. Most of them were barely more than
boys. She wondered how they could possibly hope to drive
the Normans from England.

But this was not her first concern. She must find something to cover herself besides the blanket. Not only was she
chilled, the tattered covering left her feeling too vulnerable.

Then she had to see Robert. From his treatment of her
earlier, Rose knew the meeting might prove difficult.

She looked around for a likely source of clothing. The camp consisted of a number of tents, and only two wooden structures. The fires burned low, dense smoke rising up in the air from the damp wood. The men who sat around the fires, and others who went about their work, wore long dreary faces.

Rose shuddered. No wonder Elspith had been so glad to be away from this place. It was dirty, dank and miserable.

Seeing no one was going to pay her any attention, Rose moved off in search of the needed clothing. Going behind the tents, she found a line that was hung with a few threadbare articles of clothing someone was attempting to dry.

The grey tunic was still damp, but it would have to do. She also took a shirt which had once been white but was now as grey as the tunic.

Stepping behind a bush, Rose hurriedly pulled the shirt over her head, then the tunic. The rough wool was clammy and itchy on her skin. When she saw the length of leg that was left bare by the shirt, Rose took the wool blanket and tied it around her waist. She knew she must look a sight, but she was, at least, covered.

She came out from behind the bush, determined to find Robert and speak to him. No matter how difficult he made it for her, Rose had to warn him about the traitor in his midst.

Then she would have to think of some way to effect her own and Gaston's release.

As if thinking of him had conjured up her lover, Gaston appeared at the side of the clearing. Three stripling boys led him forward. His hands were tied behind his back, and he was still naked. But his shoulders were high, and he strode before them with his usual self-assurance.

She made a move to run to him, but she was stopped by a hand on her shoulder. Edgar's expression told her very clearly that she was not to move.

Obviously they meant to keep her and Gaston separated. There was nothing to be gained in belaboring the point now.

She would first speak with her cousin. Surely he would let
them go when he knew why she had come. She turned to
Edgar with what she hoped was a tone of command. "I
must speak with Robert."

The thin, wiry man did not even deign to look at her. "He
will not see you," he answered coldly. His eyes were on the
knight as one of the boys told Gaston to halt.

Edgar went forward and spoke to the three young men.
"Take him to the shed and confine him."

Her gaze went to Gaston's face and she saw concern for
her etched on his handsome features. Rose shook her head
in answer to his unspoken question. She knew he still believed she might come to harm. With Edgar making certain
to keep them apart, Rose could not explain why she was safe
with these men, even had she wanted to.

Still now, Rose hoped the two of them could escape
without Gaston ever learning of Robert's identity.

Gaston went quietly when they led him away. He and the
men who stood guard over him disappeared into one of the
two wooden structures.

If one of the structures was used for confining prisoners,
the other building was probably where she would find
Robert.

She backed away from Edgar slowly, hoping to escape his
notice.

He swung around to face her. "Where do you think you
are going?"

Consternation halted her for a moment. Then she gathered her courage and raised her head high. "I will see
Robert. I must speak with him of a matter of grave importance to him, and to all of you."

"What is this matter?" Edgar questioned, his grey brows
rising.

Rose looked around them. She did not want to tell Edgar
here, where anyone might overhear her. There was no way
of knowing if the spy was among the men who stood about
them.

She stuck out her stubborn chin. "My words are for Robert's ears only."

Edgar bent closer to her, sneering. "Lord Robert does not wish to listen to the words of a traitor."

Rose leaned close to his face. "I am no traitor, Edgar of Brentwood." Rose would not accept his judgment of her without defiance. There was more to being right or wrong than the difference between Norman and Saxon. Though she did have some empathy for Edgar's beliefs, this was no time to try convincing him. "How dare you speak so to me? You know nothing of me, and so have no right to judge what I do."

Edgar took a step backward, his gaze unable to hold hers. Lady Rose had always been a good woman. Mayhap they had been too quick to judge.

Then his jaw hardened. There was no changing the fact that she had seemed very cozy, all bedded down with the Norman.

Even though he could not forgive what he had seen this very day, Edgar's voice was more respectful when he continued. "Lord Robert has given strict orders for you to be kept from him." His eyes flicked toward the largest of the wooden structures and away.

Rose knew a moment of elation. So she had been right. Now she knew where Robert was, it would simply be a question of getting inside.

As if in submission, she backed away from Edgar. "I will wait. Tell Robert what I have said. If he values his own life and the lives of his men, he will allow me to speak with him."

He seemed to hesitate, studying her, then nodded. "I will do as you ask." Edgar turned away and stalked across the camp to the wooden building. He was called in immediately after he knocked.

Her gaze sweeping over the camp, Rose saw that though Edgar had not ordered anyone else to watch over her, she was plainly the center of attention. Word of her liaison with

Gaston had obviously spread through the ranks. It would be no use to just go directly to the door of Robert's headquarters and beg admittance. She would be stopped before she got there. No matter that Robert's men were a group of ragtag boys, they were loyal.

Rose raised her head high. Going to a fallen tree limb, she sat down upon it to think.

When they saw she meant to behave herself, the men in the camp seemed to grow less vigilant, most going about their other duties.

After a time, she stood. One of the young men at the fire nearest her stood, also. Rose turned her back on him and went into the trees, after sending him a quelling look that forbade his following her.

A short while later, she reappeared and he settled back down to talk with his fellows once more. He did not have to be told to know what she had been about.

Now Rose had a plan. It would not do to excuse herself again soon, but the next time she slipped away she would stay gone just a bit longer. The observers would relax their guard even further. When she finally did make her move, none of them would be expecting it.

Rose spent the rest of the afternoon in the camp. Every hour or so she would go off to the woods for a time. The men finally stopped taking much notice, barely looking up as she passed by.

When it began to grow dark, Rose stood up and stretched. No one even glanced as she passed them on her way to the woods.

She could barely contain her eagerness. This time she would circle around the outside of the camp to the rear of Robert's headquarters. If she hurried, she should be able to reach her goal before anyone missed her.

In relatively short time, Rose approached the back of the building.

Staying close against the side of the wooden structure, Rose made her way toward the front, keeping an eye out for anyone passing by.

Reaching the corner, she took a deep breath and held it as she made ready to run for the door. She knew if she was seen, the men would not allow her a second chance.

With hope riding hard on her shoulders, Rose bolted toward the door. She had just stretched out her hand to grasp the wooden handle when a shout went up behind her.

Pulling at the door frantically, Rose almost fell when it swung open. She threw herself inside just as a hand grabbed the back of her tunic. Even though she'd been caught, Rose refused to admit defeat. "Robert!"

Her cousin was sitting at a crude wooden table, Edgar and two other men seated opposite him. Their conversation came to a halt as they saw Rose.

Robert did not even acknowledge her. He stood up and growled to the man who grasped her tunic from behind. "She was to be kept away."

The freckle-faced boy who held her blushed and took her arm. "We thought she had only gone to relieve herself, my lord." He began to pull at her, motioning for another man, who had come running up to them, to take her other arm.

The two began to drag Rose backward, but she would not give up. Robert was standing only a few feet away and she must make him listen.

She sank her teeth into the freckled boy's hand as she kicked at the other man. Her foot must have connected, for he yelped, doubling over to cover himself with his hands.

"Robert, please, listen to me," she begged, rushing forward as her captors released her.

Her cousin's gaze was cold as ice, but he was looking at her. His tone was foreboding. "I have nothing to say to you."

"If you don't care about yourself," she cried, "then at least, have the sense to listen to what I have to say for your men's sakes."

He eyed her vacantly, as if she were a stranger. "What could you possibly have to tell me that would save the lives of me or my men, Norman-lover?"

Rose's heart contracted with pain, but she forced herself to stare back at him, unblinking. She answered him without wavering. "What I must tell you is for your ears alone." She looked pointedly at the other men. One of them might be the very spy she had come to warn him of.

Robert folded his arms across his chest and stared down at her. "I trust my men with anything you might have to tell me."

Desperately Rose moved toward him, her gaze imploring. "Please, Robert, I have come all this way. Can you not even give me an opportunity to help you?"

His reply was distant. "When I asked your lover for information, he had no answers. Why suddenly have you found your tongue?"

She answered with complete candor, not denying that Gaston was her lover. "He followed me here. He does not know of my errand, and I could not speak in front of him."

As he looked down into Rose's wide green eyes, Robert seemed to hesitate.

Seeing this, Rose pressed her point. "After you have heard what I must tell you, then you can judge for yourself whether or not my words are important. If you do not let me speak with you..." Helplessly she shrugged.

As if he were still uncertain, Robert nodded slowly. He turned and motioned for the men who had tried to remove her to leave. The men around the table started to rise, also. Robert stopped them.

When Rose frowned at him, he said, "I trust these men with my life. Anything you might have to say is as safe with them as it would be with me alone."

Looking down at the floor, Rose nodded.

Robert sat down, and the four men gave Rose their full attention.

Rose was so relieved Robert had finally decided to listen to her that it took her a moment to organize her thoughts.

Robert cleared his throat and Rose raised her eyes to him hurriedly. Without delay she began her story, first telling of William the Conqueror's offer to assist Hubert, and ending with Hubert's plot against him.

When she was finished, Robert sat in silence for a moment. That he was shocked by her accusation that a Saxon would betray his own people was painfully obvious.

Finally he spoke. "How can I know what you say is true? Did I not see you bedded down with one of the enemy this very morning?"

Rose stamped her foot with impatience. "I told you, Gaston followed me here. I was coming to warn you of this plot, and he saw me leaving Carlisle. How can I make you believe me?"

Robert's tone was coolly reasoning. "You can start by telling me where you came by this information."

Rose put her hand over her eyes. Why had it never occurred to her that Robert might ask how she had come to know about the spy? It was a very logical question. The problem was she didn't know how to answer. There was no way she could say Elspith had learned of the conspiracy in Hubert's bed.

Since she couldn't tell the real story, Rose decided to bluff her way through. "What difference does it make?" She lowered her hand and looked at him. "The thing you should be considering is whether or not I speak the truth."

Robert narrowed his eyes and glared at her. "If I had not seen you with that Norman bastard this day, I would be much more likely to listen to what you tell me." He stood, leaning over her.

"You pigheaded—"

Edgar rose, and the cousins turned to him. Both of them had forgotten the other occupants of the room, in the heat of their argument.

Edgar spoke slowly. "I feel we must be certain that what Lady Rose tells us is a falsehood before we condemn her. I have considered this matter as she talked, and I can think of no way in which her telling us this information could be of benefit to the Normans."

With one last scowl at Rose, Robert sat down heavily. What Edgar said had the ring of sensibility. He could think of nothing that might harm them in what she had said. Was he allowing his anger toward Rose to cloud his thinking?

Rose wanted to hug the old soldier. "Robert, please listen to Edgar. I want only to help you."

"There is a boy who only recently joined us," Edgar went on. "He said he was from Mayhill, and we accepted him without question."

For a long moment, Robert sat pensive, saying nothing. Then his expression changed. His eyes became hard and remorseless. "Find him and bring him here to me."

Rose shuddered. Now that she knew her cousin would be safe, she felt a certain amount of sympathy for the boy. He was, after all, only striking back at a world that had been more than unkind.

"What will you do to him?" she asked, twisting her hands together.

He raised his golden brows. "That is none of your affair. If what you say proves to be true, he will be dealt with as he deserves."

He looked away from Rose, dismissing her. "And now I would like you to leave."

Rose's shoulders sagged and a sigh escaped her lips. There was nothing she could do now. Robert had heard what she had come to say, and still he shunned her. There would be no words of kinship between them.

Her gaze followed him, his hand clasping the hilt of the sword that rested against his chair. The hilt of the weapon was set with a bloodred ruby.

Gaston's sword!

She bit her lip as she raised her eyes to Robert's face.

Aware of her scrutiny, Robert smiled sardonically. "Your lover won't be needing this any longer." He lifted the sheathed sword and rested it across his lap. "Dead men have no reason to fight."

Chapter Sixteen

It didn't take long for Edgar to find the traitor. The boy had no idea his deceit was known. He talked easily with the older man as they approached. Clearly Edgar had not informed him of the accusations against him.

He was young, blond and fair of face. It was easy to see how he could have become the object of a sick man's lust.

Rose had not strayed far from Robert's headquarters since she had been ushered out. She watched with mixed feelings as the boy and Edgar went inside.

A short time later, Rose heard shouting from inside the building. The door burst open and the young man ran out. He looked around frantically for some way to escape.

Robert called from the doorway. "Take him."

Immediately surrounded, the boy had no choice but to yield. His hand closed on air as it went to his side. He was not even carrying his weapon.

Robert came down the steps slowly. He tapped his hand on his hip as he faced the traitor, who was held by two of his men. "Well, what should we do with you?" He studied the young man as if he were a leper, his expression both fascinated and repulsed.

One of the men cried out, "What is going on?"

Robert swung around to face his men. "I'll tell you what's going on. You all know Oren." He waved a hand at the boy.

"He came to us a few days ago, bidding us to take him into our group. He said he had taken enough of the Norman tyranny and wished to help us in our fight against them."

There were nods of assent from the crowd of men.

"It has come to my attention," Robert went on, "that Oren was not totally honest." He held up his hands to quiet the growls of anger that came. "It seems as if Oren has betrayed us, his own people, to the Normans."

The men looked even more angry now, some of them raising their fists to shake them as they shouted their condemnation.

Robert held up his hands for silence. "I have questioned the boy and he has no answer to my queries."

There was one lone call for restraint. "Let him have a chance to defend himself."

"I'll give no defense to the pack of bastards that you are," Oren shouted, jumping toward Robert and pulling a knife from the taller man's belt. "If I'm to die, at least, it will be fighting."

But they were too quick for him. Robert turned with one swift motion and knocked the knife from Oren's grasp. Then the boy was pinned to the ground, his face in the dirt.

Robert yelled, "What shall we do with him, men?"

Rose put her hands to her throat. Everything from maiming to flaying was suggested, as Robert listened, smiling. This was not the Robert she knew, but a stranger who had taken over his body. Her cousin would never have looked on benevolently as though he were enjoying the thought of torturing a prisoner, no matter how guilty.

Oren managed to turn his head from the ground so he could cry out. "I don't care what you do to me. I'll be dead and rid of the shame that's been brought on me. You all call the Normans savages, but you're none the better. With the Normans a man knows where he stands. They make no game of pretending to be your friend."

Robert and the other men laughed as one of the men ground the boy's face into the earth.

Rose could take no more of this cruelty. She stepped up beside Robert. The camp grew still as she raised her arms for attention. "You have the right to punish this man. He betrayed you to your enemies, but can you not treat him as you would wish to be treated?"

"Don't listen to her!" someone shouted. "She's the one what was bedded down with the Norman, cozy as you please."

Rose flushed, but she refused to back down. "I am also the one who came here to warn you of this man's betrayal." Rose turned to Robert. "Am I not?"

He scowled at her, but he was forced, by whatever goodness was still in him, to nod his head at the truth of her statement.

"Please listen to Oren's story and you may be able to find some compassion in your hearts." There was a silence as Rose went on to tell them of Oren's abuse at the hands of the former thane of Mayhill.

She could see some of the men shifting with discomfort at the very thought of what had happened to the boy.

"If what the Lady Rose says is, indeed, true," Robert spoke up when she had finished, "we do owe the traitor some sign of mercy. That mercy will be shown in his quick death rather than a long and lingering one."

There was a roar of approval from the men, and Oren was lifted off the ground by his captors. With a wave and a shout, Robert led the way into the forest. The men surged behind him.

Rose stood where she was. At least she had spared the boy the torture he might have suffered. No matter that he was a traitor, she had been able to warn Robert in time to prevent Oren from doing any real harm.

In the distance, she could hear the men. From the sound of their voices, she thought they must have taken Oren deeper into the forest.

Cautiously Rose looked around the camp. There was not another soul in sight. The band had been so intent on punishing Oren with all possible speed they hadn't remembered their captives.

With bated breath, she turned to the shed where Gaston was confined. Even the guard who had been standing there was gone.

Her feet padded loudly on the damp, hard-tracked earth as she ran across the camp.

"Gaston, Gaston," she panted as she halted in front of the doorway. Her heart was pounding with excitement. Rose knew this might be their one opportunity to escape. They would have to go quickly, before someone remembered she was not to be trusted.

His voice answered from the other side of the door. "Rose."

"You heard?" she asked.

"Yes."

"They have all gone," she told him.

His voice became urgent. "Are you certain?"

Rose looked around the camp once more. "I am as certain as I can be," she answered. "Besides, I am sure if someone were here, they would have prevented me from speaking with you."

"I need my sword," he said. "Have you seen it?"

"Yes." Rose nodded, though he couldn't see her. "I saw it when I was speaking with Ro...I know where it is," she finished.

"Bring it here to me. And hurry!"

Rose raced to the other building. She had no trouble finding the sword. The weapon was resting against the chair where she had seen it earlier.

It took more strength than she would have thought to lift the heavy sword and carry it. But desperation added vigor to her limbs, and she managed to stagger across the camp to the prisoner's shed.

"I have it," she told him in a breathless whisper.

''Can you lift the sword and hand it in to me through the bars?'' His confident tone encouraged her. ''I know it is heavy, sweeting, but you can do it.''

Rose pulled the sword from its scabbard. The bars were narrow slits through which food and water could be passed. The sword would fit through one of the narrow gaps. The problem was that they were on a level with her chin. Her tongue flicked out to wet her dry lips as she struggled to lift the weapon so high.

It took every ounce of Rose's strength, but she managed to get the hilt up to the opening.

By turning his hand sideways, Gaston was able to take the sword from her and pull it through. ''Good girl,'' he said. ''Now stand away from the door.''

She stepped back, hearing the sound of splintering wood as Gaston used the heavy weapon to break through the door of his prison.

Cold sweat beaded on her face and neck, and she continuously glanced over her shoulder. Hardly any time had passed since the men had left, but her presence could be remembered at any moment.

After what seemed like ages, Gaston broke through the door.

For a moment, Rose could only stand staring at him. Then she began to laugh. Gaston looked very fierce standing there with his sword at the ready, without a stitch to cover his nakedness.

His scowl was black enough to frighten the devil himself. ''Why do you laugh?''

''I am sorry.'' Rose tried to stop. ''It's just that you look so murderous, and you are not wearing anything at all.'' She blushed.

Grinning now, Gaston grabbed her close and placed a hungry kiss on her mouth. ''Another time I'll teach you that humor is not the proper emotion for you to display at seeing me this way.''

Rose flushed even more deeply, stepping back to remove the tunic she was wearing.

Gaston took the garment as she held it out to him. Picking up his scabbard, he belted it around the tunic and sheathed his sword. "Where do they keep the horses?"

Rose pointed to a spot behind Robert's headquarters. "Every man I have seen ride into camp has gone that way."

"Have I told you what a clever maid you are?" He took her hand, leading her in the direction she had indicated.

Rose felt a wave of pleasure at the praise. Then she had no time to think as she ran quickly to keep up with him. The blanket she had tied around her waist only served to hinder her, binding about her legs. With her free hand, Rose pulled it loose from her waist. The woolen blanket fell to the ground behind them.

They came to a roughly made enclosure. There were a number of horses inside, but none of them was Pegasus.

"By the blood of Christ," Gaston swore, "we can not leave without Pegasus. On his back, we are assured of outdistancing them." He let go of Rose's hand. "Stay here."

Gaston disappeared behind a group of trees and Rose felt a rush of anxiety. But she made herself wait there as he had asked her. It would do neither of them any good if Gaston were to return and find her gone. They had no time to spare in looking for each other.

She was rewarded for her patience when Gaston came back a short time later, leading the mighty war-horse. He strode to her side and lifted her into the saddle, swinging up behind her.

With a signal to the horse, they were off. She was pulled back close against Gaston's body as the destrier broke into a gallop.

They had gone only a short distance when she heard a rumbling outcry behind them, like the sound of many voices raised in fury.

She grabbed his arm. "They will catch us."

"It is getting dark," Gaston answered as he spurred their mount on. "Even they will have some difficulty in finding us in this wood after dark."

They rode on, neither of them talking. At times Rose was sure she heard the sounds of hooves not far behind them, but the riders saw no one. She made herself concentrate on the rhythm of the stallion, thinking of nothing save getting out of the wood without falling into one of the dangerous pits.

A crescent moon rose in a night sky dotted with stars, but it offered little illumination to the pair of riders.

Finally, when Pegasus stumbled, narrowly missing what might have been a very deep hole, Rose said, "Gaston, we must stop now, until daylight comes. Then I will be able to lead you from this place. Tonight I am as lost as if I had never been here before."

His voice was husky as if his throat were dry. "I must see you safely returned to Carlisle."

Rose swallowed, thinking she would give almost anything for a drink of water herself. But she forced herself to think beyond her own physical discomfort; she must make Gaston see reason. "Think of Pegasus. Even if you did not care for his life, remember we would be an easy target on foot."

He leaned over to try to see her face as he pulled on the reins, stopping the horse. "You told me those men would not harm you."

"I have helped you to escape." She shrugged. "You heard what they did to Oren. Those men do not accept betrayal with good grace."

"You are protecting that man." Gaston swung to the ground.

Rose looked down at him, her heart pounding. "Who?"

Gaston spoke softly, but she could hear something strange in his voice. "The one who was your lover. I realize after last night that you could no longer feel for him. No woman could love me as you did and still care for another."

"Oh, Gaston, all along I have tried to tell you there was room for you and no other in my heart." She wanted to read his expression, but he stood in shadow and she was unsure of his reaction. Rose didn't want to go on, but heaven help her, she still felt the need to keep Robert's identity secret. "How can you accuse me? What makes you think I have any connection to any of them?"

Now the disappointment in his tone came clearly, disappointment in her. "He threatened you, held you against your will, and still you protect him."

Swallowing past the lump in her throat, Rose looked down at her hands. "I don't know what you're talking about."

Gaston's pain exploded in anger. "The leader of the rebels, and your former lover, are one in the same. There is no use denying it. His golden coloring sets him apart. Also there is a distinctive quality to his voice. When I saw him in the crofter's hut this morning, I realized the truth."

"Gaston…" She didn't know what to say. Rose couldn't tell him the truth. She must protect Elspith. Gaston would surely tell Hubert if he learned of their true relationship. And Hubert would then use Elspith to get to Robert. Hubert would stop at nothing to capture the man who had plagued him so thoroughly for months.

His eyes compelled her to face him. "Tell me!"

Rose shook her head. Then she realized something that had been lurking at the back of her mind since they left the camp. Now Gaston knew where to find Robert.

"You can't take Hubert there," she said.

Gaston turned and his face was illuminated in the moonlight. "I must."

Rose tried to read some sign of relenting in his eyes. "But that would be wrong. You only knew where to find them because you followed me. You told me you came only to protect me."

"How can I go back to Carlisle, knowing where these devils are and not say anything? That would be wrong. They have wreaked havoc all over the countryside, against Norman and Saxon."

"Rob—he hasn't done all those things. It's true that he has done everything in his power to irritate Hubert, but he is not a cruel man. It is simply not he who is raping and killing."

Gaston noted that Rose was still being careful not to use the man's name. "Did he tell you this?"

Rose hesitated. "No."

Visibly he sought to control his anger. "Then how do you know? I for one, would not believe him if he denied what he has done. You want me to think the man incapable of cruelty, yet I heard the things he and his men planned to do to Hubert's spy. Only your pleading convinced them to be merciful."

What reply could she make? Rose was hard-pressed to understand what was going on, herself. And Robert had given her no opportunity to question him. He had been too furious with her. "I do not have an explanation," she answered slowly. "I only know he has not committed these vile acts. Please, you must keep his location a secret."

"I am sorry, Rose. There is very little I would deny you. I would gladly lay down my life to protect yours, but I can not do as you ask." He turned away, a muscle flexing in cheek.

"But—"

"No." He made a cutting motion with his hand. "You tell me you must protect your people when I ask you to leave and marry me. Now I tell you I must protect your people. This man has wrought destruction wherever he goes, and it can continue no longer." He looked up at her where she sat atop the stallion's back.

She opened her mouth to argue further.

His barely controlled voice held a warning. "Do not say any more. I believe you have allowed your former feelings for this man to cloud your reason."

Rose felt a slow ball of anger burning behind her eyes. How dare Gaston accuse her of endangering her people to protect Robert?

It mattered little that she had been the one to encourage Gaston in his suspicions from the beginning. All that mattered right now was that Gaston thought she would sacrifice her people's well-being for a man.

"You—you Norman!" she spat, her tone rife with indignation. "How dare you accuse me? Did you learn nothing of me last eve? I have given my heart into your keeping, yet I will marry your repulsive brother. And you stand there in all your self-righteousness and tell me I would do anything to protect a man whom I have loved. I have given my all to the people of Carlisle."

Gaston clenched his hands at his sides. "That was not what I said."

She ground her teeth, so angry she was shaking. "And now, do you tell me I do not understand the words that are put to me?" Rose was filled with an intense desire to place some distance between herself and Gaston. Before he could even take another breath to go on, Rose swung her legs around to the other side of the stallion and started to slip to the ground.

Unbeknownst to Rose, Pegasus was trained to lash out at anything approaching him from the wrong position. This had saved Gaston's life countless times in battle, many opponents falling prey to the flashing hooves. That same training had made Pegasus dangerous to those unfamiliar with him.

As Rose slipped from his back, the horse lunged, automatically reacting to the foreign presence beside him.

Gaston responded without thought, grabbing at the horse's reins to pull him away from the surprised girl. Gaston was strong, but the stallion was stronger. It was only by sheer force of will that Gaston was able to push Pegasus the scant inch it took to save Rose from the animal's deadly hooves.

Acting only out of a need for self-preservation, Rose rolled as Pegasus bumped her with his massive shoulder when he reared in the air.

Rose lay there on the ground, fighting to catch her breath. Too much had happened in the past few days, and this fright coming so close on the heels of her anger at Gaston had rendered her motionless with shock.

As soon as the war-horse was under control, Gaston ran to Rose. When he saw the maid's vacant stare, he feared he had been wrong in thinking she hadn't been hurt.

He gathered her into his arms, his voice hoarse with dread. "Rose, my love."

Gaston's embrace shocked Rose out of her trancelike state. She put her hands to her face and began to cry. Great wrenching sobs racked her slender body and she choked on the words that sprang to her lips. "So frightened...I was so frightened. I am frightened of everything. I want so much to be brave, but ... I can't seem to help myself."

He pulled her up onto his lap, rocking her in his arms. "You are the bravest of women. You have shown more bravery in the short time I have known you than most men do in their lives."

"Oh, Gaston, I only wish that were true," she sobbed.

"It is true. It is one of the things I love about you. You think because you feel terror you are a coward. That is not so. It is the mark of true bravery when one can overcome fear, and go on with what must be done. When you say you will marry Hubert even though you hate him, that is bravery of a kind I have rarely seen."

"But you accused me of protecting Robert at my own people's expense." She buried her head in his shoulder. "You accused me of being weak."

"That is not what I said, love. I meant you may be letting your former feelings for this man cloud your thinking. He may have changed from the way you once knew him."

Rose's sobs had subsided somewhat and she lay more quietly in his arms as she thought about what he had said.

Could it be true that she was remembering Robert as he had once been, and not as he was? He had been so very different when he looked at her today. His eyes had been cold as chips of ice.

Then she shook her head, hiccuping. Gaston could believe whatever he might, but she knew Robert had not rampaged through the countryside raping and killing. There was some other factor that eluded them all.

Gaston put his hand under her chin and turned her to face him. His voice was low and full of torment as he spoke. "If I sounded as if I were blaming you, it was only because of my own self-doubt."

Quizzically she gazed up at him. "I don't understand."

"I am so filled with jealousy I want to rid your mind and heart of any other man besides myself. Even to think of you with him causes an ache near my heart that takes away my breath."

"Gaston." She put her arms around his neck. "You need never fear that I will care for any other man. For you are my love, and will be for eternity. I could no more stop loving you than I could stop the sun from rising; and have no more desire to do so. No matter what comes after this, you must believe that, as you believe nothing else."

"Rose." He pulled her up to him, his lips meeting hers with unrestrained passion.

He laid her down on a bed of soft green moss. In a matter of seconds, her shirt had been removed, and she lay naked before him. She offered herself to Gaston openly, wanting him to know she was his and always would be.

Her hands went to his buckle, fumbling in her haste to have it undone. She wanted to see him again as she had earlier, his sinewy body bared to her gaze. As the tunic fell away, Rose's only wish was that it was day so she could feast her eyes upon his beauty.

But she let her fingers see for her, running them over the smooth skin of his shoulders, glorying in the hard ridges of muscle under her questing touch.

Gaston kissed her fiercely, then lowered his head to the full beauty of her breasts. He groaned against her skin. "I want you."

Rose opened her legs and reached up her arms. "Take me now, my love. I die for you."

Gaston moved to cover her, his velvet, hard shaft slipping into her warmth in one passionate thrust of his hips.

She cried out with the glory of it, lifting her legs to wrap them around him. He took her with him to paradise and her body convulsed under him, her joyous cries filling the night.

Gaston gave in then to the powerful force of the passion that drove him. "Rose," he moaned, feeling himself spill into her womb.

With a sob of possession, Rose held him to her heart.

This might well be their last time together.

Chapter Seventeen

When Rose and Gaston rode into Carlisle the next day, a crowd gathered around them quickly.

Rose realized what a strange-looking pair they must make: she in the shirt that didn't reach her knees; and Gaston in a tunic that did not come together over his wide chest.

In minutes, Hubert was running across the courtyard toward them, his face distorted with anger.

Looking at him, Rose could see their joint disappearance had led him to the wrong conclusion. Hubert could not be blamed for believing Rose and Gaston had gone off together. What was he to think when the two of them left without any explanation?

He strode to Gaston, who was dismounting. "Where have you been?" Hubert reached out and grabbed the edge of his brother's ill-fitting tunic with a meaty fist.

Gaston put his hand over Hubert's, his eyes never leaving his brother's as Gaston pulled his hand away slowly. "I have been to the camp of the rebels."

Hubert stepped back, blinking in surprise. This was the one thing he had not suspected. His face took on a belligerent expression, and he nodded his head in Rose's direction, his eyes taking in her disheveled appearance and bare legs. "Why is the woman with you?"

"We will talk about that later. Right now we should be returning to their hiding place. The men know we have escaped and could be changing their location at this very moment." Gaston ran his hand through his hair.

Hubert took another long look at Rose, then turned to glare at Gaston.

Gaston's eyes on his brother's were a clear grey. "We have much to talk about. But what must be said would be better said when this matter has been taken care of."

Hubert didn't answer for a long moment. He looked like a man who did battle with his own mind. Then, finally, he nodded. "We will go now."

Hubert turned to his soldiers, who had gathered. "Tell all the men to make ready now. We go to end this for once and for all."

Rose slipped down off the horse's back as the men talked. Gaston didn't even notice.

She turned to go to her bower. She must, at least, dress herself before she was confronted by Elspith. It would be hard enough to tell her what had happened.

Once in her bower, Rose called for Mary. She wanted to bathe before she dressed. The night in the hut and the day spent in Robert's camp had left her feeling chilled and grimy.

As Rose leaned back in the wooden tub, she took a deep breath and let it out on a sigh. Her hair had been washed, and Mary moved to draw the heavy mass over the side of the tub so it would dry.

"Thank you," Rose told her. "You needn't stay any longer. I can manage by myself."

Mary nodded and left the room.

Now Rose was able to relax and think. She put her hand over her mouth, stifling a yawn. She and Gaston had woken after only a few hours. They had both grown cold from sleeping on the ground with no cover. Even though it was summer, the nights could turn chilly. Though her eyes burned with fatigue, she knew it would be impossible to sleep. If Robert were captured, it would be her fault.

There had been little speech between her and Gaston after waking. It was almost as if their lovemaking of the night before had never been.

The wall that separated them seemed insurmountable. Gaston felt compelled to tell Hubert of Robert's hiding place, and Rose could not forgive him.

What was she to say to Elspith?

Without warning, the door opened. Rose let out a gasp, raising her hands to cover her breasts. She sighed with relief when she saw it was Elspith. Her relief turned to wariness as she saw the expression of outrage on her cousin's face.

Elspith came across the room to stand over the tub. "What have you done?"

"I have done nothing," Rose defended herself. She stood and took a soft linen cloth from the bench beside the tub. Stepping out of the water, she wrapped it around herself.

Elspith's golden eyes flashed. "Then why do Hubert and Gaston ride to the Pitted Wood?"

Rose closed her eyes and put her hands to her face. She wanted to reassure Elspith, but she could not. The situation was every bit as bad as it appeared. Then she raised her head, refusing to be blamed for what had happened. Rose had meant nothing but good in going to Robert's camp.

Coolly she addressed her cousin. "Sit down, please." She went across the room and poured them each a glass of the watered wine Mary had brought earlier.

As she handed one of the glasses to Elspith, she said, "You must hear me out, before you ask any questions." She paused and waited. When Elspith nodded slowly, she went on. Rose told Elspith everything that had occurred since the evening she had left Carlisle. Elspith looked as though she were hard-pressed not to interrupt, but she did not. The only thing Rose left out was the fact that she and Gaston had made love.

When she was finished, Rose sat down and waited for
Elspith to comment.

''What are we to do?'' Elspith said finally. ''Gaston will
be able to take Hubert to Robert's headquarters. How could
you have allowed this to happen?''

Rose raised her hand to her breast. ''How could I have
allowed it to happen? I went only to warn Robert. How
could I have known Gaston would follow me? Every precaution was taken to ensure my destination was kept secret.
It was Robert who captured us. I would never have taken
Gaston to the camp.''

''How would you have warned Robert without Sir Gaston
knowing?'' Elspith asked.

Rose colored. ''I would have convinced Gaston that I
must go on alone.''

Elspith saw her cousin's heightened color, but she made
no comment. What was between Rose and Gaston was none
of her concern.

But she was worried about her brother. ''If you hadn't
helped Gaston to escape, he could not have come back here
and told Hubert where to find Robert.''

Rose stood up abruptly, beginning to pace the small
room. ''I could not just sit there and allow them to kill
him.'' She rounded on Elspith. ''You did not hear the horrible things they planned to do to Oren, before I convinced
them he deserved some compassion. What would have kept
them from carrying out their wicked plans on Gaston? To
them he is nothing but a Norman. Think of your own lover.
Would you have stood by and watched while Hubert died?''

Elspith lowered her head. ''Forgive me. You can not be
blamed for what has happened.'' She raised her face to Rose
and her eyes held a sheen of tears. ''It is just that I am so
worried about what will become of Robert.''

Rose's answer was cautiously optimistic. ''We can only
wait to see what will happen. It is my hope that Robert will
have realized they are coming and move his camp. The

Normans do not have his knowledge of the area, and so may still be thwarted in their plans to capture him and his men.''

Elspith's face began to show some hope. ''Do you think such a thing would be possible?''

Rose folded her hands together. ''I can only pray that it may be so.''

Elspith's face fell again. ''But what will become of Robert if he is captured?''

''That is something we must discuss now.'' Rose leaned close to her. ''I have been thinking, and I believe we may be able to do for Robert what I was able to for Gaston.''

Elspith sucked in a quick breath then her eyes began to shine. ''Do we dare?'' She put her hands up to her cheeks.

''We dare try,'' Rose answered, nodding.

''But Hubert . . . if we were caught . . .''

''We will worry about that when, and if, the time arrives,'' Rose said. She sat down beside Elspith and began to outline her plan.

It was late the next evening when Hubert and Gaston rode up the hill to the keep.

Walking behind Hubert's horse, his hands tied before him, was Robert. He was led by a long rope that trailed behind the stallion. His clothes were dirty and torn, and a patch that looked like dried blood showed at his right side. He stumbled and fell.

Hubert did not even slow his mount, just kept on going with the same steady pace.

Elspith raised the back of her hand to her lips with a strangled cry.

Rose grasped her arm tightly, whispering a fierce warning. ''Take hold of yourself. You will only do him harm if you allow yourself to react to his suffering.''

Robert was dragged several feet, then he found his footing and managed to trudge on behind the great lord on his mighty steed.

''Yes.'' Elspith swallowed hard. ''I will take care.''

Rose released her cousin's arm and stared out at the approaching men. She and Elspith had come to this vantage point at the top of the palisade as quickly as word had reached them that Hubert was approaching Carlisle.

She forced down her own feelings of despair. The only thing to do now was make sure she and Elspith took every care to see their plans for Robert's escape were not foiled.

Her gaze went to Gaston. Rose felt her chest tighten at the sight of him sitting tall upon his destrier.

Hesitantly the two women went forward as the men came in through the gate.

Servants came forth to take their horses as Gaston and Hubert dismounted. Hubert kept a hold on the rope that led from Robert's bound wrists taking no care to move slowly in deference to the poor, tired man, who had walked all the way from Brentwood.

Robert stumbled, swaying, and almost fell again.

Elspith gasped, but a quelling glance from Rose moved her to caution. She made no sound as Hubert yanked on the rope, laughing.

As Rose looked to Gaston she could see that dark circles rimmed his misty grey eyes. She realized suddenly that he'd had very little sleep in the nights they were together, and likely none since.

It was foolish of her to care so much. He had betrayed her confidence by taking Hubert to Robert's camp. Gaston had shown his true loyalties by choosing Hubert over her.

At that moment, he turned to her, and Rose saw the fierce possession and longing in his eyes. She felt as though he claimed her with that look.

Rose shivered in reaction. Something told her Gaston was not prepared to give her up. Tremendous joy rose in her at the thought of belonging to this man, her only love. At the same time she tried to suppress the feelings of elation.

As long as Hubert ruled Carlisle, he would be her master and husband.

Only with a great effort was Rose able to turn her thoughts from Gaston. Now was not the time to bemoan her lot. She must center her attention on the task of freeing Robert.

Curiously Rose noted that only a few of Hubert's men had returned with him. With so many of his force spread throughout his lands, and more gone with William, Carlisle seemed sadly undermanned. Why would Hubert return without his soldiers?

Rose nearly laughed aloud at her thoughts. Before Hubert had come, she would not have worried over the number of troops at the keep. Hubert had infected her with his own paranoia.

Many of the people in the crowd of onlookers who had gathered were pointing at Robert and whispering amongst themselves. Rose knew most of them would recognize him even though his filthy, gaunt appearance made him look very different from the proud young thane they had known.

Robert didn't look at any of them. He kept his eyes fixed on the ground, intent on keeping his feet as Hubert strutted around the courtyard.

Rose's lips turned up, but not with amusement. She was a study in contempt as she watched her intended bridegroom. Her gaze swung away from Hubert to collide with Gaston's. His expression held a warning.

Hubert stood still and assumed a cocky stance. He pointed to Robert. "Do you see this man? He is the leader of the rebels, and I hold him prisoner, as I said I would."

Not a sound was uttered.

Hubert yanked hard on the rope, and Robert stumbled to his knees.

Rose ground her teeth in vexation. Why, by all that was holy, must Hubert be so cruel? Could it not be enough that he had captured Robert, made him come to heel as he had sworn he would?

But this was not sufficient. Hubert would always have a need to prove his manhood before everyone.

After a time, Hubert appeared to grow tired of the game. He had before him a captive who seemed truly beaten, and it took much of the thrill out of his victory. Only Rose saw the flash of defiance in Robert's eyes as he looked at his captor.

At long last, Hubert beckoned forth one of the few soldiers who stood in the crowd of onlookers. "Take him and lock him up. I shall decide how to deal with him later. I must have time to carefully consider his punishment."

The soldier leapt to do Hubert's bidding. No one would try Hubert's patience in this mood. He took the rope and led Robert away.

As Robert was led away, he passed directly in front of Rose. She wanted to step back, not wishing to face him. Surely he must blame her for his capture.

But she made herself stand there. It might be possible for her to communicate her desire to help.

Robert looked up into Rose's eyes. The naked hatred in his face rocked her to the core. She felt his animosity slice through her heart like a jagged-edged blade. Rose stepped back, recoiling from him instinctively.

Robert was so bent on making Rose see how much he detested her for what she had done, he failed even to notice his sister standing a few steps behind her.

Only Rose heard the sharp cry of pain Elspith could not repress.

In the time it takes to sigh, Robert had moved on. But his passing had left Rose feeling as though she had been trampled under careless feet.

Then, looking to where Hubert watched her, Rose took a deep breath to steady herself. She would not let Hubert see how much the encounter had shaken her. Lifting her head high, she stared back at him openly.

Hubert's brows pulled together over his nose, and he thrust out his chin. He watched her for one more moment, willing her to accept the fact that he had proved he was the stronger.

She glared back at him.

He swung on his heel and headed toward the Great Hall.

Looking to Gaston, Rose saw he was openly frowning at her. Then he too turned and went toward the Great Hall.

With a muttered curse, Rose followed them. She was determined to find out what had happened at Robert's camp and what Hubert planned to do to him.

When Rose entered the hall, Hubert had already ordered that a pitcher of wine be brought to him.

Gaston was just seating himself next to his brother.

Squaring her shoulders, Rose walked across the room and stopped before them. "What happened? Why have you returned with so few of your men? Were they killed in trying to take the raiders?"

Hubert's jaw tightened for a moment, then he smiled and ran his eyes over her with feigned indifference. He reached forward and took a long pull from his cup before he answered. "There is no reason to keep the truth from you, madam. In point of fact, it pleases me to tell you how well we have squashed these irritating bugs." He brought his fist down onto the table with a loud bang that made her jump.

Rose recovered herself quickly, facing him with steely defiance. Something told her things had not gone as smoothly as Hubert professed. Robert and his men knew the forest well.

Hubert went on, smirking unpleasantly. "Their leader delivered himself into my hands to gain the release of two of his men." Hubert chuckled unpleasantly. "Merely boys, really. A foolish move, my men will only recapture them with the rest." He leaned back and watched for her reaction.

So, he had caught her wily cousin by trickery. Robert's men were still at large. He found no chink in her armor of disdain. She raised a haughty brow. "If this is true, where are your men?"

Hubert rested his elbows on the table, leaning toward her. "They are just a few hours behind us. There were a few stray rebels to round up in the woods. And the camp must be found and burned.''

''Where are the captured rebels?'' Rose asked, her brow puckering as she frowned in pretended dismay.

Gaston cast her a look of warning, but she ignored him, bent on making Hubert look the fool he was.

Hubert went on as if to reassure himself. ''The soldiers will bring them along soon enough. I did not wish to risk their leader's escape. Without him they are like sheep...lost.'' Hubert scowled at his brother. ''Gaston returned with me, as he had no stomach for the sport.''

Rose only glanced at Gaston, then away. She could not risk the tight control she held on her emotions. Why wouldn't he wish to help? He was sure Robert's men had wreaked terrible destruction all over the lands.

But Rose had other problems to deal with. Hubert's inefficiency had dealt her cause a serious blow. With Robert separated from his followers, her plan to help them escape must be postponed. She would have to wait until Robert's men were brought to Carlisle. Never would her cousin leave them to Hubert's mercy. Meanwhile, she must think of some way to keep Hubert from venting his spleen on Robert.

For a long moment, Rose was afraid her carefully laid plans would all be for naught. Hubert had waited long to retaliate against his enemy. Desperately she hit on Hubert's love of the dramatic. She folded her arms, speaking in a conspiratorial tone. ''To effectively lesson the people to your swift retribution, you would do well to punish the rebels together.''

A great bellowing guffaw escaped Hubert. He threw up his hands, drawing the attention of the few people in the hall. ''Do you hear this? The woman thinks to lesson me in matters of punishment!'' He laughed again.

Rose clenched her hands into tight fists at her sides. Oh, how she hated this man. She forced herself to speak calmly, even though her jaw ached with the effort to control herself. ''You have shown me, my lord, how very important it is to make a show of strength. These men have created untold havoc over the past months. I but seek to assure the safety of my vassals.''

Hubert spread his hands wide, palms up. "I am happy to have taught you so well, damsel, but there is no need to worry." His eyes turned cold as a long winter. "That man has plagued me long and well. My soldiers have scattered hither and yon in search of him. I have seen my store of gold dwindle to naught." He glanced sharply over to Gaston. "I have left the care of my lands to another. The outlaw will be punished in such a way to make other dissenters reconsider their chosen course."

Her stomach tightened with anger. Even when she tried to behave as he wished, he avoided answering. This was one time she would not be put off. "When, and what will you do?"

Hubert glanced about the hall as if bored with her questioning. "This is none of your concern, woman. I will only say that without a leader any pack of dogs is less apt to turn on you." He raised his cup, dismissing her.

"What will you do to him?" Rose persisted. She bent forward, placing her hands on the table as she leaned toward Hubert.

"Away with you, woman," Hubert threatened, not looking up.

Rose's voice had risen to a demand. "You must tell me." She was tired of Hubert's overbearing ways. Didn't she, as the Lady of Carlisle, have a right to know?

Without warning, Hubert's fist snaked out.

Rose saw what was happening, but she had no time to react. He was too quick. She closed her eyes, expecting the blow to fall.

Rose opened her eyes. It had taken no more than a split second for her to realize that, for some reason Hubert had not carried through with his intent.

Now she saw why. Hubert's fist was caught and held in Gaston's strong grip.

The two brothers sat staring at each other for an infinite moment. Neither of them was willing to relent.

Finally it was Hubert who turned away. "You have interfered again in something that is not your affair."

Gaston refused to give ground, his tone even but set. "The time has come for us to talk."

Hubert stood, eyeing his brother angrily. "I will not discuss this with you."

Gaston stood firm. "Whether it be now, or at some other time, we will discuss this matter. There are things you must hear, will you or no."

Hubert's tone carried a warning. "Think carefully before you speak, brother. Some things said can never be undone." He turned and strode from the hall, calling for Elspith.

Rose could not look at Gaston. Her heart was pounding and a cold sweat had broken out on her body, chilling her. Her voice was husky. "What have you done?"

There was no sign of wavering in his face. "I will not give you up." She could feel the heat of his determination when he came to stand before her.

She looked up at him, her eyes damp with tears. "You must not do this. Please. I have taken a vow. I can not break it. If you love me as you say you do, you must not tell Hubert we have been lovers."

"I would marry you."

Rose gulped back tears, allowing him to see the true measure of her hurt. "What matter is that? I would not marry you. If you trusted me, truly believed it when you say I am honorable and brave, then you would believe me when I tell you Robert is no real threat to any of us."

She watched his face for some sign of relenting and found none. She buried her face in her hands. What was she to do now?

Gaston reached toward her. ''Rose?''

She backed away from him. She could not allow him to touch her. Rose turned, running from the hall as quickly as her feet would take her.

Could worked toward her. Slowly she
she shrank away from him. She could not allow him to
touch her. Rose stood, running from the hall as quickly as
her feet would take her.

Chapter Eighteen

Rose huddled close to the wall of the Great Hall. Not a
sound broke the stillness of night. She gave a start as she felt
a hand on her arm. Quickly she turned, then sighed with
relief when she saw Elspith.

"What is wrong?" Elspith asked.

"Nothing." Rose shook her head, forgetting Elspith
would not be able to see the gesture in the enveloping darkness. Looking up into the sky, she once again gave thanks
for the clouds that covered the moon. They would have need
of as much protection from prying eyes as was possible on
this night.

"Is everything ready?" Elspith questioned. Rose could
hear the nervous excitement in her cousin's voice.

"I have sent Mary with drugged wine. She will share the
wine with the guard so he will not suspect. I have made certain neither of them will receive a harmful dose."

Elspith squeezed Rose's arm in anticipation. "Then all we
can do is wait."

The two women watched and waited. The small shed
where Robert was being held sat only a few feet away.

After her conversation with Hubert earlier in the day,
Rose had realized they must help Robert escape this very
night.

It was as if Hubert saw Robert as a scapegoat for his own
bitterness. If he could make Robert suffer greatly, it would

be compensation, in part, for everything that had happened; his engagement to Rose, his dissatisfaction with Carlisle, his growing mistrust of Gaston.

Late in the day, Elspith had emerged from Hubert's bower. Her lips were swollen, her eyes heavy and languid after several hours in Hubert's bed.

Rose had made no comment, but the redness in her cheeks served as mention enough. She did not understand how Elspith could go so easily to the man who meant to kill her brother.

When Rose had outlined her conversation with Hubert, Elspith had agreed the two of them must go through with their plans to release Robert immediately.

Robert would not wish to go without his men, but his very life could depend on the women's ability to convince him.

When the cramps in Rose's legs had become almost unbearable, she shifted restlessly.

Elspith whispered, "Do you think enough time has passed?" It was obvious from the strain in her voice that she too was uncomfortable.

Rose knew she should not have allowed Elspith to become involved in this in her condition. But she had been afraid Robert would be unwilling to trust her if his sister was not there.

Elspith prompted, "Well?"

"Just a short time longer, to be certain they are sleeping," Rose answered.

Elspith made no comment, but Rose could hear her restless movements next to her. After a moment, she said, "You're sure Sir Gaston isn't suspicious?"

Rose's lips thinned. "Why do you ask?"

Elspith shrugged. "He seems overinterested in your movements."

Rose answered her stiffly. "Sir Gaston has other matters on his mind this night." Rose did not care to think about Sir Gaston and what he might know. With his determination to confront Hubert with his love for Rose, he threatened to undermine everything she stood for. How could he expect so much from her when he offered nothing? If only he could believe in her.

Rose shook her head, making herself concentrate on the task at hand. There would be time to think of Gaston once Robert was safely away.

Some time later, Rose stood. "I believe we have waited long enough." More than enough time had passed, but Rose wanted no problems to arise. They would not likely be given a second opportunity. Tomorrow Robert might well be dead.

With a nervous sigh, Elspith stood, too. She followed Rose as she made her way cautiously toward the shed.

Neither of them saw the raven-haired man who pressed more closely to the shadows, then moved away.

Stopping at the edge of the shed, Rose waited, listening. She couldn't hear a sound, not even from Robert inside. Her heart was pumping so loudly she was sure it drowned out any other noises.

Then, with a deep breath for courage, Rose stepped around the corner of the shed, feeling Elspith's reassuring presence right behind her.

They crept up to the bench along the front of the shed. A man sat slumped against the side of the building. The serf Mary sat beside him, her head flung back, mouth open.

A loud snore erupted from the round-bellied soldier, causing Rose to start in surprise.

Elspith gave an anxious titter as he snored again, this time even louder. Her relief was evident, as he had startled her too.

Even though both of them knew it was too dark to see clearly, they exchanged a conspiratorial grin.

Everything was going well.

Crossing to the door of the shed, Rose pulled at the bolt that held the door secure. It was a heavy bar of metal that Hubert had installed. With some difficulty, she got the rusty metal to slide.

Elspith, who was standing at her shoulder, clapped her hands softly in elation as Rose pulled open the door.

Rose went first, bending over to pass through the low, narrow doorway, wondering all the while why Robert had not come forward.

Her silent question was answered when she saw him. He was standing against one wooden wall. His hands were tied over his head and his feet were tied wide apart. He raised his head to glare at her, his eyes gleaming with hatred.

He smiled coldly. "Have you come to gloat?"

Rose recoiled from the loathing he exuded. "I . . ."

A slight sound behind her made Robert raise his eyes. A welcoming smile transformed his face. "Elspith," he whispered.

Rose was surprised at the sudden change from enemy to loving brother. She felt a sense of loss for the family closeness she and Robert had once shared.

Elspith rushed forward to raise herself up and kiss his blond-bearded cheek. "Robbie."

Rose said nothing, only coming forward to work at the knots that bound his hands. Realizing she could not undo the tight knots with her fingers, Rose took her eating knife from the small pouch at her waist.

In no time, the sharp little knife had slashed through the ropes and Robert's hands fell to his sides.

"Ohh," he exclaimed, pain assaulting him as the blood began to rush back into his arms, which had been held above him for too long. Elspith began to rub one useless limb. Her motions brought a gasp of agony to his lips, but she did not stop.

Rose squatted to cut the ropes that bound his feet. As soon as this was done, she stood and began to massage Robert's other arm. Time was their enemy, they must get him out of Carlisle before they were discovered. Robert refused to look at Rose. And as soon as he could control the movements of his arms, he snatched the one Rose was ministering to away.

Rose said nothing. She knew Robert held her responsible for his capture.

But Elspith, seeing what was happening, could not allow her brother to treat Rose so badly. "Don't, Robbie." She looked up at her brother, her golden eyes filled with pleading. "You mustn't be angry with Rose. She meant you no harm."

"But I saw her," he snarled with a gesture toward Rose, still not looking at her. "She was sleeping with that Norman."

Elspith blanched.

Rose was not sure if this was because she was surprised that Rose had slept with Gaston, or because she too had bedded down with one of the hated Normans.

But they had no leisure for discussion. Robert had to go now. "There is no time," Rose told them. "We must see him away."

Elspith put her hand over her mouth as she remembered the danger. "You are right. I was only trying to explain to him."

Rose's comment was direct. "If we can get Robert away from Carlisle safely, there will be a better time to explain. If we do not, there will be no need."

"Come." Rose motioned for Robert to follow her. She went to the door to look out.

With a gasp of despair, she took two steps backward.

"What . . ." Elspith began, then she let out a groan that came from deep within her.

In the doorway of the hut stood two of Hubert's soldiers. One was a tall gangly-looking man with very large hands. The other was a short burly man. They held their swords in their hands.

The shorter man laughed. "I knew there was something up when I saw that Blodel, here—" he motioned toward the soldier and the serf girl "—had fallen asleep at his post. He's a good man, is Blodel. In all the years I've know him, he's never slept through his watch." His lips thinned as he looked at the three inside the hut as if they had purposely conspired to ruin that perfect record. "Then when I saw the door was opened," he went on, "I called you, Ren."

The tall man nodded and moved forward.

Rose backed toward Robert and Elspith. She knew that despite the man's awkward appearance he would be a skilled swordsman. The easy way he held his weapon was proof enough.

Slowly the two soldiers continued to advance. "Lord Hubert won't be too pleased about this." The burly man looked from Rose to Elspith.

Rose took another step backward and came up against Robert. Without warning, she felt herself pulled close to him. His hand snaked around her, reaching into the pouch that held her eating knife. Then he thrust her away and backed close to the wall. He held the knife at the ready, willing to defend himself even with so small a weapon.

Ren laughed softly and Rose shivered. She knew that her assessment of the soldier had been right when he edged closer to Robert, testing the weight of his sword with pleasure.

Elspith reached toward her brother. "Robert."

"Don't get in my way," he told her. His attention never left the two soldiers as they advanced on him.

The shorter of the two men rushed at Robert's side, yelling, "He must be taken alive."

As the short man called out, Ren stopped in midthrust, giving Robert the opportunity to slash at him with the knife. A streak of red appeared on Ren's arm and he growled in anger.

At that moment, the shorter soldier came up behind Robert's back and hit him over the head with the hilt of his sword.

Rose cried out in warning, but it came too late, and she watched with regret as her cousin fell to the floor, unconscious.

"Robert." Elspith rushed forward to kneel beside her brother.

Ren took her arm and roughly pulled her to her feet as the other soldier gave Robert a vicious kick in the ribs.

Rose ran across the floor to push the man away from her prone cousin. "Leave him alone. Haven't you done enough?"

The stocky man replied, "We'll see how much needs doing when Lord Hubert learns of this." He turned to Rose with a frown of regret. "I wish you were not involved with this, Lady Rose. Claude is my cousin. Everyone knows he would be dead if it weren't for you. Why would you want to help this rebel escape after all the evil things he and his men have done?"

"But..." Elspith struggled, trying to pull her arm from Ren's grasp.

Sadly Rose shook her head. "It is no use trying to convince them he is innocent, Elspith. They refuse to listen. Robert has been found guilty without benefit of trial."

Ren made an impatient gesture. "There will be no more talk. Take her, Hugh," he instructed the other man, with a nod toward Elspith. "We'll see what Lord Hubert thinks about her part in this." He bent and lifted Robert from the floor. Once this would have been an almost impossible task for a slight man such as Ren, but Robert had lost so much weight the soldier was able to carry him easily.

Hugh, who had taken Elspith's arm when he was bid, came closely behind. He paid no attention to Elspith's pleas to be freed.

Rose had not been constrained in any way, but she followed, wondering why the soldiers had not attempted to take her. After what Hugh had said about Claude being his cousin, that might be a possible explanation.

Ren led the way directly to the Great Hall. Rose felt a sinking in the pit of her stomach, but she forced herself to step through the wide opening after them. She knew she was almost powerless to help, and yet she had to try.

There was no telling how Hubert would react to the fact that she and Elspith had tried to free Robert.

Hubert and Gaston were sitting at the high table.

As they entered, Hubert looked up, his face showing puzzlement when he saw the strange tableau before them. He stood immediately, coming around the table.

Gaston was slower to react. He came to his feet, a frown marring his brow. If Rose had not known better, she would have thought his expression one of sympathy.

There was no doubt in her mind that she must be mistaken.

Brazenly Rose lifted her chin. She would not let him intimidate her. She had only done what she must.

"What goes on here?" Hubert bellowed, rushing up to Ren, who dropped the still-unconscious Robert onto the floor without ceremony. He turned to his brother. "You passed through the courtyard but a short time ago. Did you see nothing?"

Gaston looked to Rose. "I did not."

In that moment, she guessed the truth. Gaston had known they were helping Robert to escape, and protected her. Rose's heart sang with love, a love that shone in her glistening eyes.

Hugh pushed Elspith to the forefront. "We caught them trying to help the prisoner escape, my lord."

Hubert looked down at the man on the floor. He turned to Elspith, his eyes registering surprise and hurt.

For a moment Rose was almost sorry for Hubert, but this pity evaporated quickly as he began to speak.

"What have you done?" Hubert moved forward, roughly grabbing Elspith's shoulder. He put his hand under her chin and forced her to turn her pale face up to his.

"I . . . he . . ." Elspith stuttered.

Hubert's disillusionment emerged as rage. "Speak, woman!"

"Hubert, please," Elspith whispered, tears running down her cheeks.

"I trusted you," he cried, "told you everything!" The pain in his voice was so raw Rose had to turn away. Looking at the other men, Rose could see they felt the same. Even Gaston was staring at the floor.

It was then Rose noticed Robert had regained consciousness. His attention was completely centered on Hubert and Elspith. There was a feral gleam of hatred in his eyes. He made her think of an animal who has been run to ground and, finding no safety, turns to defend its life.

Only it was not himself he sought to protect, but his sister.

Rose realized that to Robert, it must appear as though Hubert were about to harm Elspith. The thunderous expression on Hubert's face and his threatening demeanor warned of a foreboding violence.

Rose did not believe Hubert would injure Elspith; he loved her too well. Even as she took a breath to shout a warning, Hubert screamed, "Speak!"

Robert leapt. As he pushed Elspith out of the way, Robert flew at Hubert's throat.

The two men tumbled to the ground as they grappled. Hubert brought his huge arms up to wrap them around Robert's chest and squeezed.

Ren and Hugh ran to Hubert's assistance. Robert's hands dropped away from the powerful knight's throat as he gasped for breath.

"He is mine," Hubert growled, tightening his arms even more.

Robert was no match for the well-honed Hubert. His life of deprivation in the forest had sapped his strength and skill until he was a mere shell of his former self.

Rose started forward to help Robert herself, but she found her shoulders held from behind. Her struggles to free herself were useless against Gaston's strength.

She lifted her gaze in desperation, pleading with Gaston. "Hubert will kill him!"

Gaston did not answer, and there was no change in his tight-lipped expression.

Elspith stood, the back of her hand pressed to her mouth as she watched the scene in horror.

Keeping his stranglehold on Robert, Hubert rose slowly to his feet. The muscles in his thick neck bulged with the effort he was making to squeeze the very life from his enemy.

For that was what it appeared he would do. Robert's hands hung useless at his sides, and his face had turned a mottled purple.

"Please!" Elspith screamed, finding her voice and running forward to pull at Hubert's arms. "You are killing him."

Ren hurried to pull her away.

With a loud grunt of exasperation, Hubert lifted Robert, tossing him away as if he weighed no more than a child.

Sobbing hysterically, Elspith broke free from Ren and ran to her brother. She fell to his side, wrapping her arms around the still form.

Hubert's brow wrinkled in confusion, and he took a step toward her. "Elspith?"

She looked up at him, near blinded by her tears. "He is my brother!" she cried, cradling Robert's head against her breast. "He is my brother."

Rose felt Gaston's fingers tighten on her shoulders.

"Your brother?" Hubert muttered.

"What is going on?" Gaston swung Rose around to face him, Elspith's confession breaking the inertia that had held them all. "How did the sister of your former lover come to be a serving woman at Carlisle? The time for explanations has come."

Rose looked up into his eyes, knowing the time had, indeed, come to talk. Her love for Gaston was a deep, open wound in her heart. Gaston had decided to trust her, no matter how damning the evidence against her beliefs.

Rose began without preamble. "Robert is the former Lord of Brentwood."

"The Lord of Brentwood?" Hubert interrupted. He turned to Elspith. "This means *you* are the Lady of Brentwood."

She bowed her head. "Yes."

Robert stirred in his sister's arms. He opened his eyes and tried to sit up, his gaze searching for Hubert. "Where is he?"

Elspith held Robert's shoulders, trying to make him lie down. "Stay. You only do yourself harm."

Robert resisted her efforts to quiet him. "I will kill him."

There was steely determination in his voice, but Rose knew Robert would be no match for Hubert. That much had already been proved.

Insistently she pressed him back, her voice soft. "You must not, for he is the father of my unborn child."

For a long moment there was a deathly silence in the hall.

Hubert was the first to react. He went to Elspith and drew her up beside him. "You are with child?"

She answered slowly, "I carry your child."

"You filthy whoreson," Robert screamed, leaping to his feet.

Hubert moved to stand before Elspith, his body protecting her in case she was inadvertently harmed by her brother's rage.

Robert swung at Hubert, who blocked the blow easily and knocked Robert backward with one tap from his massive fist.

Hugh jumped to take hold of Robert, only to find out he was much stronger in his mad state. It was only when Ren moved to help him that they were able to subdue the young man.

Hubert turned to Rose, having heard what Gaston said to her. "What is this about the man being your lover?" He looked a little dazed, as if events were happening too quickly for him to be able to sort them out.

"And why have you not told me of this, Gaston? The lady is my affianced wife." He scowled at his brother.

Putting his arm around her, Gaston pulled Rose close against his side. "This lady will never be your wife."

At that moment, chaos erupted outside.

"Fire!" a voice shouted. "We are under attack."

Gaston was the first to react, running to the entrance of the hall. He drew his sword as he went.

Ren and Hugh looked at each other. Their combined gazes turned to Robert, then to Hubert for instructions.

Hubert recovered himself quickly. Going to Robert, he slapped him, hard, across the face. "Your men have attacked the keep, though I don't understand how they have escaped my soldiers." His hand went to his sword. "Call them off, or I will kill you now."

Leaving Elspith to protect Robert, Rose ran to the doorway after Gaston. Carlisle was her first concern.

What was happening did not make sense. There were few amongst Robert's men who would have the courage or the cunning to lead an attack upon the keep.

In the courtyard, Rose wasted no time in issuing orders to everyone with earshot. As every structure was made from wood, there were already several fires burning that needed to be put out.

Moments later, when Hubert dragged Robert from the hall, Rose was beating at a hay fire started by a flaming arrow. He pushed her cousin up the ladder to the palisade and thrust him to the forefront.

Hubert stood behind him and hollered down to the men below. "If you do not stop this attack, your leader will die a slow and painful death here before your very eyes." He waited for a response.

To Hubert's surprise, a volley of arrows and rancorous laughter came back to him.

Hubert shook Robert roughly. "What goes on here?"

Horrified, Rose ran up onto the palisade and halted before Hubert. Rage made her voice unsteady. "Those are not his men out there. How would they overpower your soldiers? They are poorly armed and weak with malnutrition.

I have known something was wrong from the outset. Robert would never allow his men to maim, rape and torture his fellow Saxons.''

Hubert shook Robert again. ''Does the woman speak true?''

''I will tell you nothing, Norman,'' Robert snarled.

Hubert drew back his hand, meaning to quell the Saxon with a mighty blow. He halted in midswing when Elspith stepped between them. For a moment, Hubert was surprised by her sudden appearance, and he scowled, regarding her with impatience. ''Get you gone from here to a safer place.''

With an unusual show of strength, she shook her head. ''No. Robert is not responsible for the attacks on Saxons. If only for the love you bear me—'' her voice broke, but she would not let herself cry ''—you must let him go.''

Hubert bellowed, ''Then who are these men?''

Gaston came running in time to hear the last remark. ''Who they are matters less than that they have broken through the west side of the palisade. We haven't enough men to hold them.''

Rose's gaze ran over him hungrily, relief flooding her when she saw he was unscathed. But she knew her happiness could be short-lived. Unless they could manage to withstand this attack, all their lives might be forfeit.

Gaston seemed to be the only one amongst the men who understood the immediate danger that surmounted their feud. She turned to him. ''We will be of little help to you. Unless the men in the village see the smoke, they will not come to our aid. Most of them will have gone to their beds.''

There was a cry from the courtyard below, and they looked down to see a group of Saxons run into view. They were a ragtag-looking band, with their mix-matched weapons and dirty clothes. None of them owned a sword, they carried only rakes or hoes.

With one last glare for Robert, Hubert pushed him aside and made his way to the courtyard, his sword in his hand.

Rose turned to Gaston, her eyes pleading with him to be careful. He pulled her close, to place a quick kiss on her willing lips. "I must rejoin the fighting." Then he was gone, calling back as he ran, "Stay where you are. I will return for you."

Rose knew she would be wise to heed his instructions. In the courtyard below them, Norman and Saxon labored together to turn back the aggressors. She would not be safe on the ground.

Elspith ran to her brother. "You must help us."

Robert folded his arms across his chest and watched the scene of destruction below with a smile. "Why would I help? Everything belongs to the Norman. I have no sorrow in seeing him lose all he possesses, as I have."

A surge of anger like none she had ever felt rushed through Rose, firing her blood. Without thought, she went to Robert and struck him across the face.

His smile disappeared, and he raised his hand to touch the spot. Anger lit his golden eyes. "Why did you strike me?"

"You fool. Can you not see that Saxon lives will be lost here, too? Instead of wishing ill on Hubert, you should be down there helping to fight off these raiders. If I am not far off the mark, they have caused much suffering amongst your people and mine over the past months. Hubert matters little. It is the people we have an obligation to protect."

Robert looked to Elspith, who folded her arms across her chest and glared at him. "Do not look to me for support," she told him. "Rose speaks true. You, as well as the rest of us, must come to accept the Normans and go on."

His expression was ambiguous as he turned to Rose. "They will never trust me with a weapon. What can I do?"

She faced him squarely. "Someone must go to the village and get help. It is our only hope."

Robert answered at last. "If only for the two of you, I will do it. But first I will see the both of you to safety."

"There is no safety," Rose stated.

At that moment, one of the raiders came up the ladder of the walkway and hurried toward them, a long knife in his hand.

With the practiced skill of a soldier, Robert sidestepped, grabbed the knife, then threw his weight against the assailant, pushing him over the palisade.

"Come," Robert told them. He managed to hold all attackers at bay, until they reached the Great Hall. "You must go inside," he ordered. "At least the hall will offer some protection."

Over Robert's shoulder, Rose saw Gaston engaged in combat. Her breath stopped as his opponent charged, but Gaston was the more agile of the two. He brought his sword forward, felling the other man. As if sensing her nearness, he glanced around, then motioned for her to go inside.

When she didn't obey, he raced through the melee, dispatching adversaries as he came. Finally he reached her side.

His eyes flicked to Robert and away, dismissing him. Gaston's love and concern for Rose were clearly written on his face as he looked at her. "Why have you left the palisade?"

"It was being overrun. Robert brought us to the hall."

"Maida is inside with some of the serving women," he told her. "For the moment it is safe, but I know not how much longer. If only it were not made of wood, we are too susceptible to fire." He cast a desperate glance about them. "There are too many of them. With so many soldiers gone we stand little chance. From the way these men fight, I would say they are deserters from Harold's army."

He moved closer, his eyes on hers as he took out a knife and handed it to her. "If I should fall, you must find the courage to use this. These men are vicious dogs. The things they have done to other women in the district are unspeakable. I would not have you used by them."

Swallowing hard, Rose took the knife. "You will not fall, my love. I could not bear it."

He pulled her close to him for a long moment, then kissed her hard. "I will fight while there is breath in my body."

Rose pointed to Robert. "There may be help coming. Robert will go to the village and bring the men."

Gaston once more glanced toward Robert and away. "Why would he help us?"

"Because Saxon lives are being lost," Rose said simply.

Just then a man lunged at him from behind, and she screamed his name in warning. "Gaston!"

Gaston turned, swinging his sword. The man fell and Gaston shouted, "You must get inside. Now!"

He took her hand and pulled her after him to the door. He pounded on the heavy oaken door with the hilt of his sword, shouting out, "It is Sir Gaston."

Just then, Rose heard Elspith call out. She turned to see a man, sword raised, coming at Gaston's back. Before he could complete his downward stroke, he fell, Robert's knife protruding from his back.

Gaston said nothing as he turned to Robert, but his eyes held less contempt than they had.

Beating at the oak door again, Gaston shouted for someone to open. There was the sound of wood rubbing against wood as the bar was lifted, and then they were inside.

Maida came forward to envelope Rose in her arms. She drew back, smiling, her gaze going to Elspith. "Only the Lord knows how grateful I am to see you two well." Then her eyes came to rest upon Robert and she drew in a breath of surprise as she turned to Gaston.

Rose nearly laughed. So much had happened this night. All their precautions to hide Elspith's relationship to Robert seemed ridiculous now. "He knows," Rose told her.

"He knows?" Maida muttered.

Rose turned to Gaston.

He seemed restless to be away. And though one part of her wished he could stay here, in relative safety, she knew he could not. His duty called him. She reached up to touch his beloved face. There was no point in hiding anything now.

Gaston had all but told Hubert of their relationship. What would happen would happen. There was no need for her to mask her feelings anymore. "You must not stay here worrying over us, love. I know you are needed to help save Carlisle."

He pressed her palm to his lips, his eyes deep with emotion. "Remember what I told you. Don't let them take you or any of the women, can you prevent it."

"I understand." Putting her arms around his neck, she kissed him with all the longing in her heart. As she watched him leave, she whispered, "Go with God, my love."

As the door closed behind Gaston, she noticed Robert was gone. He must have slipped out before the knight. She only hoped he would succeed in bringing help from the village.

Elspith was standing alone, her eyes round and frightened in a white face. Rose went to her and made her sit down. She could not worry about Elspith now. She must help the women to ready bandages and medicines. Maida had the foresight to bring Rose's bag of medications with her when she came to the hall. In the event that this battle ended with the attacker's defeat, there would be many wounded. If it did not...Rose would not allow herself to think on that.

Sometime later, a loud scream pierced the hum of women's voices.

Hysterically a woman screeched, "Fire! We are on fire."

At the far end of the hall fire had broken out. Someone must have set the blaze from outside, but it was quickly burning through.

Over the din that had broken out, Rose shouted, "Get buckets of water."

The women used every bit of water in the hall and were not able to even dampen the flames that licked along the old, dry wood. Already the smoke was beginning to make their eyes water and their throats burn.

There was no choice for them but to open the door and go out into the courtyard. Running to the door, Rose drew up the wooden bar. "Come this way," she beckoned.

She stood back as the women hurried out of the hall. As the last of them left, Rose followed. She realized then being outside was little better than inside.

Fires were burning everywhere, all along the palisade, the outbuildings, even her bower was in flames. Her heart contracted with the knowledge that everything of her former life was gone. She fought back tears, forcing herself to put this new grief aside for now. She looked away. From the tight ring of fighting around the Great Hall, Rose knew the men were making a final stand to protect their women.

She had to step over dead bodies as she moved away from the door, though she did not know where she could go. There seemed to be nothing left of safety.

Rose felt an arm go around her waist from behind and she was pulled back against a male form. She tried to twist around in the arms that held her, but the grip was too tight.

With a cry of rage, she kicked at the man's legs. He laughed.

She was half dragged across the courtyard to a place where the fighting was less intense, and dumped onto the ground.

Looking up at her assailant, Rose let out a cry of horror. She would never forget that face as long as she lived. The long wicked scar that ran down his right cheek made this man easily identifiable. She could still recall his face as he had bent over her that day in the forest.

"How could it be you?" She tried to scoot away as he knelt in front of her. "I saw Gaston kill you with my very own eyes."

"You assume too much," he snarled, reaching down a hand to unfasten the cloth that covered his loins. "It was my brother who was struck down, though he wasn't dead when you left him. He managed to crawl all the way back to camp before he died in my arms."

Her gaze went to the scar that turned up the side of his mouth. "But I saw..."

He slapped her, making her head snap back on her slender neck. His hand went to the scar, his thick fingers tracing the ridge. "Twins, we were, and raised by our uncle after our parents died. As alike as two peas, until I fell from a horse and got this. Our uncle, he didn't see the sense in us being different after looking alike for so long. One night when he was drunk, he grabbed Thom up onto his lap and used his knife to give my brother a scar that matched mine. No one could tell us apart."

He looked down at her, an evil light shining in his face as he rubbed his side. "When the sword entered his body, I felt it, too. My men have been ordered to take your lover alive." He smiled. "I want him to watch as I take my pleasure of you, before he dies a slow lingering death."

"No." Rose screamed as he grabbed at her knees with his scabby hands.

He worked to pry her legs apart. "I will have you now, and then, too. I may want you many times before I tire of you." His hand stroked the smooth skin on her legs where he had raised her gown. "The battle is almost won, so there is time. My men will finish off the few who are left."

Rose backed away, her words meant to distract him. "So they are your men."

"Of course." He smiled confidently, following her.

He reached out and grabbed a handful of her long hair, successfully stopping her. "I shall have what you so freely gave the Norman that day in the glebe."

Hot color stained Rose's cheeks when she realized this savage had witnessed her and Gaston's lovemaking. "How did you come to be there?"

His expression was insolent. "I came upon the little lordling's band of rabble rousers and followed them. One can never know too much about one's competition. It was quite amusing to see them scramble when you and your Norman friends arrived at the church. After that it took me an inordinate amount of time to decide if having you was worth killing the priest. The old fellow did himself a very good turn by leaving.'' His gaze left her feeling soiled as it followed the line of her body. ''Alas, the Norman returned and I had to forgo the pleasure of taking you myself.'' He shrugged. ''But why should I be denied the sight of you?''

''You filthy animal!'' Outrage added strength to her limbs and she kicked out at him, catching him in the chest. Her head jerked as his hand came away from her hair.

With a grunt of pain, the scarred man fell backward. But he was quickly after her again. He fell on her, determined to carry out his threats. Holding her with one hand, he threw her gown up with the other while he forced her legs apart with his knee.

Rose fought him with all her might, but his madness over the death of his brother had given him the strength of three men. Her muscles strained as they gave way and her legs parted. ''No!''

He laughed, his face flushed with lust and the knowledge that victory was at hand. She felt his hard member pressing against her thigh, and the bile rose in her throat.

''Hold!''

Rose looked over her assailant's shoulder to see Gaston running toward them. Tears streamed down her face with the effort it had cost her to fight the much larger man. ''Thank God,'' a voice sounded in her head, ''Thank God.''

Turning to see what had brought such an expression of joy to Rose's face, her attacker growled out his fury. He leapt to his feet, picking up the sword he had dropped as he attacked Rose. He smiled coldly as he hefted his weapon. ''Don't think this has done more than put off our pleasure.''

He ran at Gaston as one crazed.

But Gaston's rage at seeing Rose assaulted knew no bounds. He rushed forward, his sword held high over his head, with a battle cry that chilled the blood of all those who heard it.

Rose's limbs shook with reaction that made her weak, and she could only watch, horrified.

The two men set upon each other like wild animals. Their swords clashed loudly, drowning out the other sounds of battle around them. They lunged and sidestepped, each wanting nothing more than the other's death.

Finally, by slashing with his sword and stepping into the blow, Gaston was able to knock the other man's weapon from his hand.

Without pause, the scarred man turned, grabbing Rose's arm and pulling her up before him. "Now, drop your sword," he ordered.

Gaston looked to Rose, who shook her head no, only to be clouted on the shoulder by her assailant's fist. Her eyes watered with the pain.

Reluctantly Gaston's grip on his sword hilt loosened and the weapon slid to the ground, the red glow of many fires reflected in the blade.

The man who held her laughed. "I have longed for this day, prayed for it."

"I don't believe it is God who has brought you here," Gaston said. "Mayhap the devil."

He only laughed the louder. Then he stopped, his hand moving up to cup Rose's breast. "What matter who has brought me here, if I get what I desire?"

Gaston started forward, but he stopped when the man squeezed Rose's breast cruelly, making her cry out.

"Do not hurt her more," Gaston pleaded. "I will do as you say."

The maniac let out a bark of amusement. "I care not what you do, beyond that you shall watch me take your woman. After that," he snarled, "you will pay with your life for what you have done to me."

"I don't understand, what have I done to you?" Gaston asked, in desperation.

"What have you done to me?" he screeched, holding Rose at arm's length and shaking her in his wrath. "You killed my brother—my twin. I am sworn to avenge him." He pushed Rose away as he grabbed Gaston's sword, raising it high as he rushed forward.

Stumbling backward, Rose felt the hardness of Gaston's knife in her shoe. Without stopping to think, she took it out and ran at the madman.

Just as he swung the sword at Gaston's head, she leapt at him, burying the knife in the back of his neck. For a long moment, he stood there, the sword poised above Gaston. Then he tumbled to the ground to lie still.

Gaston held out his arms, and she ran into them, knowing there was no place she would rather be.

When he felt how she trembled, he held her even more tightly. "It's all right, my sweet. He can not harm you."

Just then there was a shout from outside the burning palisade. Robert ran into the courtyard. Behind him came the men from the village. They were armed only with farming implements and household knives, but their expressions were determined.

They poured through the opening and quickly engaged in the struggle.

After seeing Rose safely to the storage cellar, where the other women waited, Gaston rejoined the fighting once more.

It seemed like an eternity until he, at last, returned to fetch her. Rose leapt up to throw herself into his arms, raining kisses on his smoke-blackened face. "Hold me, hold me," she cried.

Gaston was more than happy to comply. He wrapped his arms around her with such enthusiasm that she felt as though her ribs would crack. But she gloried in his fierce possession.

She stopped kissing him for a moment to inquire, "Has Carlisle been secured?"

Gaston held her away for a moment to laugh bitterly as he gestured around them. "What is left of Carlisle—" he gave a mock bow "—has been secured, though many have per-ished in the struggle."

Rose's eyes darkened with a sheen of tears as she took in the destruction. She pressed close to his warmth, knowing she could not have come through this without his strength. "Thank God, you have been spared."

Gaston gave her another bone-crushing hug.

Over Gaston's shoulder, Rose became aware of Hubert's presence. He was watching them, his dark face unreadable. "Dear heaven," she whispered, pulling away.

Gaston turned to follow the direction of her gaze. On seeing his brother, he drew Rose back into the haven of his arms. "No," he said firmly when she tried to resist him. "I will pretend no more. You are mine and I will fight Hubert if need be to keep you."

"Gaston, he is your brother."

"And you are my love."

Gaston turned to face Hubert as he slowly advanced toward them. He came to a halt, and Rose felt her heart come up into her throat. During the thick of battle, Rose had thought she was resigned to facing Hubert with the truth of their love. But looking at him now, she realized it might prove more difficult than she thought. He held her lands and people in his sway.

Hubert looked at the two of them for a long time before his gaze moved to take in the ruined keep.

It was then Rose realized that a crowd had gathered. Everyone watched Hubert de Thorne for his reaction. It came as no surprise to the people that Sir Gaston loved their lady. They had seen the truth long ago.

But Hubert was known as a hard man, and their eyes were filled with trepidation.

Rose's gaze came to rest on Elspith, where she stood at the edge of the crowd. Her hands were folded before her and she would not lift her attention from the ground.

Hubert raised his hands high for silence, though it was not necessary as not a voice was heard. "People of Carlisle," he began. "Many unforeseen things have taken place this day. Not the least of which is that I have found I am to be a father."

All eyes turned to Elspith, and she hunched her shoulders, still refusing to look up.

"As you all know," Hubert went on, drawing their stares back to him, "I have been plagued by problems since almost the very day I arrived here at Carlisle. These problems have drained my resources until the well is nearly dry. And now," he said as he looked at the pile of rubble around them, "I find myself faced with the task of rebuilding the whole of what I have accomplished and more. It is a responsibility I would gladly disavow."

There was a muttering in the crowd. "My problem now," Hubert raised his voice to silence them, "is that I must find a man who would take on the task and still have King William's blessing. He must also be a man I can trust, since this property lies betwixt my others, Mayhill and Brentwood."

He turned to Rose and Gaston, who awaited whatever he might say. "I offer these lands to my brother Gaston de Thorne and charge him with the responsibility of rebuilding them. He shall become Lord of Carlisle, should he choose, under only one condition. And that condition is that he will continue work on the proper fortress King William has ordered be built on this crossroad to the north."

Gaston stepped forward, his face solemn as he clasped his brother's arm. "I accept your offer most gladly. I shall strive to be worthy of the honor you have done me."

A great deafening cheer went up in the crowd. If they must be ruled by a Norman, Gaston was a worthy choice. He had proved himself to be a just and fair leader.

Rose held herself still as Gaston and Hubert clasped hands. She was afraid to believe what she most desired could come to her.

Hubert held up his arms again, and there was silence. "I find I am engaged to marry one woman while another car-

ries my unborn child," he said. "In all decency I ask this
lady—" he pointed to Rose "—to release me from my
pledge so I might marry the woman who bears my child, and
whom I love."

Elspith raised her golden eyes to Hubert, and it was as if
stars shone in them.

"I release you from your pledge!" Rose cried happily,
running toward Gaston and throwing herself into his outstretched arms. He caught her and swung her high in the air,
to the sound of more cheers.

He set her to the ground and Rose blushed at the smiling
faces around them. It seemed that their secret had not been
nearly so well kept as she and Gaston had thought.

Rose glanced over at Elspith to see that Robert had
stepped between her and Hubert. He said something to his
sister, and she watched him for a long moment before she
stepped around him and went to Hubert's side.

Robert looked on with disdain as Hubert caught her close
and kissed her.

Rose felt pity for Robert, knowing how hard his new life
would be unless he came to accept it. She knew only time
would tell.

Gaston bent and whispered in her ear, his voice full of
concern. "You look troubled, love."

Rose gazed up at him, forgetting all else save the fact that
they would now be together. "It was only a shadow on the
sun." She looked up to see dawn spreading its golden fingers across the sky.

* * * * *

Author's Note

In 1067 the Normans and the Saxons spoke two different languages. Over time, as victor and vanquished became one people, their languages mingled and ultimately evolved into the English spoken today.

In view of this melding, I have chosen to overlook the issue for the sake of telling Rose and Gaston's story. As their languages have integrated, so have their descendants.

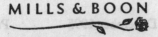

GET 4 BOOKS
AND A MYSTERY GIFT

Return the coupon below and we'll send you 4 Legacy of Love novels and a mystery gift absolutely FREE! We'll even pay the postage and packing for you.

We're making you this offer to introduce you to the benefits of Reader Service: FREE home delivery of brand-new Legacy of Love novels, at least a month before they are available in the shops, FREE gifts and a monthly Newsletter packed with information.

Accepting these FREE books and gift places you under no obligation to buy, you may cancel at any time, even after receiving just your free shipment. Simply complete the coupon below and send it to:

MILLS & BOON READER SERVICE, FREEPOST, CROYDON, SURREY, CR9 3WZ.

No stamp needed

Yes, please send me 4 free Legacy of Love novels and a mystery gift. I understand that unless you hear from me, I will receive 4 superb new titles every month for just £2.50* each postage and packing free. I am under no obligation to purchase any books and I may cancel or suspend my subscription at any time, but the free books and gifts will be mine to keep in any case. (I am over 18 years of age)

2EP5M

Ms/Mrs/Miss/Mr _____

Address _____

_____

_____

_____ Postcode _____